PENGUIN (logo) CLASSICS

THE PENGUIN BOOK OF GASLIGHT CRIME

MICHAEL SIMS has edited two other collections for Penguin Classics: *The Annotated Archy and Mehitabel* and *Arsène Lupin, Gentleman-Thief*. His research for the latter inspired *The Penguin Book of Gaslight Crime*. His most recent nonfiction book is *Apollo's Fire: A Journey through the Extraordinary Wonders of an Ordinary Day*, which National Public Radio chose as one of the Best Science Books of 2007. He is also the author of *Adam's Navel: A Natural and Cultural History of the Human Form*, which was a *New York Times* Notable Book and a *Library Journal* Best Science Book; and *Darwin's Orchestra: An Almanac of Nature in History and the Arts*. His writing has appeared in *New Statesman, Gourmet, Orion,* the *Washington Post,* and many other periodicals in the United States and abroad. Learn more at www.michaelsimsbooks.com.

The Penguin Book of Gaslight Crime

CON ARTISTS, BURGLARS, ROGUES, AND SCOUNDRELS FROM THE TIME OF SHERLOCK HOLMES

Edited with an Introduction and Notes by
MICHAEL SIMS

PENGUIN BOOKS

PENGUIN BOOKS

Published by the Penguin Group
Penguin Group (USA) Inc., 375 Hudson Street, New York, New York 10014, U.S.A.
Penguin Group (Canada), 90 Eglinton Avenue East, Suite 700, Toronto,
Ontario, Canada M4P 2Y3 (a division of Pearson Penguin Canada Inc.)
Penguin Books Ltd, 80 Strand, London WC2R 0RL, England
Penguin Ireland, 25 St Stephen's Green, Dublin 2, Ireland (a division of Penguin Books Ltd)
Penguin Group (Australia), 250 Camberwell Road, Camberwell, Victoria 3124,
Australia (a division of Pearson Australia Group Pty Ltd)
Penguin Books India Pvt Ltd, 11 Community Centre, Panchsheel Park, New Delhi – 110 017, India
Penguin Group (NZ), 67 Apollo Drive, Rosedale, North Shore 0632,
New Zealand (a division of Pearson New Zealand Ltd)
Penguin Books (South Africa) (Pty) Ltd, 24 Sturdee Avenue,
Rosebank, Johannesburg 2196, South Africa

Penguin Books Ltd, Registered Offices:
80 Strand, London WC2R 0RL, England

First published in Penguin Books 2009

3   5   7   9   10   8   6   4

Selection, introduction and notes copyright © Michael Sims, 2009
All rights reserved

LIBRARY OF CONGRESS CATALOGING IN PUBLICATION DATA
The Penguin book of Gaslight crime : con artists, burglars, rogues, and scoundrels from the time of
Sherlock Holmes / edited with an introduction and notes by Michael Sims.
p. cm.
Includes bibliographical references.
ISBN 978-0-14-310566-4
1. Criminals—Fiction.   2. Thieves—Fiction.   3. Detective and mystery stories, English.   4. Detective
and mystery stories, American.   5. English fiction—19th century.   6. English fiction—20th century.
7. American fiction—19th century.   8. American fiction—20th century.   I. Sims, Michael, 1958–
PR1309.C7P46 2009
823'.0872—dc22   2008037363

Printed in the United States of America
Set in Sabon

Contents

Acknowledgments

First I want to thank the anthologists and scholars who helped lure me into this entertaining subset of crime fiction, primarily Ellery Queen and Otto Penzler. Throughout my work on this collection, Otto advised and encouraged. I also especially want to thank anthologist Douglas G. Greene; Roger Johnson, BSI, editor of *The Sherlock Holmes Journal* in England; Steven Womack, detective novelist and always the best man; and Larry Woods, longtime friend, encyclopedia of mystery fiction, and co-owner (with the charming Saralee) of BookMan/BookWoman in Nashville, where I first discovered some of these authors and characters. For other help, including comments on the text or the story lineup, my thanks to Alan Bostick, Maria Browning, Michael Dirda, Jon Erickson, Casey Gill, Karissa Kilgore, Jane Langton, Michele Slung, and Art Taylor. Thanks to Cesare Muccari and his excellent staff at the Greensburg Hempfield Area Library, especially those indefatigable book detectives, Cindy Dull and Linda Matey. As always, the enterprising crew at Penguin has been superb. My thanks to executive editor Elda Rotor, editorial assistant Lauren Fanelli, publicity director Maureen Donnelly, production editor Jennifer Tait, copy editor Randee Marullo, and publicist Courtney Allison (not to be confused with the private eye). And perpetual gratitude to my wife, Laura Sloan Patterson, the actual trained scholar in the family, who continues to encourage and assist my forays into dusty corners of literary history.

Introduction

Fools and Their Money

"A fool and his money are soon parted," wrote Thomas Tusser, the sixteenth-century Englishman who also made the astute observation that Christmas comes but once a year. As history and the daily news demonstrate, there are as many species of thieves in the world as there are of foolishness. Not surprisingly, one is often drawn to the other. The book you hold in your hand is populated with clever thieves who make their living by separating fools from their money as efficiently and as often as possible.

When I first became interested in crime fiction's little subgenre of caper stories, I went looking for an anthology about these charming miscreants. To my surprise, I searched in vain. No such volume existed. Although the important detectives of the era had been herded into a lineup again and again, the great con artists and burglars had mostly eluded capture. So eventually I suggested to Penguin that together we remedy this oversight. In the present volume, for the first time, the best crooks of the gaslight era are gathered in one place.

Our party includes distinguished guests from outside the field of mystery and detection. Who but the dustiest of scholars remembers that American Nobel Prize winner Sinclair Lewis and British novelist Arnold Bennett wrote an occasional crime story? Most collections of short fiction by O. Henry omit his crime stories, other than the sentimental account of safecracker Jimmy Valentine, and thereby miss the adventures of his itinerant con men in small-town America. William Hope Hodgson, renowned for his supernatural fiction, also wrote a volume of stories about a wily smuggler.

Fans of Victorian and Edwardian detective stories may find their favorite authors working here on the other side of the law. Some of the great thieves of this era were chronicled by people known for their popular crime fighters. For example, the prolific Edgar Wallace, nowadays remembered mostly for his detective J. G. Reeder, provides one of the adventures of a con woman nicknamed Four Square Jane. And of course the legendary thieves are here—A. J. Raffles, Colonel Clay, Simon Carne, Get-Rich-Quick Wallingford, the Infallible Godahl. I omit the suave Arsène Lupin because I have already devoted an entire volume to his adventures: *Arsène Lupin, Gentleman-Thief* (Penguin Books, 2007). I have included a single quirky detective story, the first adventure of Robert Barr's Frenchman Eugene Valmont, because all the action in it is masterminded by an offstage thief.

This volume gathers stories about the thieves of the gaslight era, so I ought to define both *gaslight* and *thief.* The taxonomy of genre fiction is no more precise than that of the larger world of literature. Such terms as *gaslight, noir,* and *hard-boiled*—like *modernist* or *surreal*—are labels applied after the fact and for diverse reasons. One writer may employ "gaslight era" to represent the heyday of Arthur Conan Doyle and the next writer may use it to approximate Queen Victoria's entire reign from 1837 to 1901. Technically, the real-life period of gas lighting began in 1807, when London's Pall Mall first lit up like a fairy-tale kingdom. Edison invented the incandescent bulb—the filament lamp that replaced gas lighting—in 1879, but probably no city finished replacing all its gas lamps until after World War I. Some places (London, Berlin, even Cincinnati) still employ gaslight streetlamps in certain historical neighborhoods.

Therefore I felt comfortable using the term to cover stories that appeared between the mid-1890s and the early 1920s—pretty much the era of Sherlock Holmes. For me *gaslight* invokes a mood and a voice, both of them romantically luminous with distilled scenes from Robert Louis Stevenson, Charles Dickens, and Arthur Conan Doyle. The term implies an urban setting, minus the honking stench of our modern highways; sophisticated characters, but not twenty-first-century cynics. The moment I envision a gaslight lamp, the special-effects department in my brain surrounds it with London fog. Then it cues the rattle of a hansom cab across cobblestones and the whinny of a horse—even though several stories in this volume occur elsewhere in Europe or in the United States, and the later adventures include telephones and motorcars.

In these pages our own daily world fades away: no television, no jet planes, no computers. Escapism? Of course. Can it be that we are nostalgic for an era that none of us experienced? After all, "Nostalgia," says the Chilean novelist Alberto Fuguet, "has nothing to do with memory." From our perspective we know what awaits these characters around the curve in the twentieth century: airborne bombing, genocide, poison gas, nuclear weapons. The gaslight era is close enough to seem familiar and far enough away to feel safe. Furthermore, the authors wrote with enviable freedom from technical research. "Stories from that era," observes the crime-fiction collector Larry Woods, "legitimately avoid the mystery/detective structural problems of technology, since almost all the forensic technology known to the modern reader was then in its infancy or had not yet achieved wide practical application." Perhaps it is no coincidence that, in the (fictional) heyday of criminal masterminds, the pinnacle of crime-fighting technology was Sherlock Holmes's magnifying glass.

And what about the term *thief*? These pages are decidedly not populated with the usual suspects. The criminals herein arm themselves with wit rather than with guns. You will run into con games and burglaries, art forgery and diamond smuggling, but you will not stumble over a corpse in the library. I exclude Percival Pollard's character Lingo Dan, for example, because he is not only a thief but also a murderer. Likewise Fantomas, as well as Madame Sara & Co. The threat of death requires no talent. As the term *con artist* implies, these tales are about skill and imagination; this is a gathering of rogues, not villains. You need not be afraid to invite them to dinner—but don't let them wander about the house unattended.

Prior to the earliest story here, which appeared in 1896,

there had been burglars who claimed gentlemanly status, but whose quick revolvers disqualified them for the present volume. As far back as 1882, *The Silver King,* the first popular success by the later renowned playwright Henry Arthur Jones (in collaboration with Henry Herman), featured a gentleman cracksman nicknamed The Spider. He strolls onstage in "faultless evening dress" but is quick to shoot when threatened. Another well-armed burglar, calling himself Jack Sheppard in honor of the eighteenth-century London brigand immortalized in novels and even in John Gay's *Beggar's Opera,* appeared in a single story in 1895. Not that my ethics on this point are unimpeachable. While mostly eschewing personal violence, some of these characters are not above despicable machinations that put people at risk. In one story, the con man even goes so far as to create an international incident that might have led to war.

Although this anthology emerges from my wide reading in the genre and era, supplemented by advice from scholars in the field, the contents page reflects my own taste. I barred the door against a few once-popular thieves because I found them, well, boring. Authors who lack sophistication themselves have a difficult time convincing us of their characters' urbanity. Between World War I and World War II, for example, Frank L. Packard recounted the rough-and-tumble adventures of Jimmie Dale (alias the Gray Seal) in a painfully inept style. Consider this sample: "Tight-lipped, Jimmie Dale's eyes travelled from Burton's shaking shoulders to the motionless form on the floor." Mr. Dale's athletic eyes were not invited to our party. Other characters who did not pass muster include Bertram Atkey's Smiler Bunn and John Kendrick Bangs's Mrs. Raffles.

Some once-popular characters turned out to work better on-screen than on the page. The year 1919 brought Jack Boyle's sole novel about Boston Blackie, a half-reformed criminal and secret crusader for justice; his decades of fame grew out of ongoing film adaptations. In the mid-1920s, Englishman Bruce Graeme launched a series about Richard Verrell, a masked cracksman nicknamed Blackshirt. A bestselling author, he steals for fun—until a woman discovers his identity and calls him up to make him steal (and solve crimes) on demand. Blackshirt too gained in translation to the screen.

Surprisingly, in this anthology you will find only one story about a female thief. During the gaslight era there were plenty of female detectives. C. L. (Catherine Louisa) Pirkis launched the career of Loveday Brooke in 1894. Three years later George R. Sims introduced Dorcas Dene. Around the turn of the century, the prolific L. T. Meade, in collaboration with Robert Eustace, published several stories about Miss Florence Cusack. Baroness Orczy, creator of the Scarlet Pimpernel, published the collection *Lady Molly of Scotland Yard* in 1910. Orczy also created the villainess Madame Sara, while Meade gave us the equally dastardly Madame Koluchy. Apparently, in the unwritten rules of the time, women could write about or commit or solve murders, but lesser crimes were left mostly to men. The only female thief in our collection—not counting a collaborator whose identity must remain secret until you stumble upon it as you read—is the brilliant Four Square Jane, who was created by a man, Edgar Wallace. Soon afterward, but a bit beyond the purview of this collection, came Sophie Lang, Fidelity Dove, and their colleagues.

The majority of these stories come from a series about the character. In most cases I have read and reread every entry in the series to determine which one best represents the character and author. A note placing both in context precedes each story, so that you won't have to flip back and forth between the story and this introduction to fish around for background information. Stories appear in order of publication.

Although this era's stories make us think of the term *gentleman thief*, not every malefactor in *The Penguin Book of Gaslight Crime* is an aristocrat (and, of course, the last thief in the book isn't male). J. Rufus Wallingford raised himself from poverty; Captain Gault commands a ship. Author O. Henry, in particular, portrays the more working-class side of the criminal life.

Part of the fun of these capers lies in the way that they reflect the growing skepticism about official Victorian virtues. Some of our lawbreaking protagonists are explicitly critical of the business and social worlds on which they prey. O. Henry, who was adept at skewering Gilded Age business-speak, once described a meeting of a burglar, a con man, and a financier as a conference of "labor and trade and capital." In his malapropriate way, O. Henry's con man Jeff Peters remarks about his partner Andy Tucker that nowhere in the world could you find three people "with brighter ideas about down-treading the proletariat than the firm of Peters, Satan and Tucker, incorporated." In one story, Peters deliberately sets out to hunt *Midas americanus,* the Pittsburgh millionaire.

Aside from profit, incidentally, motives in these stories include financing true love and balancing the scales of justice. A few of the criminals are actually vexed by a Robin Hood urge to redistribute wealth beyond their own coffers. Four Square Jane robs "people with bloated bank balances."

"Thieves respect property," wrote G. K. Chesterton a century ago. "They merely wish the property to become their property that they may the more perfectly respect it." Chesterton, creator of the popular detective Father Brown, was himself a man of stern morals in his fiction. While trying to convert the criminal Flambeau from his life of thievery, Father Brown assures him that "There is still youth and humour in you; don't fancy they will last in that trade. . . . Many a man I've known started like you to be an honest outlaw, a merry robber of the rich, and ended stamped with slime."

Although one or two of the characters in this book wind up slimed, most would disagree with the priest. They remain quite merry despite—or perhaps because of—years of robbing the rich. Theirs was the first great era in which fictional crime was allowed to pay. Impatient with Victorian ideals of proper behavior, Edwardian-era crime fiction permitted a whole range of outrageous behavior, and along the way it lampooned the crass values of an increasingly materialistic society. "I think a lot of people were happy about those who could get something for nothing," remarks the noted anthologist and scholar Otto Penzler. "Anarchy was in the air."

In crime-fiction circles, this kind of anarchy led to the period of gleeful irreverence chronicled in this book. "His conscience was sufficiently elastic to give him no trouble," writes Guy Boothby of aristocrat Simon Carne. "To him it was scarcely a robbery he was planning, but an artistic trial of skill, in which he pitted his wits and cunning against the forces of society in general." Not that every con attempted meets with success. One story (and of course I'm not going to tell you which) fails spectacularly; the nature of its failure becomes the point of the story.

But mostly these authors and their characters are having fun: burgling London and Paris, conning New York and Ostend, laughing all the way to the bank—not that they would ever trust a bank. I had always intended *The Penguin Book of Gaslight Crime* to read like a holiday jaunt into the past. As I assembled the final manuscript, I was pleased to find that the first words in the first story are "Let us take a trip."

—MICHAEL SIMS

Suggestions for Further Reading

Several histories of detective stories include small amounts of useful information about gaslight thief tales, but the sources below focus on the authors and topics particularly relevant to *The Penguin Book of Gaslight Crime*. The list features books available through libraries, omitting articles of narrow focus that appear in specialist journals. More in-depth sources can be found cited within the books listed below or in source guides online.

William Vivian Butler, *The Durable Desperadoes: A Critical Study of Some Enduring Heroes* (London: Macmillan, 1973).

Frank Wadleigh Chandler, *The Literature of Roguery* (New York: Houghton Mifflin, 1907).

Edward Clodd, *Grant Allen: A Memoir* (London: Grant Richards, 1900). About the creator of Colonel Clay.

Dictionary of Literary Biography, various volumes, and the numerous sources listed therein.

Richard Lancelyn Green, introduction and notes to *Raffles: The Amateur Cracksman* (London: Penguin, 2003), by E. W. Hornung.

Howard Haycraft, *Murder for Pleasure: The Life and Times of the Detective Story*, rev. ed. (New York: Carroll & Graf, 1984).

Margaret Lane, *Edgar Wallace: The Biography of a Phenomenon* (London: Heinemann, 1938). About the creator of Four Square Jane.

Gerald Langford, *Alias O. Henry: A Biography of William Sidney Porter* (London: Macmillan, 1957). About the creator of Jeff Peters.

Richard Lingeman, *Sinclair Lewis: Rebel from Main Street* (New York: Random House, 2002).

George Orwell, "Raffles and Miss Blandish," from *Horizon*, August 28, 1944, available online at http://www.netcharles .com/orwell/essays/raffles.htm or in various Orwell essay collections.

Nick Rance, "The Immorally Rich and the Richly Immoral: Raffles and the Plutocracy," in *Twentieth Century Suspense* (London: Macmillan, 1990).

Peter Rowland, *Raffles and His Creator* (London: Nekta, 1999). About E. W. Hornung, the creator of A. J. Raffles.

Norman St. Barbe Sladen, *The Real Le Queux* (London: Nicholson and Watson, 1938). About William Le Queux, the creator of Count Bindo de Ferraris.

Chris Steinbrunner and Otto Penzler, *Encyclopedia of Mystery and Detection* (New York: McGraw-Hill, 1976).

Colin Watson, *Snobbery with Violence: English Crime Stories and Their Audience,* rev. ed. (London: Macmillan, 1979).

ONLINE INTRODUCTIONS
AND READING GUIDES

http://www.classiccrimefiction.com/history-articles.htm
http://gadetection.pbwiki.com/
http://www.philsp.com/homeville/fmi/ostart.htm#TOC
http://www.mysterylist.com/

The Penguin Book of
Gaslight Crime

GRANT ALLEN

Before his Colonel Clay series was collected in *An African Millionaire* in 1897, Grant Allen had been publishing books for two decades. More than fifty volumes had already appeared and dozens more would follow; any almost random selection of their titles demonstrates the variety of his interests. Allen's self-published first book, *Physiological Aesthetics,* was followed by such equally weighty tomes as *The Colour-Sense* and *The Evolution of the Idea of God.* He also wrote popular novels, including *A Bride from the Desert, The Type-writer Girl* (under a female pseudonym), and *For Maimie's Sake,* which boasted the eye-catching subtitle *A Tale of Love and Dynamite.* Allen was a free-thinker about both religion and marriage. His most notorious novel was the 1895 succès de scandale *The Woman Who Did,* about a well-educated young woman (pointedly not a guttersnipe) who chose to have a child outside of wedlock.

Perhaps Allen's diverse interests and impatience with narrow social conventions emerged from his varied upbringing. He was born Charles Grant Blairfindie Allen in Ontario, to an Irish father who had immigrated some years before and a Scottish-French mother from a distinguished Canadian family. At first home-schooled by his father and later assigned a Yale tutor, he attended both English and French universities before becoming a classics major at Oxford. After teaching Greek and Latin in several British schools, he spent three years as a professor of moral and mental philosophy in Jamaica. When the school failed, he settled in England and launched a writing career.

Allen worked so hard that his severe writer's cramp became a cautionary fable among fellow writers. Colleagues on both sides of his career held him in high esteem. When he was briefly in financial straits, his friend Charles Darwin lent him money, and shortly after Darwin's death in 1882 Allen wrote a charming biography of his friend for Andrew Lang's series of "English Worthies." When Allen himself died with his picaresque detective novel *Hilda Wade* unfinished, his friend Arthur Conan Doyle completed it for him.

Allen came relatively late to crime fiction, partly because he couldn't survive by writing only science-related nonfiction, but he was soon adept at the conjuror's sleight of hand and distracting patter that distinguishes the masters in the field. He also simply wrote a fine sentence—sly, literate, precise. He invented two noteworthy detectives, both women, both (like Colonel Clay) nonstop travelers: Miss Lois Cayley, who is out for adventure, and Hilda Wade, who is out to avenge her father's murder.

But Allen is remembered now mostly for his ingenious Colonel Clay, the first series character who was a criminal yet appeared in the role of hero rather than villain. Clay dares to rob the same victim again and again during the course of a dozen clever and amusing episodes. In one of them, he impersonates a detective hired to find the notorious Colonel Clay, a plot device that Maurice Leblanc would steal a few years later in a novel about the equally protean Arsène Lupin. Allen seems to have based Clay's victim, Charles Vandrift, on notorious South African diamond millionaire Barney Barnato, who also inspired Raffles's unscrupulous opponent in a story by E. W. Hornung.

First published in *The Strand Magazine* in July 1896, "The Episode of the Diamond Links" is only the second caper in the series, and occurs not long after the encounter with the Mexican Seer who is mentioned in the story. It is narrated by Vandrift's brother-in-law and secretary.

THE EPISODE OF THE DIAMOND LINKS

"Let us take a trip to Switzerland," said Lady Vandrift. And any one who knows Amelia will not be surprised to learn that we *did* take a trip to Switzerland accordingly. Nobody can drive Sir Charles, except his wife. And nobody at all can drive Amelia.

There were difficulties at the outset, because we had not ordered rooms at the hotels beforehand, and it was well on in the season; but they were overcome at last by the usual application of a golden key; and we found ourselves in due time pleasantly quartered in Lucerne, at the most comfortable of European hostelries, the Schweitzerhof.

We were a square party of four—Sir Charles and Amelia, myself and Isabel. We had nice big rooms, on the first floor, overlooking the lake; and as none of us was possessed with the faintest symptom of that incipient mania which shows itself in the form of an insane desire to climb mountain heights of disagreeable steepness and unnecessary snowiness, I will venture to assert we all enjoyed ourselves. We spent most of our time sensibly in lounging about the lake on the jolly little steamers; and when we did a mountain climb, it was on the Rigi or Pilatus—where an engine undertook all the muscular work for us.

As usual, at the hotel, a great many miscellaneous people showed a burning desire to be specially nice to us. If you wish to see how friendly and charming humanity is, just try being a well-known millionaire for a week, and you'll learn a thing or two. Wherever Sir Charles goes he is surrounded by charming and disinterested people, all eager to make his distinguished acquaintance, and all familiar with several excellent investments, or several deserving objects of Christian charity. It is my

business in life, as his brother-in-law and secretary, to decline
with thanks the excellent investments, and to throw judicious
cold water on the objects of charity. Even I myself, as the great
man's almoner, am very much sought after. People casually
allude before me to artless stories of "poor curates in Cum-
berland, you know, Mr. Wentworth," or widows in Cornwall,
penniless poets with epics in their desks, and young painters
who need but the breath of a patron to open to them the doors
of an admiring Academy. I smile and look wise, while I admin-
ister cold water in minute doses; but I never report one of these
cases to Sir Charles, except in the rare or almost unheard-of
event where I think there is really something in them.

Ever since our little adventure with the Seer at Nice, Sir
Charles, who is constitutionally cautious, has been even more
careful than usual about possible sharpers. And, as chance
would have it, there sat just opposite us at *table d'hôte* at the
Schweitzerhof—'tis a fad of Amelia's to dine at *table d'hôte;*
she says she can't bear to be boxed up all day in private rooms
with "too much family"—a sinister-looking man with dark hair
and eyes, conspicuous by his bushy overhanging eyebrows. My
attention was first called to the eyebrows in question by a nice
little parson who sat at our side, and who observed that they
were made up of certain large and bristly hairs, which (he told
us) had been traced by Darwin to our monkey ancestors. Very
pleasant little fellow, this fresh-faced young parson, on his
honeymoon tour with a nice wee wife, a bonnie Scotch lassie
with a charming accent.

I looked at the eyebrows close. Then a sudden thought
struck me. "Do you believe they're his own?" I asked of the curate; "or are they only stuck on—a make-up disguise? They
really almost look like it."

"You don't suppose——" Charles began, and checked himself suddenly.

"Yes, I do," I answered; "the Seer!" Then I recollected my
blunder, and looked down sheepishly. For, to say the truth,
Vandrift had straightly enjoined on me long before to say nothing of our painful little episode at Nice to Amelia; he was afraid
if *she* once heard of it, *he* would hear of it for ever after.

"What Seer?" the little parson inquired, with parsonical curiosity.

I noticed the man with the overhanging eyebrows give a queer sort of start. Charles's glance was fixed upon me. I hardly knew what to answer.

"Oh, a man who was at Nice with us last year," I stammered out, trying hard to look unconcerned. "A fellow they talked about, that's all." And I turned the subject.

But the curate, like a donkey, wouldn't let me turn it.

"Had he eyebrows like that?" he inquired, in an undertone. I was really angry. If this *was* Colonel Clay, the curate was obviously giving him the cue, and making it much more difficult for us to catch him, now we might possibly have lighted on the chance of doing so.

"No, he hadn't," I answered testily; "it was a passing expression. But this is not the man. I was mistaken, no doubt." And I nudged him gently.

The little curate was too innocent for anything. "Oh, I see," he replied, nodding hard and looking wise. Then he turned to his wife and made an obvious face, which the man with the eyebrows couldn't fail to notice.

Fortunately, a political discussion going on a few places farther down the table spread up to us and diverted attention for a moment. The magical name of Gladstone saved us. Sir Charles flared up. I was truly pleased, for I could see Amelia was boiling over with curiosity by this time.

After dinner, in the billiard-room, however, the man with the big eyebrows sidled up and began to talk to me. If he *was* Colonel Clay, it was evident he bore us no grudge at all for the five thousand pounds he had done us out of. On the contrary, he seemed quite prepared to do us out of five thousand more when opportunity offered; for he introduced himself at once as Dr. Hector Macpherson, the exclusive grantee of extensive concessions from the Brazilian Government on the Upper Amazons. He dived into conversation with me at once as to the splendid mineral resources of his Brazilian estate—the silver, the platinum, the actual rubies, the possible diamonds. I listened and smiled; I knew what was coming. All he needed to develop this magnificent concession was a little more capital. It was sad to see thousands of pounds' worth of platinum and car-loads of rubies just crumbling in the soil or carried away by the river, for want of a few hundreds to work them with properly. If he knew of anybody, now, with money to invest, he could recommend him—nay, offer him—a unique opportunity of earning, say, 40 per cent on his capital, on unimpeachable security.

"I wouldn't do it for every man," Dr. Hector Macpherson remarked, drawing himself up; "but if I took a fancy to a fellow who had command of ready cash, I might choose to put him in the way of feathering his nest with unexampled rapidity."

"Exceedingly disinterested of you," I answered drily, fixing my eyes on his eyebrows.

The little curate, meanwhile, was playing billiards with Sir Charles. His glance followed mine as it rested for a moment on the monkey-like hairs.

"False, obviously false," he remarked with his lips; and I'm bound to confess I never saw any man speak so well by movement alone; you could follow every word though not a sound escaped him.

During the rest of that evening Dr. Hector Macpherson stuck to me close as a mustard-plaster. And he was almost as irritating. I got heartily sick of the Upper Amazons. I have positively waded in my time through ruby mines (in prospectuses, I mean) till the mere sight of a ruby absolutely sickens me. When Charles, in an unwonted fit of generosity, once gave his sister Isabel (whom I had the honour to marry) a ruby necklet (inferior stones), I made Isabel change it for sapphires and amethysts, on the judicious plea that they suited her complexion better. (I scored one, incidentally, for having considered Isabel's complexion.) By the time I went to bed I was prepared to sink the Upper Amazons in the sea, and to stab, shoot, poison, or otherwise seriously damage the man with the concession and the false eyebrows.

For the next three days, at intervals, he returned to the charge. He bored me to death with his platinum and his rubies. He didn't want a capitalist who would personally exploit the thing; he would prefer to do it all on his own account, giving the capitalist peference debentures of his bogus company, and a lien on the concession. I listened and smiled; I listened and yawned; I listened and was rude; I ceased to listen at all; but still he droned on with it. I fell asleep on the steamer one day, and woke up in ten minutes to hear him droning yet, "And the yield of platinum per ton was certified to be——" I forget how many pounds, or ounces, or penny-weights. These details of assays have ceased to interest me: like the man who "didn't believe in ghosts," I have seen too many of them.

The fresh-faced little curate and his wife, however, were quite different people. He was a cricketing Oxford man; she was a breezy Scotch lass, with a wholesome breath of the Highlands about her. I called her "White Heather." Their name was Brabazon. Millionaires are so accustomed to being beset by harpies of every description, that when they come across a young couple who are simple and natural, they delight in the purely human relation. We picnicked and went on excursions a great deal with the honeymooners. They were so frank in their young love, and so proof against chaff, that we all really liked them. But whenever I called the pretty girl "White Heather," she looked so shocked, and cried: "Oh, Mr. Wentworth!" Still, we were the best of friends. The curate offered to row us in a boat on the lake one day, while the Scotch lassie assured us she could take an oar almost as well as he did. However, we did not accept their offer, as row-boats exert an unfavourable influence upon Amelia's digestive organs.

"Nice young fellow, that man Brabazon," Sir Charles said to me one day, as we lounged together along the quay; "never talks about advowsons or next presentations. Doesn't seem to me to care two pins about promotion. Says he's quite content in his country curacy; enough to live upon, and needs no more; and his wife has a little, a very little, money. I asked him about his poor to-day, on purpose to test him: these parsons are always trying to screw something out of one for their poor; men in my position know the truth of the saying that we have that class of the population always with us. Would you believe it, he says he hasn't any poor at all in his parish! They're all well-to-do farmers or else able-bodied labourers, and his one terror is that somebody will come and try to pauperise them. 'If a philanthropist were to give me fifty pounds to-day for use at Empingham,' he said, 'I assure you, Sir Charles, I shouldn't know what to do with it. I think I should buy new dresses for Jessie, who wants them about as much as anybody else in the village—that is to say, not at all.' There's a parson for you, Sey, my boy. Only wish we had one of his sort at Seldon."

"He certainly doesn't want to get anything out of you," I answered.

That evening at dinner a queer little episode happened. The man with the eyebrows began talking to me across the table in his usual fashion, full of his wearisome concession on the Upper Amazons. I was trying to squash him as politely as possible, when I caught Amelia's eye. Her look amused me. She was engaged in making signals to Charles at her side to observe the little curate's curious sleeve-links. I glanced at them, and saw at once they were a singular possession for so unobtrusive a person. They consisted each of a short gold bar for one arm of the link, fastened by a tiny chain of the same material to what seemed to my tolerably experienced eye—a first-rate diamond. Pretty big diamonds, too, and of remarkable shape, brilliancy, and cutting. In a moment I knew what Amelia meant. She owned a diamond *rivière,* said to be of Indian origin, but short by two stones for the circumference of her tolerably ample neck. Now, she had long been wanting two diamonds like these to match her set; but owing to the unusual shape and antiquated cutting of her own gems, she had never been able to complete the necklet, at least without removing an extravagant amount from a much larger stone of the first water.

The Scotch lassie's eyes caught Amelia's at the same time, and she broke into a pretty smile of good-humoured amusement. "Taken in another person, Dick, dear!" she exclaimed, in her breezy way, turning to her husband. "Lady Vandrift is observing your diamond sleeve-links."

"They're very fine gems," Amelia observed incautiously. (A most unwise admission if she desired to buy them.)

But the pleasant little curate was too transparently simple a soul to take advantage of her slip of judgment. "They *are* good stones," he replied; "very good stones—considering. They're not diamonds at all, to tell you the truth. They're best old-fashioned Oriental paste. My great-grandfather bought them, after the siege of Seringapatam, for a few rupees, from a Sepoy who had looted them from Tippoo Sultan's palace. He thought, like you, he had got a good thing. But it turned out, when they came to be examined by experts, they were only paste—very wonderful paste; it is supposed they had even imposed upon Tippoo himself, so fine is the imitation. But they are worth—well, say, fifty shillings at the utmost."

While he spoke Charles looked at Amelia, and Amelia looked at Charles. Their eyes spoke volumes. The *rivière* was also supposed to have come from Tippoo's collection. Both drew at once an identical conclusion. These were two of the same stones, very likely torn apart and disengaged from the rest in the *mêlée* at the capture of the Indian palace.

"Can you take them off?" Sir Charles asked blandly. He spoke in the tone that indicates business.

"Certainly," the little curate answered, smiling. "I'm accustomed to taking them off. They're always noticed. They've been kept in the family ever since the siege, as a sort of valueless heirloom, for the sake of the picturesqueness of the story, you know; and nobody ever sees them without asking, as you do, to examine them closely. They deceive even experts at first. But they're paste, all the same; unmitigated Oriental paste, for all that."

He took them both off, and handed them to Charles. No man in England is a finer judge of gems than my brother-in-law. I watched him narrowly. He examined them close, first with the naked eye, then with the little pocket-lens which he always carries. "Admirable imitation," he muttered, passing them on to Amelia. "I'm not surprised they should impose upon inexperienced observers."

But from the tone in which he said it, I could see at once he had satisfied himself they were real gems of unusual value. I know Charles's way of doing business so well. His glance to

Amelia meant, "These are the very stones you have so long been in search of."

The Scotch lassie laughed a merry laugh. "He sees through them now, Dick," she cried. "I felt sure Sir Charles would be a judge of diamonds."

Amelia turned them over. I know Amelia, too; and I knew from the way Amelia looked at them that she meant to have them. And when Amelia means to have anything, people who stand in the way may just as well spare themselves the trouble of opposing her.

They were beautiful diamonds. We found out afterwards the little curate's account was quite correct: these stones *had* come from the same necklet as Amelia's *rivière*, made for a favourite wife of Tippoo's, who had presumably as expansive personal charms as our beloved sister-in-law's. More perfect diamonds have seldom been seen. They have excited the universal admiration of thieves and connoisseurs. Amelia told me afterwards that, according to legend, a Sepoy stole the necklet at the sack of the palace, and then fought with another for it. It was believed that two stones got split in the scuffle, and were picked up and sold by a third person—a looker-on—who had no idea of the value of his booty. Amelia had been hunting for them for several years to complete her necklet.

"They are excellent paste," Sir Charles observed, handing them back. "It takes a first-rate judge to detect them from the reality. Lady Vandrift has a necklet much the same in character, but composed of genuine stones; and as these are so much like them, and would complete her set, to all outer appearance, I wouldn't mind giving you, say, £10 for the pair of them."

Mrs. Brabazon looked delighted. "Oh, sell them to him, Dick," she cried, "and buy me a brooch with the money! A pair of common links would do for you just as well. Ten pounds for two paste stones! It's quite a lot of money."

She said it so sweetly, with her pretty Scotch accent, that I couldn't imagine how Dick had the heart to refuse her. But he did, all the same.

"No, Jess, darling," he answered. "They're worthless, I know; but they have for me a certain sentimental value, as I've often told you. My dear mother wore them, while she lived, as earrings; and as soon as she died I had them set as links in order that I might always keep them about me. Besides, they have historical and family interest. Even a worthless heirloom, after all, *is* an heirloom."

Dr. Hector Macpherson looked across and intervened. "There is a part of my concession," he said, "where we have reason to believe a perfect new Kimberley will soon be discovered. If at any time you would care, Sir Charles, to look at my diamonds—when I get them—it would afford me the greatest pleasure in life to submit them to your consideration."

Sir Charles could stand it no longer. "Sir," he said, gazing across at him with his sternest air, "if your concession were as full of diamonds as Sindbad the Sailor's valley, I would not care to turn my head to look at them. I am acquainted with the nature and practice of salting." And he glared at the man with the overhanging eyebrows as if he would devour him raw. Poor Dr. Hector Macpherson subsided instantly. We learnt a little later that he was a harmless lunatic, who went about the world with successive concessions for ruby mines and platinum reefs, because he had been ruined and driven mad by speculations in the two, and now recouped himself by imaginary grants in Burmah and Brazil, or anywhere else that turned up handy. And his eyebrows, after all, were of Nature's handicraft. We were sorry for the incident; but a man in Sir Charles's position is such a mark for rogues that, if he did not take means to protect himself promptly, he would be for ever overrun by them.

When we went up to our *salon* that evening, Amelia flung herself on the sofa. "Charles," she broke out in the voice of a tragedy queen, "those are real diamonds, and I shall never be happy again till I get them."

"They are real diamonds," Charles echoed. "And you shall have them, Amelia. They're worth not less than three thousand pounds. But I shall bid them up gently."

So, next day, Charles set to work to higgle with the curate. Brabazon, however, didn't care to part with them. He was no money-grubber, he said. He cared more for his mother's gift and a family tradition than for a hundred pounds, if Sir Charles

were to offer it. Charles's eye gleamed. "But if I give you *two*
hundred!" he said insinuatingly. "What opportunities for good!
You could build a new wing to your village school-house!"

"We have ample accommodation," the curate answered. "No,
I don't think I'll sell them."

Still, his voice faltered somewhat, and he looked down at
them inquiringly.

Charles was too precipitate.

"A hundred pounds more or less matters little to me," he
said; "and my wife has set her heart on them. It's every man's
duty to please his wife—isn't it, Mrs. Brabazon?—I offer you
three hundred."

The little Scotch girl clasped her hands.

"Three hundred pounds! Oh, Dick, just think what fun we
could have, and what good we could do with it! Do let him
have them."

Her accent was irrestible. But the curate shook his head.

"Impossible," he answered. "My dear mother's ear-rings!
Uncle Aubrey would be so angry if he knew I'd sold them. I
daren't face Uncle Aubrey."

"Has he expectations from Uncle Aubrey?" Sir Charles asked
of White Heather.

Mrs. Brabazon laughed. "Uncle Aubrey! Oh, dear, no. Poor
dear old Uncle Aubrey! Why, the darling old soul hasn't a
penny to bless himself with, except his pension. He's a retired
post captain." And she laughed melodiously. She was a charming woman.

"Then I should disregard Uncle Aubrey's feelings," Sir Charles
said decisively.

"No, no," the curate answered. "Poor dear old Uncle
Aubrey! I wouldn't do anything for the world to annoy him.
And he'd be sure to notice it."

We went back to Amelia. "Well, have you got them?" she
asked.

"No," Sir Charles answered. "Not yet. But he's coming round,
I think. He's hesitating now. Would rather like to sell them himself, but is afraid what 'Uncle Aubrey' would say about the
matter. His wife will talk him out of his needless consideration

for Uncle Aubrey's feelings; and to-morrow we'll finally clench the bargain."

Next morning we stayed late in our *salon,* where we always breakfasted, and did not come down to the public rooms till just before *déjeûner,* Sir Charles being busy with me over arrears of correspondence. When we *did* come down the *concierge* stepped forward with a twisted little feminine note for Amelia. She took it and read it. Her countenance fell. "There, Charles," she cried, handing it to him, "you've let the chance slip. I shall *never* be happy now! They've gone off with the diamonds."

Charles seized the note and read it. Then he passed it on to me. It was short, but final:—

> "*Thursday,* 6 *a.m.*
>
> "DEAR LADY VANDRIFT—*Will* you kindly excuse our having gone off hurriedly without bidding you good-bye? We have just had a horrid telegram to say that Dick's favourite sister is *dangerously* ill of fever in Paris. I wanted to shake hands with you before we left—you have all been so sweet to us—but we go by the morning train, absurdly early, and I wouldn't for worlds disturb you. Perhaps some day we may meet again—though, buried as we are in a North-country village, it isn't likely; but in any case, you have secured the grateful recollection of
> Yours very cordially,   JESSIE BRABAZON.
>
> "P.S.—Kindest regards to Sir Charles and those *dear* Wentworths, and a kiss for yourself, if I may venture to send you one."

"She doesn't even mention where they've gone," Amelia exclaimed, in a very bad humour.

"The *concierge* may know," Isabel suggested, looking over my shoulder.

We asked at his office.

Yes, the gentleman's address was the Rev. Richard Peploc Brabazon, Holme Bush Cottage, Empingham, Northumberland.

Any address where letters might be sent at once, in Paris?

For the next ten days, or till further notice, Hôtel des Deux Mondes, Avenue de l'Opéra.

Amelia's mind was made up at once.

"Strike while the iron's hot," she cried. "This sudden illness, coming at the end of their honeymoon, and involving ten days' more stay at an expensive hotel, will probably upset the curate's budget. He'll be glad to sell now. You'll get them for three hundred. It was absurd of Charles to offer so much at first; but offered once, of course we must stick to it."

"What do you propose to do?" Charles asked. "Write, or telegraph?"

"Oh, how silly men are!" Amelia cried. "Is this the sort of business to be arranged by letter, still less by telegram? No. Seymour must start off at once, taking the night train to Paris; and the moment he gets there, he must interview the curate or Mrs. Brabazon. Mrs. Brabazon's the best. She has none of this stupid, sentimental nonsense about Uncle Aubrey."

It is no part of a secretary's duties to act as a diamond broker. But when Amelia puts her foot down, she puts her foot down—a fact which she is unnecessarily fond of emphasising in that identical proposition. So the self-same evening saw me safe in the train on my way to Paris; and next morning I turned out of my comfortable sleeping-car at the Gare de Strasbourg. My orders were to bring back those diamonds, alive or dead, so to speak, in my pocket to Lucerne; and to offer any needful sum, up to two thousand five hundred pounds, for their immediate purchase.

When I arrived at the Deux Mondes I found the poor little curate and his wife both greatly agitated. They had sat up all night, they said, with their invalid sister; and the sleeplessness and suspense had certainly told upon them after their long railway journey. They were pale and tired, Mrs. Brabazon, in particular, looking ill and worried—too much like White Heather. I was more than half ashamed of bothering them about the diamonds at such a moment, but it occurred to me that Amelia was probably right—they would now have reached the end of the sum set apart for their Continental trip, and a little ready cash might be far from unwelcome.

I broached the subject delicately. It was a fad of Lady Vandrift's, I said. She had set her heart upon those useless trinkets.

And she wouldn't go without them. She must and would have them. But the curate was obdurate. He threw Uncle Aubrey still in my teeth. Three hundred?—no, never! A mother's present; impossible, dear Jessie! Jessie begged and prayed; she had grown really attached to Lady Vandrift, she said; but the curate wouldn't hear of it. I went up tentatively to four hundred. He shook his head gloomily. It wasn't a question of money, he said. It was a question of affection. I saw it was no use trying that tack any longer. I struck out a new line. "These stones," I said, "I think I ought to inform you, are really diamonds. Sir Charles is certain of it. Now, is it right for a man of your profession and position to be wearing a pair of big gems like those, worth several hundred pounds, as ordinary sleeve-links? A woman?—yes, I grant you. But for a man, is it manly? And you a cricketer!"

He looked at me and laughed. "Will nothing convince you?" he cried. "They have been examined and tested by half a dozen jewellers, and we know them to be paste. It wouldn't be right of me to sell them to you under false pretences, however unwilling on my side. I *couldn't* do it."

"Well, then," I said, going up a bit in my bids to meet him, "I'll put it like this. These gems are paste. But Lady Vandrift has an unconquerable and unaccountable desire to possess them. Money doesn't matter to her. She is a friend of your wife's. As a personal favour, won't you sell them to her for a thousand?"

He shook his head. "It would be wrong," he said,—"I might even add, criminal."

"But we take all risk," I cried.

He was absolute adamant. "As a clergyman," he answered, "I feel I cannot do it."

"Will *you* try, Mrs. Brabazon?" I asked.

The pretty little Scotchwoman leant over and whispered. She coaxed and cajoled him. Her ways were winsome. I couldn't hear what she said, but he seemed to give way at last. "I should love Lady Vandrift to have them," she murmured, turning to me. "She *is* such a dear!" And she took out the links from her husband's cuffs and handed them across to me.

"How much?" I asked.

"Two thousand?" she answered, interrogatively. It was a big rise, all at once; but such are the ways of women.

"Done!" I replied. "Do you consent?"

The curate looked up as if ashamed of himself.

"I consent," he said slowly, "since Jessie wishes it. But as a clergyman, and to prevent any future misunderstanding, I should like you to give me a statement in writing that you buy them on my distinct and positive declaration that they are made of paste—old Oriental paste—not genuine stones, and that I do not claim any other qualities for them."

I popped the gems into my purse, well pleased.

"Certainly," I said, pulling out a paper. Charles, with his unerring business instinct, had anticipated the request, and given me a signed agreement to that effect.

"You will take a cheque?" I inquired.

He hesitated.

"Notes of the Bank of France would suit me better," he answered.

"Very well," I replied. "I will go out and get them."

How very unsuspicious some people are! He allowed me to go off—with the stones in my pocket!

Sir Charles had given me a blank cheque, not exceeding two thousand five hundred pounds. I took it to our agents and cashed it for notes of the Bank of France. The curate clasped them with pleasure. And right glad I was to go back to Lucerne that night, feeling that I had got those diamonds into my hands for about a thousand pounds under their real value!

At Lucerne railway station Amelia met me. She was positively agitated.

"Have you bought them, Seymour?" she asked.

"Yes," I answered, producing my spoils in triumph.

"Oh, how dreadful!" she cried, drawing back. "Do you think they're real? Are you sure he hasn't cheated you?"

"Certain of it," I replied, examining them. "No one can take me in, in the matter of diamonds. Why on earth should you doubt them?"

"Because I've been talking to Mrs. O'Hagan, at the hotel, and she says there's a well-known trick just like that—she's read of it in a book. A swindler has two sets—one real, one false; and he makes you buy the false ones by showing you the real, and pretending he sells them as a special favour."

"You needn't be alarmed," I answered. "I am a judge of diamonds."

"I shan't be satisfied," Amelia murmured, 'till Charles has seen them."

We went up to the hotel. For the first time in her life I saw Amelia really nervous as I handed the stones to Charles to examine. Her doubt was contagious. I half feared, myself, he might break out into a deep monosyllabic interjection, losing his temper in haste, as he often does when things go wrong. But he looked at them with a smile, while I told him the price.

"Eight hundred pounds less than their value," he answered, well satisfied.

"You have no doubt of their reality?" I asked.

"Not the slightest," he replied, gazing at them. "They are genuine stones, precisely the same in quality and type as Amelia's necklet."

Amelia drew a sigh of relief. "I'll go upstairs," she said slowly, "and bring down my own for you both to compare with them."

One minute later she rushed down again, breathless. Amelia is far from slim, and I never before knew her exert herself so actively.

"Charles, Charles!" she cried, "do you know what dreadful thing has happened? Two of my own stones are gone. He's stolen a couple of diamonds from my necklet, and sold them back to me."

She held out the *rivière*. It was all too true. Two gems were missing—and these two just fitted the empty places!

A light broke in upon me. I clapped my hand to my head. "By Jove," I exclaimed, "the little curate is—Colonel Clay!"

Charles clapped his own hand to his brow in turn. "And Jessie," he cried, "White Heather—that innocent little Scotchwoman! I often detected a familiar ring in her voice, in spite of the charming Highland accent. Jessie is—Madame Picardet!"

We had absolutely no evidence; but, like the Commissary at Nice, we felt instinctively sure of it.

Sir Charles was determined to catch the rogue. This second deception put him on his mettle. "The worst of the man is," he said, "he has a method. He doesn't go out of his way to cheat us; he makes us go out of ours to be cheated. He lays a trap, and we tumble headlong into it. To-morrow, Sey, we must follow him on to Paris."

Amelia explained to him what Mrs. O'Hagan had said. Charles took it all in at once, with his usual sagacity. "That explains," he said, "why the rascal used this particular trick to draw us on by. If we had suspected him he could have shown the diamonds were real, and so escaped detection. It was a blind to draw us off from the fact of the robbery. He went to Paris to be out of the way when the discovery was made, and to get a clear day's start of us. What a consummate rogue! And to do me twice running!"

"How did he get at my jewel-case, though?" Amelia exclaimed.

"That's the question," Charles answered. "You *do* leave it about so!"

"And why didn't he steal the whole *rivière* at once, and sell the gems?" I inquired.

"Too cunning," Charles replied. "This was much better business. It isn't easy to dispose of a big thing like that. In the first place, the stones are large and valuable; in the second place, they're well known—every dealer has heard of the Vandrift *rivière,* and seen pictures of the shape of them. They're marked gems, so to speak. No, he played a better game—took a couple of them off, and offered them to the only one person on earth who was likely to buy them without suspicion. He came here, meaning to work this very trick; he had the links made right to the shape beforehand, and then he stole the stones and slipped them into their places. It's a wonderfully clever trick. Upon my soul, I almost admire the fellow."

For Charles is a business man himself, and can appreciate business capacity in others.

How Colonel Clay came to know about that necklet, and to appropriate two of the stones, we only discovered much later. I will not here anticipate that disclosure. One thing at a time is a good rule in life. For the moment he succeeded in baffling us altogether.

However, we followed him on to Paris, telegraphing beforehand to the Bank of France to stop the notes. It was all in vain. They had been cashed within half an hour of my paying them. The curate and his wife, we found, quitted the Hôtel des Deux Mondes for parts unknown that same afternoon. And, as usual with Colonel Clay, they vanished into space, leaving no clue behind them. In other words, they changed their disguise, no doubt, and reappeared somewhere else that night in altered characters. At any rate, no such person as the Reverend Richard Peploe Brabazon was ever afterwards heard of—and, for the matter of that, no such village exists as Empingham, Northumberland.

We communicated the matter to the Parisian police. They were *most* unsympathetic. "It is no doubt Colonel Clay," said the official whom we saw; "but you seem to have little just ground of complaint against him. As far as I can see, messieurs, there is not much to choose between you. You, Monsieur le Chevalier, desired to buy diamonds at the price of paste. You, madame, feared you had bought paste at the price of diamonds. You, monsieur the secretary, tried to get the stones from an unsuspecting person for half their value. He took you all in, that brave Colonel Caoutchouc—it was diamond cut diamond."

Which was true, no doubt, but by no means consoling.

We returned to the Grand Hotel. Charles was fuming with indignation. "This is really too much," he exclaimed. "What an audacious rascal! But he will never again take me in, my dear Sey. I only hope he'll try it on. I should love to catch him. I'd know him another time, I'm sure, in spite of his disguises. It's absurd my being tricked twice running like this. But never again while I live! Never again, I declare to you!"

"Jamais de la vie!" a courier in the hall close by murmured responsive. We stood under the verandah of the Grand Hotel, in the big glass courtyard. And I verily believe that courier was really Colonel Clay himself in one of his disguises.

But perhaps we were beginning to suspect him everywhere.

GUY BOOTHBY

Guy Boothby's character Simon Carne was the first memorable "gentleman thief," a title for which Grant Allen's Colonel Clay was not born in the right circumstances to qualify. Carne is well bred, independently wealthy, and on equal footing with aristocrats and international diplomats. His peers fall prey to his charm, for he is both con artist and burglar—as well as, of course, a master of disguise. Carne might have dined with other such characters in this volume, including Arnold Bennett's millionaire Cecil Thorold, but he would never have crossed paths with, say, O. Henry's rustic con men.

Like Grant Allen, Guy Newell Boothby immigrated from the colonies to make his mark in England. The grandson of a judge and the son of an assemblyman, he was born in Adelaide, on Australia's southern coast. One of his earliest jobs was serving as secretary to the mayor of the city. In 1890, while in his early twenties, he joined with musician Cecil James Sharp, who was later renowned as a music folklorist, and wrote the libretto for a comic opera. He also performed opera himself. Over the next few years he traveled across the island continent with his brother, including a journey from Cooktown, on the northeast coast, back down to Adelaide, and in 1894 published an account of the trips in his first book, *On the Wallaby*. Travel remained a favorite preoccupation.

Following the success of his first novel at about the same time, he moved to London and devoted himself to writing. Between 1895 and 1901 he published five shamelessly melodramatic novels about Dr. Nikola, a sinister criminal mastermind in the Professor

Moriarty mode, spiced with a dash of Fu Manchu. Boothby died of pneumonia at the young age of thirty-seven, leaving behind a wife and three children. During his brief life, he wrote more than fifty books.

The first Simon Carne story, "The Duchess of Wiltshire's Diamonds," appeared in the February 1897 issue of *Pearson's Magazine,* under the series title "A Prince of Swindlers," which the next year also became the title of the collected adventures.

THE DUCHESS OF WILTSHIRE'S DIAMONDS

To the reflective mind the rapidity with which the inhabitants of the world's greatest city seize upon a new name or idea, and familiarize themselves with it, can scarecely prove otherwise than astonishing. As an illustraton of my meaning let me take the case of Klimo—the now famous private detective, who has won for himself the right to be considered as great as Lecocq, or even the late lamented Sherlock Holmes.

Up to a certain morning London had never even heard his name, nor had it the remotest notion as to who or what he might be. It was as sublimely ignorant and careless on the subject as the inhabitants of Kamtchatka or Peru. Within twenty-four hours, however, the whole aspect of the case was changed. The man, woman, or child who had not seen his posters, or heard his name, was counted an ignoramous unworthy of intercourse with human beings.

Princes became familiar with it as their trains bore them to Windsor to luncheon with the Queen; the nobility noticed and commented upon it as they drove about the town; merchants, and business men generally, read it as they made their ways by omnibus or underground, to their various shops and counting-houses; street boys called each other by it as a nickname; music hall artists introduced it into their patter, while it was even rumoured that the Stock Exchange itself had paused in the full flood tide of business to manufacture a riddle on the subject.

That Klimo made his profession pay him well was certain, first from the fact that his advertisements must have cost a good round sum, and, second, because he had taken a mansion in Belverton Street, Park Lane, next door to Porchester House, where, to the dismay of that aristocratic neighbourhood, he advertised that he was prepared to receive and be consulted by his clients. The invitation was responded to with alacrity, and from that day forward, between the hours of twelve and two, the pavement upon the north side of the street was lined with carriages, every one containing some person desirous of testing the great man's skill.

I must here explain that I have narrated all this in order to show the state of affairs in Belverton Street and Park Lane when Simon Carne arrived, or was supposed to arrive, in England. If my memory serves me correctly, it was on Wednesday, the 3rd of May, that the Earl of Amberley drove to Victoria to meet and welcome the man whose acquaintance he had made in India under such peculiar circumstances, and under the spell of whose fascination he and his family had fallen so completely.

Reaching the station, his lordship descended from his carriage, and made his way to the platform set apart for the reception of the Continental express. He walked with a jaunty air, and seemed to be on the best of terms with himself and the world in general. How little he suspected the existence of the noose into which he was so innocently running his head!

As if out of compliment to his arrival, the train put in an appearance within a few moments of his reaching the platform. He immediately placed himself in such a position that he could make sure of seeing the man he wanted, and waited patiently until he should come in sight. Carne, however, was not among the first batch; indeed, the majority of passengers had passed before his lordship caught sight of him.

One thing was very certain, however great the crush might have been, it would have been difficult to mistake Carne's figure. The man's infirmity and the peculiar beauty of his face rendered him easily recognisable. Possibly, after his long sojourn in India, he found the morning cold, for he wore a long fur coat, the collar of which he had turned up round his ears, thus making a fitting frame for his delicate face. On seeing Lord Amberly he hastened forward to greet him.

"This is most kind and friendly of you," he said, as he shook the other by the hand. "A fine day and Lord Amberley to meet me. One could scarcely imagine a better welcome."

As he spoke, one of his Indian servants approached and salaamed before him. He gave him an order, and received an answer in Hindustani, whereupon he turned again to Lord Amberley.

"You may imagine how anxious I am to see my new dwelling," he said. "My servant tells me that my carriage is here, so may I hope that you will drive back with me and see for yourself how I am likely to be lodged?"

"I shall be delighted," said Lord Amberley, who was longing for the opportunity, and they accordingly went out into the station yard together to discover a brougham, drawn by two magnificent horses, and with Nur Ali, in all the glory of white raiment and crested turban, on the box, waiting to receive them. His lordship dismissed his Victoria, and when Jowur Singh had taken his place beside his fellow servant upon the box, the carriage rolled out of the station yard in the direction of Hyde Park.

"I trust her ladyship is quite well," said Simon Carne politely, as they turned into Gloucester Place.

"Excellently well, thank you," replied his lordship. "She bade me welcome you to England in her name as well as my own, and I was to say that she is looking forward to seeing you."

"She is most kind, and I shall do myself the honour of calling upon her as soon as circumstances will permit," answered Carne. "I beg you will convey my best thanks to her for her thought of me."

While these polite speeches were passing between them they were rapidly approaching a large hoarding, on which was displayed a poster setting forth the name of the now famous detective, Klimo.

Simon Carne, leaning forward, studied it, and when they had passed, turned to his friend again.

"At Victoria and on all the hoardings we meet I see an enormous placard, bearing the word 'Klimo.' Pray, what does it mean?"

His lordship laughed.

"You are asking a question which, a month ago, was on the lips of nine out of every ten Londoners. It is only within the last fortnight that we have learned who and what 'Klimo' is."

"And pray what is he?"

"Well, the explanation is very simple. He is neither more nor less than a remarkably astute private detective, who has succeeded in attracting notice in such a way that half London has been induced to patronize him. I have had no dealings with the man myself. But a friend of mine, Lord Orpington, has been the victim of a most audacious burglary, and, the police having failed to solve the mystery, he has called Klimo in. We shall therefore see what he can do before many days are past. But, there, I expect you will soon know more about him than any of us."

"Indeed! And why?"

"For the simple reason that he has taken No. 1, Belverton Terrace, the house adjoining your own, and sees his clients there."

Simon Carne pursed up his lips, and appeared to be considering something.

"I trust he will not prove a nuisance," he said at last. "The agents who found me the house should have acquainted me with the fact. Private detectives, on however large a scale, scarcely strike one as the most desirable of neighbours—particularly for a man who is so fond of quiet as myself."

At this moment they were approaching their destination. As the carriage passed Belverton Street and pulled up, Lord Amberley pointed to a long line of vehicles standing before the detective's door.

"You can see for yourself something of the business he does," he said. "Those are the carriages of his clients, and it is probable that twice as many have arrived on foot."

"I shall certainly speak to the agent on the subject," said Carne, with a shadow of annoyance upon his face. "I consider the fact of this man's being so close to me a serious drawback to the house."

Jowur Singh here descended from the box and opened the door in order that his master and guest might alight, while portly

Ram Gafur, the butler, came down the steps and salaamed before them with Oriental obsequiousness. Carne greeted his domestics with kindly condescension, and then, accompanied by the ex-Viceroy, entered his new abode.

"I think you may congatulate yourself upon having secured one of the most desirable residences in London," said his lordship ten minutes or so later, when they had explored the principal rooms.

"I am very glad to hear you say so," said Carne. "I trust your lordship will remember that you will always be welcome in the house as long as I am its owner."

"It is very kind of you to say so," returned Lord Amberley warmly. "I shall look forward to some months of pleasant intercourse. And now I must be going. Tomorrow, perhaps, if you have nothing better to do, you will give us the pleasure of your company at dinner. Your fame has already gone abroad, and we shall ask one or two nice people to meet you, including my brother and sister-in-law, Lord and Lady Gelpington, Lord and Lady Orpington, and my cousin, the Duchess of Wiltshire, whose interest in china and Indian art, as perhaps you know, is only second to your own."

"I shall be most glad to come."

"We may count on seeing you in Eaton Square, then, at eight o'clock?"

"If I am alive you may be sure I shall be there. Must you really go? Then good-bye, and many thanks for meeting me."

His lordship having left the house, Simon Carne went upstairs to his dressing-room, which it was to be noticed he found without inquiry, and rang the electric bell, beside the fireplace, three times. While he was waiting for it to be answered he stood looking out of the window at the long line of carriages in the street below.

"Everything is progressing admirably," he said to himself. "Amberley does not suspect any more than the world in general. As a proof he asks me to dinner tomorrow evening to meet his brother and sister-in-law, two of his particular friends, and above all Her Grace of Wiltshire."

At this moment the door opened, and his valet, the grave and respectable Belton, entered the room. Carne turned to greet him impatiently.

"Come, come, Belton," he said, "we must be quick. It is twenty minutes to twelve, and if we don't hurry, the folk next door will become impatient. Have you succeeded in doing what I spoke to you about last night?"

"I have done everything, sir."

"I am glad to hear it. Now lock that door and let us get to work. You can let me have your news while I am dressing."

Opening one side of a massive wardrobe, that completely filled one end of the room, Belton took from it a number of garments. They included a well-worn velvet coat, a baggy pair of trousers—so old that only a notorious pauper or a millionaire could have afforded to wear them—a flannel waistcoat, a Gladstone collar, a soft silk tie, and a pair of embroidered carpet slippers upon which no old clothes man in the most reckless way of business in Petticoat Lane would have advanced a single halfpenny. Into these he assisted his master to change.

"Now give me the wig, and unfasten the straps of this hump," said Carne, as the other placed the garments just referred to upon a neighbouring chair.

Belton did as he was ordered, and then there happened a thing the like of which no one would have believed. Having unbuckled a strap on either shoulder, and slipped his hand beneath the waistcoat, he withdrew a large *papier-mâché* hump, which he carried away and carefully placed in a drawer of the bureau. Relieved of his burden, Simon Carne stood up as straight and well-made a man as any in Her Majesty's dominions. The malformation, for which so many, including the Earl and Countess of Amberley, had often pitied him, was nothing but a hoax intended to produce an effect which would permit him additional facilities of disguise.

The hump discarded, and the grey wig fitted carefully to his head in such a manner that not even a pinch of his own curly locks could be seen beneath it, he adorned his cheeks with a pair of *crépu*-hair whiskers, donned the flannel vest and the velvet coat previously mentioned, slipped his feet in the carpet slippers, placed a pair of smoked glasses upon his nose, and declared himself ready to proceed about his business. The man who would have known him for Simon Carne would have been as astute as, well, shall we say, as the private detective—Klimo himself.

"It's on the stroke of twelve," he said, as he gave a final glance at himself in the pier-glass above the dressing-table, and arranged his tie to his satisfaction. "Should any one call, instruct Ram Gafur to tell them that I have gone out on business, and shall not be back until three o'clock."

"Very good, sir."

"Now undo the door and let me go in."

Thus commanded, Belton went across to the large wardrobe which, as I have already said, covered the whole of one side of the room, and opened the middle door. Two or three garments were seen inside suspended on pegs, and these he removed, at the same time pushing towards the right the panel at the rear. When this was done a large aperture in the wall between the two houses was disclosed. Through this door Carne passed, drawing it behind him.

In No. 1, Belverton Terrace, the house occupied by the detective, whose presence in the street Carne seemed to find so objectionable, the entrance thus constructed was covered by the peculiar kind of confessional box in which Klimo invariably sat to receive his clients, the rearmost panels of which opened in the same fashion as those in the wardrobe in the dressing-room. These being pulled aside, he had but to draw them to again after him, take his seat, ring the electric bell to inform his house-keeper that he was ready, and then welcome his clients as quickly as they cared to come.

Punctually at two o'clock the interviews ceased, and Klimo, having reaped an excellent harvest of fees, returned to Porchester House to become Simon Carne once more.

Possibly it was due to the fact that the Earl and Countess of Amberley were brimming over with his praise, or it may have been the rumour that he was worth as many millions as you have fingers upon your hand that did it; one thing, however, was self evident, within twenty-four hours of the noble earl's meeting him at Victoria Station, Simon Carne was the talk, not only fashionable, but also of unfashionable London.

That his household were, with one exception, natives of India, that he had paid a rental for Porchester House which ran into five figures, that he was the greatest living authority upon china and Indian art generally, and that he had come over to England in search of a wife, were among the smallest of the *canards* set afloat concerning him.

During dinner next evening Carne put forth every effort to please. He was placed on the right hand of his hostess and next to the Duchess of Wiltshire. To the latter he paid particular attention, and to such good purpose that when the ladies returned to the drawing-room afterwards, Her Grace was full of his praises. They had discussed china of all sorts, Carne had promised her a specimen which she had longed for all her life, but had never been able to obtain, and in return she had promised to show him the quaintly carved Indian casket in which the famous necklace, of which he had, of course, heard, spent most of its time. She would be wearing the jewels in question at her own ball in a week's time, she informed him, and if he would care to see the case when it came from her bankers on that day, she would be only too pleased to show it to him.

As Simon Carne drove home in his luxurious brougham afterwards, he smiled to himself as he thought of the success which was attending his first endeavour. Two of the guests, who were stewards of the Jockey Club, had heard with delight his idea of purchasing a horse, in order to have an interest in the Derby. While another, on hearing that he desired to become the possessor of a yacht, had offered to propose him for the R.C.Y.C. To crown it all, however, and much better than all, the Duchess of Wiltshire had promised to show him her famous diamonds.

"But satisfactory as my progress has been hitherto," he said to himself, "it is difficult to see how I am to get possession of the stones. From what I have been able to discover, they are only brought from the bank on the day the Duchess intends to wear them, and they are taken back by His Grace the morning following.

"While she has got them on her person it would be mani-
festly impossible to get them from her. And as, when she takes
them off, they are returned to their box and placed in a safe,
constructed in the wall of the bedroom adjoining, and which
for the occasion is occupied by the butler and one of the under
footmen, the only key being in the possession of the Duke himself, it would be equally foolish to hope to appropriate them. In
what manner, therefore, I am to become their possessor passes
my comprehension. However, one thing is certain, obtained
they must be, and the attempt must be made on the night of the
ball if possible. In the meantime I'll set my wits to work upon a
plan."

Next day Simon Carne was the recipient of an invitation to
the ball in question, and two days later he called upon the
Duchess of Wiltshire, at her residence in Belgrave Square, with
a plan prepared. He also took with him the small vase he had
promised her four nights before. She received him most gra-
ciously, and their talk fell at once into the usual channel. Having examined her collection, and charmed her by means of one
or two judicious criticisms, he asked permission to include
photographs of certain of her treasures in his forthcoming
book, then little by little he skilfully guided the conversation on
to the subject of jewels.

"Since we are discussing gems, Mr. Carne," she said, "perhaps
it would interest you to see my famous necklace. By good fortune I have it in the house now, for the reason that an alteration
is being made to one of the clasps by my jewellers."

"I should like to see it immensely," answered Carne. "At one
time and another I have had the good fortune to examine the
jewels of the leading Indian princes, and I should like to be able
to say that I have seen the famous Wiltshire necklace."

"Then you shall certainly have the honour," she answered
with a smile. "If you will ring that bell I will send for it."

Carne rang the bell as requested, and when the butler entered he was given the key of the safe and ordered to bring the
case to the drawing-room.

"We must not keep it very long," she observed while the man
was absent. "It is to be returned to the bank in an hour's time."

"I am indeed fortunate," Carne replied, and turned to the description of some curious Indian wood carving, of which he was making a special feature in his book. As he explained, he had collected his illustrations from the doors of Indian temples, from the gateways of palaces, from old brass work, and even from carved chairs and boxes he had picked up all sorts of odd corners. Her Grace was most interested.

"How strange that you should have mentioned it," she said. "If carved boxes have any interest for you, it is possible my jewel case itself may be of use to you. As I think I told you during Lady Amberley's dinner, it came from Benares, and has carved upon it the portraits of nearly every god in the Hindu Pantheon."

"You raise my curiosity to fever heat," said Carne.

A few moments later the servant returned, bringing with him a wooden box, about sixteen inches long, by twelve wide, and eight deep, which he placed upon a table beside his mistress, after which he retired.

"This is the case to which I have just been referring," said the Duchess, placing her hand on the article in question. "If you glance at it you will see how exquisitely it is carved."

Concealing his eagerness with an effort, Simon Carne drew his chair up to the table, and examined the box.

It was with justice she had described it as a work of art. What the wood was of which it was constructed Carne was unable to tell. It was dark and heavy, and, though it was not teak, closely resembled it. It was literally covered with quaint carving, and of its kind was an unique work of art.

"It is most curious and beautiful," said Carne when he had finished his examination. "In all my experience I can safely say I have never seen its equal. If you will permit me I should very much like to include a description and an illustration of it in my book."

"Of course you may do so; I shall be only too delighted," answered Her Grace. "If it will help you in your work I shall be glad to lend it to you for a few hours, in order that you may have the illustration made."

This was exactly what Carne had been waiting for, and he accepted the offer with alacrity.

"Very well, then," she said. "On the day of my ball, when it will be brought from the bank again, I will take the necklace out and send the case to you. I must make one proviso, however, and that is that you let me have it back the same day."

"I will certainly promise to do that," replied Carne.

"And now let us look inside," said his hostess.

Choosing a key from a bunch she carried in her pocket, she unlocked the casket, and lifted the lid. Accustomed as Carne had all his life been to the sight of gems, what he then saw before him almost took his breath away. The inside of the box, both sides and bottom, was quilted with the softest Russia leather, and on this luxurious couch reposed the famous necklace. The fire of the stones when the light caught them was sufficient to dazzle the eyes, so fierce was it.

As Carne could see, every gem was perfect of its kind, and there were no fewer than three hundred of them. The setting was a fine example of the jeweller's art, and last, but not least, the value of the whole affair was fifty thousand pounds, a mere fleabite to the man who had given it to his wife, but a fortune to any humbler person.

"And now that you have seen my property, what do you think of it?" asked the Duchess as she watched her visitor's face.

"It is very beautiful," he answered, "and I do not wonder that you are proud of it. Yes, the diamonds are very fine, but I think it is their abiding place that fascinates me more. Have you any objection to my measuring it?"

"Pray do so, if it is likely to be of any assistance to you," replied Her Grace.

Carne therefore produced a small ivory rule, ran it over the box, and the figures he thus obtained he jotted down in his pocket-book.

Ten minutes later, when the case had been returned to the safe, he thanked the Duchess for her kindness and took his departure, promising to call in person for the empty case on the morning of the ball.

Reaching home he passed into his study, and, seating himself at his writing table, pulled a sheet of note paper towards him and began to sketch, as well as he could remember it, the box he had seen. Then he leant back in his chair and closed his eyes.

"I have cracked a good many hard nuts in my time," he said reflectively, "but never one that seemed so difficult at first sight as this. As far as I see at present, the case stands as follows: the box will be brought from the bank where it usually reposes to Wiltshire House on the morning of the dance. I shall be allowed to have possession of it, without the stones of course, for a period possibly extending from eleven o'clock in the morning to four or five, at any rate not later than seven, in the evening. After the ball the necklace will be returned to it, when it will be locked up in the safe, over which the butler and a footman will mount guard.

"To get into the room during the night is not only too risky, but physically out of the question; while to rob Her Grace of her treasure during the progress of the dance would be equally impossible. The Duke fetches the casket and takes it back to the bank himself, so that to all intents and purposes I am almost as far off the solution as ever."

Half an hour went by and found him still seated at his desk, staring at the drawing on the paper, then an hour. The traffic of the streets rolled past the house unheeded. Finally Jowur Singh announced his carriage, and, feeling that an idea might come to him with a change of scene, he set off for a drive in the park.

By this time his elegant mail phaeton, with its magnificent horses and Indian servant on the seat behind, was as well-known as Her Majesty's state equipage, and attracted almost as much attention. To-day, however, the fashionable world noticed that Simon Carne looked preoccupied. He was still working out his problem, but so far without much success. Suddenly something, no one will ever be able to say what, put an idea into his head. The notion was no sooner born in his brain than he left the park and drove quickly home. Ten minutes had scarcely elapsed before he was back in his study again, and had ordered that Wajib Baksh should be sent to him.

When the man he wanted put in an appearance, Carne handed him the paper upon which he had made the drawing of the jewel case.

"Look at that," he said, "and tell me what thou seest there."

"I see a box," answered the man, who by this time was well accustomed to his master's ways.

"As thou say'st, it is a box," said Carne. "The wood is heavy and thick, though what wood it is I do not know. The measurements are upon the paper below. Within, both the sides and bottom are quilted with soft leather, as I have also shown. Think now, Wajib Baksh, for in this case thou wilt need to have all thy wits about thee. Tell me is it in thy power, oh most cunning of all craftsmen, to insert such extra sides within this box that they, being held by a spring, shall lie so snug as not to be noticeable to the ordinary eye? Can it be so arranged that, when the box is locked, they will fall flat upon the bottom, thus covering and holding fast what lies beneath them, and yet making the box appear to the eye as if it were empty. Is it possible for thee to do such a thing?"

Wajib Baksh did not reply for a few moments. His instinct told him what his master wanted, and he was not disposed to answer hastily, for he also saw that his reputation as the most cunning craftsman in India was at stake.

"If the Heaven-born will permit me the night for thought," he said at last, "I will come to him when he rises from his bed and tell him what I can do, and he can then give his orders as it pleases him."

"Very good," said Carne. "Then to-morrow morning I shall expect thy report. Let the work be good, and there will be many rupees for thee to touch in return. As to the lock and the way it shall act, let that be the concern of Hiram Singh."

Wajib Baksh salaamed and withdrew, and Simon Carne for the time being dismissed the matter from his mind.

Next morning, while he was dressing, Belton reported that the two artificers desired an interview with him. He ordered them to be admitted, and forthwith they entered the room. It was noticeable that Wajib Baksh carried in his hand a heavy box, which, upon Carne's motioning him to do so, he placed upon the table.

"Have ye thought over the matter?" he asked, seeing that the men waited for him to speak.

"We have thought of it," replied Hiram Singh, who always acted as spokesman for the pair. "If the Presence will deign to look, he will see that we have made a box of the size and shape such as he drew upon the paper."

"Yes, it is certainly a good copy," said Carne condescendingly, after he had examined it.

Wajib Baksh showed his white teeth in appreciaton of the compliment, and Hiram Singh drew closer to the table.

"And now, if the Sahib will open it, he will in his wisdom be able to tell if it resembles the other that he has in his mind."

Carne opened the box as requested, and discovered that the interior was an exact counterfeit of the Duchess of Wiltshire's jewel case, even to the extent of the quilted leather lining which had been the other's principal feature. He admitted that the likeness was all that could be desired.

"As he is satisfied," said Hiram Singh, "it may be that the Protector of the Poor will deign to try an experiment with it. See, here is a comb. Let it be placed in the box, so—now he will see what he will see."

The broad, silver-backed comb, lying upon his dressing-table, was placed on the bottom of the box, the lid was closed, and the key turned in the lock. The case being securely fastened, Hiram Singh laid it before his master.

"I am to open it, I suppose?" said Carne, taking the key and replacing it in the lock.

"If my master pleases," replied the other.

Carne accordingly turned it in the lock, and, having done so, raised the lid and looked inside. His astonishment was complete. To all intents and purposes the box was empty. The comb was not to be seen, and yet the quilted sides and bottom were, to all appearances, just the same as when he had first looked inside.

"This is the most wonderful," he said. And indeed it was as clever a conjuring trick as any he had ever seen.

"Nay, it is very simple," Wajib Baksh replied. "The Heaven-born told me that there must be no risk of detection."

He took the box in his own hands and running his nails down the centre of the quilting, divided the false bottom into two pieces; these he lifted out, revealing the comb lying upon the real bottom beneath.

"The sides, as my lord will see," said Hiram Singh, taking a step forward, "are held in their appointed places by these two springs. Thus, when the key is turned the springs relax, and the sides are driven by others into their places on the bottom, where the seams in the quilting mask the join. There is but one disadvantage. It is as follows: When the pieces which form the bottom are lifted out in order that my lord may get at whatever lies concealed beneath, the springs must of necessity stand revealed. However, to any one who knows sufficient of the working of the box to lift out the false bottom, it will be an easy matter to withdraw the springs and conceal them about his person."

"As you say that is an easy matter," said Carne, "and I shall not be likely to forget. Now one other question. Presuming I am in a position to put the real box into your hands for say eight hours, do you think that in that time you can fit it up so that detection will be impossible?"

"Assuredly, my lord," replied Hiram Singh with conviction. "There is but the lock and the fitting of the springs to be done. Three hours at most would suffice for that."

"I am pleased with you," said Carne. "As a proof of my satisfaction, when the work is finished you will each receive five hundred rupees. Now you can go."

According to his promise, ten o'clock on the Friday following found him in his hansom driving towards Belgrave Square. He was a little anxious, though the casual observer would scarcely have been able to tell it. The magnitude of the stake for which he was playing was enough to try the nerve of even such a past master in his profession as Simon Carne.

Arriving at the house he discovered some workmen erecting an awning across the footway in preparation for the ball that was to take place at night. It was not long, however, before he found himself in the boudoir, reminding Her Grace of her promise to permit him an opportunity of making a drawing of the famous jewel case. The Duchess was naturally busy, and within a quarter of an hour he was on his way home with the box placed on the seat of the carriage beside him.

"Now," he said, as he patted it good-humouredly, "if only the notion worked out by Hiram Singh and Wajib Baksh holds good, the famous Wiltshire diamonds will become my property before very many hours are passed. By this time to-morrow, I suppose, London will be all agog concerning the burglary."

On reaching his house he left his carriage, and himself carried the box into the study. Once there he rang his bell and ordered Hiram Singh and Wajib Baksh to be sent to him. When they arrived he showed them the box upon which they were to exercise their ingenuity.

"Bring the tools in here," he said, "and do the work under my own eyes. You have but nine hours before you, so you must make the most of them."

The men went for their implements, and as soon as they were ready set to work. All through the day they were kept hard at it, with the result that by five o'clock the alterations had been effected and the case stood ready. By the time Carne returned from his afternoon drive in the Park it was quite prepared for the part it was to play in his scheme. Having praised the men, he turned them out and locked the door, then went across the room and unlocked a drawer in his writing table. From it he took a flat leather jewel case, which he opened. It contained a necklace of counterfeit diamonds, if anything a little larger than the one he intended to try to obtain. He had purchased it that morning in the Burlington Arcade for the purpose of testing the apparatus his servants had made, and this he now proceeded to do.

Laying it carefully upon the bottom he closed the lid and turned the key. When he opened it again the necklace was gone, and even though he knew the secret he could not for the life of him see where the false bottom began and ended. After that he reset the trap and tossed the necklace carelessly in. To his delight it acted as well as on the previous occasion. He could scarcely contain his satisfaction. His conscience was sufficiently elastic to give him no touble. To him it was scarcely a robbery he was planning, but an artistic trial of skill, in which he pitted his wits and cunning against the forces of society in general.

At half-past seven he dined, and afterwards smoked a meditative cigar over the evening paper in the billiard room. The invitations to the ball were for ten o'clock, and at nine-thirty he went to his dressing-room.

"Make me tidy as quickly as you can," he said to Belton when the latter appeared, "and while you are doing so listen to my final instructions.

"To-night, as you know, I am endeavouring to secure the Duchess of Wiltshire's necklace. To-morrow morning all London will resound with the hubbub, and I have been making my plans in such a way as to arrange that Klimo shall be the first person consulted. When the messenger calls, if call he does, see that the old woman next door bids him tell the Duke to come personally at twelve o'clock. Do you understand?"

"Perfectly, sir."

"Very good. Now give me the jewel case, and let me be off. You need not sit up for me."

Precisely as the clocks in the neighbourhood were striking ten Simon Carne reached Belgrave Square, and, as he hoped, found himself the first guest.

His hostess and her husband received him in the anteroom of the drawing-room.

"I come laden with a thousand apologies," he said as he took Her Grace's hand, and bent over it with that ceremonious politeness which was one of the man's chief characteristics. "I am most unconscionably early, I know, but I hastened here in order that I might personally return the jewel case you so kindly lent me. I must trust to your generosity to forgive me. The drawings took longer than I expected."

"Please do not apologise," answered Her Grace. "It is very kind of you to have brought the case yourself. I hope the illustrations have proved successful. I shall look forward to seeing them as soon as they are ready. But I am keeping you holding the box. One of my servants will take it to my room."

She called a footman to her, and bade him take the box and place it upon her dressing-table.

"Before it goes I must let you see that I have not damaged it either externally or internally," said Carne with a laugh. "It is such a valuable case that I should never forgive myself if it had even received a scratch during the time it has been in my possession."

So saying he lifted the lid and allowed her to look inside. To all appearance it was exactly the same as when she had lent it to him earlier in the day.

"You have been most careful," she said. And then, with an air of banter, she continued: "If you desire it, I shall be pleased to give you a certificate to that effect."

They jested in this fashion for a few moments after the servant's departure, during which time Carne promised to call upon her the following morning at 11 o'clock, and to bring with him the illustrations he had made and a queer little piece of china he had had the good fortune to pick up in a dealer's shop the previous afternoon. By this time fashionable London was making its way up the grand staircase, and with its appearance further conversation became impossible.

Shortly after midnight Carne bade his hostess good-night and slipped away. He was perfectly satisfied with his evening's entertainment, and if the key of the jewel case were not turned before the jewels were placed in it, he was convinced they would become his property. It speaks well for his strength of nerve when I record the fact that on going to bed his slumbers were as peaceful and untroubled as those of a little child.

Breakfast was scarcely over next morning before a hansom drew up at his front door and Lord Amberley alighted. He was ushered into Carne's presence forthwith, and on seeing that the latter was surprised at his early visit, hastened to explain.

"My dear fellow," he said, as he took possession of the chair the other offered him, "I have come round to see you on most important business. As I told you last night at the dance, when you so kindly asked me to come and see the steam yacht you have purchased, I had an appointment with Wiltshire at half-past nine this morning. On reaching Belgrave Square, I found the whole house in confusion. Servants were running hither and thither with scared faces, the butler was on the borders of lunacy, the Duchess was well-nigh hysterical in her boudier, while her husband was in his study vowing vengeance against all the world."

"You alarm me," said Carne, lighting a cigarette with a hand that was as steady as a rock. "What on earth has happened?"

"I think I might safely allow you fifty guesses and then wager a hundred pounds you'd not hit the mark; and yet in a certain measure it concerns you."

"Concerns me? Good gracious! What have I done to bring all this about?"

"Pray do not look so alarmed," said Amberley. "Personally you have done nothing. Indeed, on second thoughts, I don't know that I am right in saying that it concerns you at all. The fact of the matter is, Carne, a burglary took place last night at Wiltshire House, *and the famous necklace has disappeared.*"

"Good heavens! You don't say so?"

'But I *do*. The circumstances of the case are as follows: When my cousin retired to her room last night after the ball, she unclasped the necklace, and, in her husband's presence, placed it carefully in her jewel case, which she locked. That having been done, Wiltshire took the box to the room which contained the safe, and himself placed it there, locking the iron door with his own key. The room was occupied that night, according to custom, by the butler and one of the footmen, both of whom have been in the family since they were boys.

"Next morning, after breakfast, the Duke unlocked the safe and took out the box, intending to convey it to the Bank as usual. Before leaving, however, he placed it on his study-table and went upstairs to speak to his wife. He cannot remember exactly how long he was absent, but he feels convinced that he was not gone more than a quarter of an hour at the very utmost.

"Their conversation finished, she accompanied him downstairs, where she saw him take up the case to carry it to his carriage. Before he left the house, however, she said: 'I suppose you have looked to see that the necklace is all right?' 'How

could I do so?' was his reply. 'You know you possess the only
key that will fit it.'

"She felt in her pockets, but to her surprise the key was not
there."

"If I were a detective I should say that that is a point to be remembered," said Carne with a smile. "Pray, where did she find
her keys?"

"Upon her dressing-table," said Amberley. "Though she has
not the slightest recollection of leaving them there."

"Well, when she had procured the keys, what happened?"

"Why, they opened the box, and, to their astonishment and
dismay, *found it empty. The jewels were gone!*"

"Good gracious! What a terrible loss! It seems almost impossible that it can be true. And pray, what did they do?'

"At first they stood staring into the empty box, hardly believ-
ing the evidence of their own eyes. Stare how they would, however, they could not bring them back. The jewels had, without
doubt, disappeared, but when and where the robbery had taken
place it was impossible to say. After that they had up all the servants and questioned them, but the result was what they might
have foreseen, no one from the butler to the kitchenmaid could
throw any light upon the subject. To this minute it remains as
great a mystery as when they first discovered it."

"I am more concerned than I can tell you," said Carne.
"How thankful I ought to be that I returned the case to Her
Grace last night. But in thinking of myself I am forgetting to
ask what has brought you to me. If I can be of any assistance I
hope you will command me."

"Well, I'll tell you why I have come," replied Lord Amberley.
"Naturally, they are most anxious to have the mystery solved
and the jewels recovered as soon as possible. Wiltshire wanted
to send to Scotland Yard there and then, but his wife and I
eventually persuaded him to consult Klimo. As you know, if the
police authorities are called in first, he refuses the business altogether. Now, we thought, as you are his next door neighbour,
you might possibly be able to assist us."

"You may be very sure, my lord, I will do everything that lies
in my power. Let us go in and see him at once."

As he spoke he rose and threw what remained of his cigarette into the fireplace. His visitor having imitated his example, they procurred their hats and walked round from Park Lane into Belverton Street to bring up at No. 1. After they had rung the bell the door was opened to them by the old woman who invariably received the detective's clients.

"Is Mr. Klimo at home?" asked Carne. "And if so, can we see him?"

The old lady was a little deaf, and the question had to be repeated before she could be made to understand what was wanted. As soon, however, as she realized their desire, she informed them that her master was absent from town, but would be back as usual at twelve o'clock to meet his clients.

"What on earth's to be done?" said the Earl, looking at his companion in dismay. "I am afraid I can't come back again, as I have a most important appointment at that hour."

"Do you think you could entrust the business to me?" asked Carne. "If so, I will make a point of seeing him at twelve o'clock, and could call at Wiltshire House afterwards and tell the Duke what I have done."

"That's very good of you," replied Amberley. "If you are sure it would not put you to too much trouble, that would be quite the best thing to be done."

"I will do it with pleasure," Carne replied. "I feel it my duty to help in whatever way I can."

"You are very kind," said the other. "Then, as I understand it, you are to call upon Klimo at twelve o'clock, and afterwards to let my cousins know what you have succeeded in doing. I only hope he will help us to secure the thief. We are having too many of these burglaries just now. I must catch this hansom and be off. Good-bye, and many thanks."

"Good-bye," said Carne, and shook him by the hand.

The hansom having rolled away, Carne retraced his steps to his own abode.

"It is really very strange," he muttered as he walked along, "how often chance condescends to lend her assistance to my little schemes. The mere fact that His Grace left the box unwatched in his study for a quarter of an hour may serve to throw the police off on quite another scent. I am also glad that they decided to open the case in the house, for if it had gone to the bankers' and had been placed in the strong room unexamined, I should never have been able to get possession of the jewels at all."

Three hours later he drove to Wiltshire House and saw the Duke. The Duchess was far too much upset by the catastrophe to see any one.

"This is really most kind of you, Mr. Carne," said His Grace when the other had supplied an elaborate account of his interview with Klimo. "We are extremely indebted to you. I am sorry he cannot come before ten o'clock to-night, and that he makes this stipulation of my seeing him alone, for I must confess I should like to have had some one else present to ask any questions that might escape me. But if that's his usual hour and custom, well, we must abide by it, that's all. I hope he will do some good, for this is the greatest calamity that has ever befallen me. As I told you just now, it has made my wife quite ill. She is confined to her bedroom and quite hysterical."

"You do not suspect any one, I suppose?" inquired Carne.

"Not a soul," the other answered. "The thing is such a mystery that we do not know what to think. I feel convinced, however, that my servants are as innocent as I am. Nothing will ever make me think them otherwise. I wish I could catch the fellow, that's all. I'd make him suffer for the trick he's played me."

Carne offered an appropriate reply, and after a little further conversation upon the subject, bade the irate nobleman goodbye and left the house. From Belgrave Square he drove to one of the clubs of which he had been elected a member, in search of Lord Orpington, with whom he had promised to lunch, and afterwards took him to a ship-builder's yard near Greenwich, in order to show him the steam yacht he had lately purchased.

It was close upon dinner time before he returned to his own residence. He brought Lord Orpington with him, and they dined in state together. At nine the latter bade him good-bye, and at ten Carne retired to his dressing-room and rang for Belton.

"What have you to report," he asked, "with regard to what I bade you do in Belgrave Square?"

"I followed your instructions to the letter," Belton replied. "Yesterday morning I wrote to Messrs. Horniblow and Jimson, the house agents in Piccadilly, in the name of Colonel Braithwaite, and asked for an order to view the residence to the right of Wiltshire House. I asked that the order might be sent direct to the house, where the Colonel would get it upon his arrival. This letter I posted myself in Basingstoke, as you desired me to do.

"At nine o'clock yesterday morning I dressed myself as much like an elderly army officer as possible, and took a cab to Belgrave Square. The caretaker, an old fellow of close upon seventy years of age, admitted me immediately upon hearing my name, and proposed that he should show me over the house. This, however, I told him was quite unnecessary, backing my speech with a present of half a crown, whereupon he returned to his breakfast perfectly satisfied, while I wandered about the house at my own leisure.

"Reaching the same floor as that upon which is situated the room in which the Duke's safe is kept, I discovered that your supposition was quite correct, and that it would be possible for a man, by opening the window, to make his way along the coping from one house to the other, without being seen. I made certain that there was no one in the bedroom in which the butler slept, and then arranged the long telescope walking-stick you gave me, and fixed one of my boots to it by means of the screw in the end. With this I was able to make a regular succession of footsteps in the dust along the ledge, between one window and the other.

"That done, I went downstairs again, bade the caretaker good-morning, and got into my cab. From Belgrave Square I drove to the shop of the pawnbroker whom you told me you had discovered was out of town. His assistant inquired my business, and was anxious to do what he could for me. I told him, however, that I must see his master personally, as it was about the sale of some diamonds I had had left me. I pretended to be annoyed that he was not at home, and muttered to myself, so that the man could hear, something about its meaning a journey to Amsterdam.

"Then I limped out of the shop, paid off my cab, and, walking down a by-street, removed my moustache, and altered my appearance by taking off my great coat and muffler. A few streets further on I purchased a bowler hat in place of the old-fashioned topper I had hitherto been wearing, and then took a cab from Piccadilly and came home."

"You have fulfilled my instructions admirably," said Carne. "And if the business comes off, as I expect it will, you shall receive your usual percentage. Now I must be turned into Klimo and be off to Belgrave Square to put His Grace upon the track of this burglar."

Before he retired to rest that night Simon Carne took something, wrapped in a red silk handkerchief, from the capacious pocket of the coat Klimo had been wearing a few moments before. Having unrolled the covering, he held up to the light the magnificent necklace which for so many years had been the joy and pride of the ducal house of Wiltshire. The electric light played upon it, and touched it with a thousand different hues.

"Where so many have failed," he said to himself, as he wrapped it in the handkerchief again and locked it in his safe, "it is pleasant to be able to congratulate oneself on having succeeded."

Next morning all London was astonished by the news that the famous Wiltshire diamonds had been stolen, and a few hours later Carne learnt from an evening paper that the detectives who had taken up the case, upon the supposed retirement from it of Klimo, were still completely at fault.

That evening he was to entertain several friends to dinner. They included Lord Amberley, Lord Orpington, and a prominent member of the Privy Council. Lord Amberley arrived late, but filled to overflowing with importance. His friends noticed his state, and questioned him.

"Well, gentlemen," he answered, as he took up a commanding position upon the drawing-room hearthrug, "I am in a position to inform you that Klimo has reported upon the case, and the upshot of it is that the Wiltshire Diamond Mystery is a mystery no longer."

"What do you mean?" asked the others in a chorus.

"I mean that he sent in his report to Wiltshire this afternoon, as arranged. From what he said the other night, after being alone in the room with the empty jewel case and a magnifying glass for two minutes or so, he was in a position to describe the *modus operandi*, and, what is more, to put the police on the scent of the burglar."

"And how *was* it worked?" asked Carne.

"From the empty house next door," replied the other. "On the morning of the burglary a man, purporting to be a retired army officer, called with an order to view, got the caretaker out of the way, clambered along to Wiltshire House by means of the parapet outside, reached the room during the time the servants were at breakfast, opened the safe, and abstracted the jewels."

"But how did Klimo find all this out?" asked Lord Orpington.

"By his own inimitable cleverness," replied Lord Amberley. "At any rate it has been proved that he was correct. The man *did* make his way from next door, and the police have since discovered that an individual answering to the description given, visited a pawnbroker's shop in the city about an hour later, and stated that he had diamonds to sell."

"If that is so it turns out to be a very simple mystery after all," said Lord Orpington as they began their meal.

"Thanks to the ingenuity of the cleverest detective in the world," remarked Amberley.

"In that case here's a good health to Klimo," said the Privy Councillor, raising his glass.

"I will join you in that," said Simon Carne. "Here's a very good health to Klimo and his connection with the Duchess of Wiltshire's diamonds. May he always be equally successful!"

"Hear, hear to that," replied his guests.

E. W. HORNUNG

For at least the first half of the twentieth century, one thief's reputation dwarfed that of his rivals as surely as Sherlock Holmes towered above other detectives. From his first appearance in 1898, the cricket-playing, safe-cracking A. J. Raffles caught the public's imagination almost as much as Holmes had a few years earlier. Between the two there were connections beyond mere analogy. The thief's creator, E. W. Hornung, was married to Arthur Conan Doyle's sister Constance.

Aside from their vivid evocation of Victorian England, the primary similarity between the Holmes and Raffles stories is their narration by a dim-witted sidekick who exhibits canine devotion. As his Watson, Raffles has the adoring Bunny. Raffles is neither always a gentleman nor always successful. Although he invokes "art for art's sake" as his motto, he is a small-time crook who steals mostly when desperate for cash. Sometimes he resorts to fisticuffs, especially when his adversary is a member of the lower classes.

To forestall public outcry against this depraved antihero, the Raffles stories appeared under the series title "In the Chains of Crime," complete with a melodramatic illustration—of Bunny rather than Raffles chained to a cowled skeletal figure of death. The recurring description before each story foretold the miscreant's doom: "Being the confessions of a late prisoner of the crown, and sometime accomplice of the more notorious A. J. Raffles, cricketer and criminal, whose fate is unknown."

The first story appeared in *Cassell's* in June 1898. When the book version was published the next year, the *Spectator* remarked that moralists must inevitably denounce the stories as "new, ingenious, artistic, but most reprehensible." After Hornung's death, Conan Doyle said in his autobiography, "I think there are few finer examples of short story writing in our language than these"—although he couldn't resist adding, "You must not make the criminal a hero." In real life the moral tables were turned; Hornung deeply disapproved of Conan Doyle's illicit affair during his wife's terminal illness and also found his brother-in-law's vocal support of spiritualist charlatans unworthy.

The first round of these stories ends with Raffles, to escape capture on a ship, leaping overboard and abandoning the loyal Bunny to suffer in prison—yet, upon his release, Bunny is eager to play dogsbody again. The second volume finds Raffles dying in the Boer War, unmasking a spy even though doing so means his own arrest. Hornung would return to Raffles in later stories, but he would be careful to describe them as new accounts of old adventures. The thief also appears in a single novel, *Mr. Justice Raffles*.

"Nine Points of the Law" was first published in *Cassell's* in September 1898, as the fourth story in the series. The next year it appeared as the sixth story in *The Amateur Cracksman*. It may have been inspired partly by one of Grant Allen's Colonel Clay stories, "The Episode of the Old Master."

NINE POINTS OF THE LAW

"Well," said Raffles, "what do you make of it?"

I read the advertisement once more before replying. It was in the last column of the *Daily Telegraph*, and it ran:—

Two thousand pounds reward.—The above sum may be earned by anyone qualified to undertake delicate mission and prepared to run certain risk.—Apply by telegram, Security, London.

"I think," said I, "it's the most extraordinary advertisement that ever got into print!"

Raffles smiled.

"Not quite all that, Bunny; still, extraordinary enough, I grant you."

"Look at the figure!"

"It is certainly large."

"And the mission—and the risk!"

"Yes; the combination is frank; to say the least of it. But the really original point is requiring applications by telegram to a telegraphic address! There's something in the fellow who thought of that, and something in his game; with one word he chokes off the million who answer an advertisement every day—when they can raise the stamp. My answer cost me five bob; but then I prepaid another."

"You don't mean to say that you've applied?"

"Rather," said Raffles. "I want two thousand pounds as much as any man."

"Put your own name?"

"Well—no, Bunny, I didn't. In point of fact, I smell something interesting and illegal, and you know what a cautious chap I am. I signed myself Saumarez, care of Hickey, 28, Conduit Street; that's my tailor, and after sending the wire I went round and told him what to expect. He promised to send the reply along the moment it came—and, by Jove, that'll be it!"

And he was gone before a double-knock on the outer door had done ringing through the rooms, to return next minute with an open telegram and a face full of news.

"What do you think?" said he. "Security's that fellow Addenbrooke, the police-court lawyer, and he wants to see me *instanter!*"

"And you're going to him now?"

"This minute," said Raffles, brushing his hat; "and so are you."

"But I came in to drag you out to lunch."

"You shall lunch with me when we've seen this fellow. Come on, Bunny, and we'll choose your name on the way. Mine's Saumarez, and don't you forget it."

Mr. Bennett Addenbrooke occupied substantial offices in Wellington Street, Strand, and was out when we arrived; but he had only just gone "over the way to the court;" and five minutes sufficed to produce a brisk, fresh-coloured, resolute-looking man, with a very confident, rather festive air, and black eyes that opened wide at the sight of Raffles.

"Mr.—Saumarez?" exclaimed the lawyer.

"My name," said Raffles, with dry effrontery.

"Not up at Lord's, however!" said the other, slyly. "My dear sir, I have seen you take far too many wickets to make any mistake!"

For a moment Raffles looked venomous; then he shrugged and smiled, and the smile grew into a little cynical chuckle.

"So you have bowled me out in my turn?" said he. "Well, I don't think there's anything to explain. I am harder up than I wished to admit under my own name, that's all, and I want that thousand pounds reward."

"Two thousand," said the solicitor. "And the man who is not above an *alias* happens to be just the sort of man I want; so don't let that worry you my dear sir. The matter, however, is of a strictly private and confidential character." And he looked very hard at me.

"Quite so," said Raffles. "But there was something about a risk?"

"A certain risk is involved."

"Then surely three heads will be better than two. I said I wanted that thousand pounds; my friend here wants the other. Must you have his name too? Bunny, give him your card."

Mr. Addenbrooke raised his eyebrows over my name, address, and club; then he drummed on my card with his finger-nail, and his embarrassment expressed itself in a puzzled smile.

"The fact is, I find myself in a difficulty," he confessed at last. "Yours is the first reply I have received; people who can afford to send long telegrams don't rush to the advertisements in the *Daily Telegraph;* but, on the other hand, I was not quite prepared to hear from men like yourselves. Candidly, and on consideration, I am not sure that you *are* the stamp of men for me—men who belong to good clubs! I rather intended to appeal to the—er—adventurous classes."

"We are adventurers," said Raffles gravely.

"But you respect the law?"

The black eyes gleamed shrewdly.

"We are not professional rogues, if that's what you mean," said Raffles calmly. "But on our beam-ends we are; we would do a good deal for a thousand pounds apiece."

"Anything," I murmured.

The solicitor rapped his desk.

"I'll tell you what I want you to do. You can but refuse. It's illegal, but it's illegality in a good cause; that's the risk, and my client is prepared to pay for it. He will pay for the attempt, in case of failure; the money is as good as yours once you consent to run the risk. My client is Sir Bernard Debenham, of Broom Hall, Esher."

"I know his son," I remarked.

"Then," said the solicitor, "you have the privilege of know-ing one of the most complete young blackguards about town, and the *fons et origo* of the whole trouble. As you know the son, you may know the father also—at all events, by reputa-tion; and in that case I needn't tell you that he is a very pecu-liar man. He lives alone in a storehouse of treasures which no eyes but his ever behold. He is said to have the finest collec-tion of the pictures in the south of England, though nobody ever sees them to judge; pictures, fiddles, and furniture are his hobby, and he is undoubtedly very eccentric. Nor can one deny that there has been considerable eccentricity in his treatment of his son. For years Sir Bernard paid his debts, and the other day, without the slightest warning, not only refused to do so any more, but absolutely stopped the lad's allowance. Well, I'll tell you what has happened. But, first of all, you must know, or you may remember, that I appeared for young Debenham in a little scrape he got into a year or two ago. I got him off all right, and Sir Bernard paid me handsomely on the nail. And no more did I hear or see of either of them until one day last week."

The lawyer drew his chair nearer ours, and leant forward with a hand on either knee.

"On Tuesday of last week I had a telegram from Sir Bernard; I was to go to him at once. I found him waiting for me in the drive; without a word he led me to the picture-gallery, which was locked and darkened, drew up a blind, and stood simply pointing to an empty picture-frame. It was a long time before I could get a word out of him. Then at last he told me that the frame had contained one of the rarest and most valuable pic-tures in England—in the world—an original Velasquez. I have checked this," said the lawyer, "and it seems literally true; the picture was a portrait of the Infanta Maria Teresa, said to be one of the artist's greatest works, and second only to his por-trait of one of the Popes in Rome—so they told me at the Na-tional Gallery, where they had its history by heart. They say there that the picture is practically priceless. And young Deben-ham has sold it for five thousand pounds!"

"The deuce he has!" said Raffles.

I inquired who had bought it.

"A Queensland legislator of the name of Craggs—the Hon. John Montagu Craggs, M.L.C., to give him his full title. Not that we knew anything about him on Tuesday last; we didn't even know for certain that young Debenham had stolen the picture. But he had gone down for money on the Monday evening, had been refused, and it was plain enough that he had helped himself in this way; he had threatened revenge, and this was obviously it. Indeed, when I hunted him up in town on the Tuesday night, he confessed as much in the most brazen manner imaginable. But he wouldn't tell me who was the purchaser, and finding out that took the rest of the week; but find it out I did, and a nice time I've had of it ever since! Backwards and forwards between Esher and the Métropole, where the Queenslander is staying, sometimes twice a day; threats, offers, prayers, entreaties, not one of them a bit of good!"

"But," said Raffles, "surely it's a clear case? The sale was illegal; you can pay him back his money and force him to give the picture up."

"Exactly; but not without an action and a public scandal, and that my client declines to face. He would rather lose even his picture than have the whole thing get into the papers; he has disowned his son, but he will not disgrace him; yet his picture he must have by hook or crook, and there's the rub! I am to get it back by fair means or foul. He gives me *carte blanche* in the matter, and, I verily believe, would throw in a blank cheque if asked. He offered one to the Queenslander, but Craggs simply tore it in two; the one old boy is as much a character as the other, and between the two of them I'm at my wits' end."

"So you put that advertisement in the paper?" said Raffles, in the dry tones he had adopted throughout the interview.

"As a last resort. I did."

"And you wish us to *steal* this picture?"

It was magnificently said; the lawyer flushed from his hair to his collar.

"I knew you were not the men!" he groaned. "I never thought of men of your stamp! But it's *not* stealing," he exclaimed heatedly; "it's recovering stolen property. Besides, Sir Bernard will pay him his five thousand as soon as he has the picture; and, you'll see, old Craggs will be just as loth to let it come out as Sir Bernard himself. No, no—it's an enterprise, an adventure, if you like—but not stealing."

"You yourself mentioned the law," murmured Raffles.

"And the risk," I added.

"We pay for that," he said once more.

"But not enough," said Raffles, shaking his head. "My good sir, consider what it means to us. You spoke of those clubs; we should not only get kicked out of them, but put in prison like common burglars. It's true we're hard up, but it simply isn't worth it at the price—double your stakes, and I for one am your man."

Addenbrooke wavered.

"Do you think you could bring it off?"

"We could try."

"But you have no——"

"Experience? No; not as thieves."

"And you would really run the risk for four thousand pounds?"

Raffles looked at me. I nodded.

"We would," said he, "and blow the odds!"

"It's more than I can ask my client to pay," said Addenbrooke, growing firm.

"Then it's more than you can expect us to risk."

"You are in earnest?"

"God wot!"

"Say three thousand if you succeed!"

"No, four."

"Then nothing if you fail——"

"Double or quits?" said Raffles. "Well, that's sporting. Done!"

Addenbrooke opened his lips, half rose, then sat back in his chair, and looked long and shrewdly at Raffles—never once at me.

"I know your bowling," he said reflectively. "I go up to Lord's whenever I want an hour's real rest, and I've seen you bowl again and again—yes, and take the best wickets in England on a plumb pitch. I don't forget the last Gentlemen and Players; I was there. You're up to every trick—every one . . . I'm inclined to think you would bowl out this old Australian if anybody can. Why! I believe you're my very man!" . . .

The bargain was clinched at the Café Royal, where Bennett Addenbrooke insisted on playing host at an extravagant luncheon. I remember that he took his whack of champagne with the nervous freedom of a man at high pressure, and have no doubt I kept him in countenance by an equal indulgence; but Raffles, ever an exemplar in such matters, was more abstemious even than his wont, and very poor company to boot. I can see him now, his eyes in his plate—thinking—thinking. I can see the solicitor glancing from him to me in an apprehension of which I did my best to disabuse him by reassuring looks. At the close Raffles apologised for his preoccupation, called for an A B C time-table, and announced his intention of catching the 3.20 to Esher.

"You must excuse me, Mr. Addenbrooke," said he, "but I have my own idea, and for the moment I should much prefer to keep it to myself. It may end in fizzle, so I would rather not speak about it to either of you just yet. But speak to Sir Bernard I must, so will you write me one line to him on your card? Of course, if you wish, you must come down with me and hear what I say; but I really don't see the point."

And, as usual, Raffles had his way, though Bennett Addenbrooke was visibly provoked, and I myself shared his annoyance to no small extent. I could only tell him that it was in the nature of Raffles to be self-willed and secretive, but that no man of my acquaintance had half his audacity and determination—that I, for my part would trust him through and through, and let him gang his own gait every time. More I dared not say, even to remove those chill misgivings with which I knew that the lawyer went his way.

That day I saw no more of Raffles, but a telegram reached me when I was dressing for dinner:—

"Be in your rooms to-morrow from noon and keep rest of day clear.—RAFFLES."

It had been sent off from Waterloo at 6.42.

So Raffles was back in town; at an earlier stage of our relations I should have hunted him up then and there, but now I knew better. His telegram meant that he had no desire for my society that night or the following forenoon; that when he wanted me I should see him soon enough.

And see him I did, towards one o'clock next day. I was watching for him from my window in Mount Street, when he drove up furiously in a hansom, and jumped out without a word to the man. I met him next minute at the lift gates, and he fairly pushed me back into my rooms.

"Five minutes, Bunny!" he cried. "Not a second more."

And he tore off his coat before flinging himself into the nearest chair.

"I'm fairly on the rush," he panted; "having the very dickens of a time! Not a word till I tell you all I've done. I settled my plan of campaign yesterday at lunch. The first thing was to get in with this man Craggs; you can't break into a place like the Métropole—it's got to be done from the inside. Problem one, How to get at the fellow. Only one sort of pretext would do—it must be something to do with this blessed picture, so that I might see where he'd got it, and all that. Well, I couldn't go and ask to see it out of curiosity, and I couldn't go as a second representative of the other old chap, and it was thinking how I could go that made me such a bear at lunch. But I saw my way before we got up. If I could only lay hold of a copy of the picture I might ask leave to go and compare it with the original. So down I went to Esher to find out if there was a copy in existence, and was at Broom Hall for one hour and a half yesterday afternoon. There was no copy there, but they must exist, for Sir Bernard himself (such a rum old boy!) has allowed a couple to be made since the picture has been in his possession. He hunted up the painters' addresses, and the rest of the evening I spent in hunting up the painters themselves; but their work had been done on commission—one copy had gone out of the country, and I'm still on the track of the other."

"Then you haven't seen Craggs yet?"

"Oh yes, I have seen him and made friends with him, and if possible he's the funnier old cuss of the two. I took the bull by the horns this morning, went in and lied like Ananias, and it was just as well I did—the old ruffian sails for Australia by to-morrow's boat. I told him a man wanted to sell me a copy of the celebrated Infanta Maria Teresa of Velasquez, that I'd been down to the supposed owner of the picture, only to find that he had just sold it to him. You should have seen his face when I told him that! He grinned all round his wicked old head. 'Did *old* Debenham admit it?' says he; and when I said he had, he chuckled to himself for about five minutes. He was so pleased that he did just what I hoped he would do; he showed me the great picture—luckily it isn't by any means a large one—and took special pride in showing me the case he's got it in. It's an iron map-case in which he brought over the plans of his land in Brisbane; he wants to know who would suspect it of containing an Old Master, too? But he's had it fitted with a new Chubb's lock, and I managed to take an interest in the key while he was gloating over the canvas. I had the wax in the palm of my hand, and I shall make my duplicate this afternoon."

Raffles looked at his watch and jumped up, saying he had given me a minute too much.

"By the way," he added, "you've got to dine with him at the Métropole to-night!"

"I?"

"Yes; don't look so scared. Both of us are invited—I swore you were dining with me; but I shan't be there."

His clear eye was upon me, bright with meaning and with mischief. I implored him to tell me what his meaning was.

"You will dine in his private sitting-room," said Raffles; "it adjoins his bed-room. You must keep him sitting as long as possible, Bunny, and talking all the time!"

In a flash I saw his plan.

"You're going for the picture while we're at dinner?"

"Exactly."

"If he hears you!"

"He shan't."

"But if he did!"

And I fairly trembled at the thought.

"If he did," said Raffles, "there would be a collision, that's all. You had better take your revolver. I shall certainly take mine."

"But it's ghastly!" I cried. "To sit and talk to an utter stranger and know that you're at work in the next room!"

"Two thousand apiece," said Raffles, quietly.

"Upon my soul I believe I shall give it away!"

"Not you, Bunny. I know you better than you know yourself."

He put on his coat and his hat.

"What time have I to be there?" I asked him with a groan.

"Quarter to eight. There will be a telegram from me saying I can't turn up. He's a terror to talk, you'll have no difficulty in keeping the ball rolling; but head him off his picture for all you're worth. If he offers to show it you, say you must go. He locked up the case elaborately this afternoon, and there's no earthly reason why he should unlock it again in this hemisphere."

"Where shall I find you when I get away?"

"I shall be down at Esher. I hope to catch the 9.55."

"But surely I can see you again this afternoon?" I cried in a ferment, for his hand was on the door. "I'm not half coached up yet! I know I shall make a mess of it!"

"Not you," he said again, "but I shall if I waste any more time. I've got a deuce of a lot of rushing about to do yet. You won't find me at my rooms. Why not come down to Esher yourself by the last train? That's it—down you come with the latest news. I'll tell old Debenham to expect you; he shall give us both a bed. By Jove! he won't be able to do us too well if he's got his picture!"

"If!" I groaned, as he nodded his adieu; and he left me limp with apprehension, sick with fear, in a perfectly pitiable condition of pure stage-fright.

For, after all, I had only to act my part; unless Raffles failed where he never did fail, unless Raffles the neat and noiseless was for once clumsy and inept, all I had to do was indeed to "smile and smile and be a villain." I practised that smile half the afternoon. I rehearsed putative parts in hypothetical conversations. I got up stories. I dipped in a book on Queensland at the club. And at last it was 7.45 and I was making my bow to a somewhat elderly man with a small bald head and a retreating brow.

"So you're Mr. Raffles's friend?" said he, overhauling me rather rudely with his light small eyes. "Have you seen anything of him? I expected him early to show me something, but he's never come."

No more, evidently, had has telegram, and my troubles were beginning early. I said I had not seen Raffles since one o'clock, telling the truth with unction while I could; even as we spoke there came a knock at the door, it was the telegram at last, and, after reading it himself, the Queenslander handed it to me.

"Called out of town!" he grumbled "Sudden illness of near relative! What near relatives has he got?"

Now, Raffles had none, and for an instant I quailed before the perils of invention; then I replied that I had never met any of his people, and again felt fortified by my veracity.

"Thought you were bosom pals?" said he, with (as I imagined) a gleam of suspicion in his crafty little eyes.

"Only in town," said I. "I've never been to his place."

"Well," he growled, "I suppose it can't be helped. Don't know why he couldn't come and have his dinner first. Like to see the death-bed that *I'd* go to without *my* dinner; it's a full-skin billet, if you ask me. Well, we must just dine without him, and he'll have to buy his pig in a poke after all. Mind touching that bell? Suppose you know what he came to see me about? Sorry I shan't see him again, for his own sake. I liked Raffles— took to him amazingly. He's a cynic. I like cynics. I'm one myself. Rank bad form of his mother or his aunt to go and kick the bucket to-day."

I connect these specimens of his conversation, though they were doubtless detached at the time, and interspersed with remarks of mine here and there. They filled the interval until dinner was served, and they gave me an impression of the man which his every subsequent utterance confirmed. It was an impression which did away with all remorse for my treacherous presence at his table. He was that terrible type, the Silly Cynic, his aim a caustic commentary on all things and all men, his achievement mere vulgar irreverence and unintelligent scorn. Ill-bred and ill-informed, he had (on his own showing) fluked into fortune on a rise in land; yet cunning he possessed, as well as malice, and he chuckled till he choked over the misfortunes of less astute speculators in the same boom. Even now I cannot feel much compunction for my behaviour to the Hon. J. M. Craggs, M.L.C.

But never shall I forget the private agonies of the situation, the listening to my host with one ear and for Raffles with the other! Once I heard him—though the rooms were divided by the old-fashioned folding-doors, and though the dividing door was not only shut but richly curtained, I could have sworn I heard him once. I spilt my wine and laughed at the top of my voice at some coarse sally of my host's. And I heard nothing more, though my ears were on the strain. But later, to my horror, when the waiter had finally withdrawn, Craggs himself sprang up and rushed to his bedroom without a word. I sat like stone till he returned.

"Thought I heard a door go," he said. "Must have been mistaken . . . imagination . . . gave me quite a turn. Raffles tell you priceless treasure I got in there?"

It was the picture at last; up to this point I had kept him to Queensland and the making of his pile. I tried to get him back there now, but in vain. He was reminded of his great ill-gotten possession. I said that Raffles had just mentioned it, and that set him off. With the confidential garrulity of a man who has been drinking freely he plunged into his darling topic, and I looked past him at the clock. It was only a quarter to ten.

In common decency I could not go yet. So there I sat (we were still at port) and learnt what had originally fired my host's ambition to possess what he was pleased to call a "real, genuine, twin-screw, double-funnelled, copper-bottomed Old Master"; it was to "go one better" than some rival legislator of pictorial proclivities. But even an epitome of his monologue would be so much weariness; suffice it that it ended inevitably in the invitation I had dreaded all the evening.

"But you must see it. Next room. This way."

"Isn't it packed up?" I inquired hastily.

"Lock and key. That's all."

"Pray don't trouble," I urged.

"Trouble be hanged!" said he. "Come along."

And all at once I saw that to resist him further would be to heap suspicion upon myself against the moment of impending discovery. I therefore followed him into his bedroom without further protest, and suffered him first to show me the iron map-case which stood in one corner; he took a crafty pride in this receptacle, and I thought he would never cease descanting on its innocent appearance and its Chubb's lock. It seemed an interminable age before the key was in the latter. Then the ward clicked, and my pulse stood still.

"By Jove!" I cried the next instant.

The canvas was in its place among the maps!

"Thought it would knock you," said Craggs, drawing it out and unrolling it for my benefit. "Grand thing, ain't it? Wouldn't think it had been painted two hundred and thirty years? But it has, *my* word! Old Johnson's face will be a treat when he sees it; won't go bragging about *his* pictures much more. Why, this one's worth all the pictures in Colony o' Queensland put together. Worth fifty thousand pounds, my boy—and I got it for five!"

He dug me in the ribs, and seemed in the mood for further confidences. My appearance checked him, and he rubbed his hands.

"If you take it like that," he chuckled, "how will old Johnson take it? Go out and hang himself to his own picture-rods, I hope!"

Heaven knows what I contrived to say at last. Struck speechless first by my relief, I continued silent from a very different cause. A new tangle of emotions tied my tongue. Raffles had failed—Raffles had failed! Could I not succeed? Was it too late? Was there no way?

"So long," he said, taking a last look at the canvas before he rolled it up—"so long till we get to Brisbane."

The flutter I was in as he closed the case!

"For the last time," he went on, as his keys jingled back into his pocket. "It goes straight into the strong-room on board."

For the last time! If I could but send him out to Australia with only its legitimate contents in his precious map-case! If I could but succeed where Raffles had failed!

We returned to the other room. I have no notion how long he talked, or what about. Whisky and soda-water became the order of the hour. I scarcely touched it, but he drank copiously, and before eleven I left him incoherent. And the last train for Esher was the 11.50 out of Waterloo.

I took a hansom to my rooms. I was back at the hotel in thirteen minutes. I walked upstairs. The corridor was empty; I stood an instant on the sitting-room threshold, heard a snore within, and admitted myself softly with my master-key.

Craggs never moved; he was stretched on the sofa fast asleep. But not fast enough for me. I saturated my handkerchief with the chloroform I had brought, and I laid it gently over his mouth. Two or three stertorous breaths, and the man was a log.

I removed the handkerchief; I extracted the keys from his pocket. In less than five minutes I put them back, after winding the picture about my body beneath my Inverness cape. I took some whisky and soda-water before I went.

The train was easily caught—so easily that I trembled for ten minutes in my first-class smoking carriage, in terror of every footstep on the platform, in unreasonable terror till the end. Then at last I sat back and lit a cigarette, and the lights of Waterloo reeled out behind.

Some men were returning from the theatre. I can recall their conversation even now. They were disappointed with the piece they had seen. It was one of the late Savoy operas, and they spoke wistfully of the days of *Pinafore* and *Patience*. One of them hummed a stave, and there was an argument as to whether the air was out of *Patience* or the *Mikado*. They all got out at Surbiton, and I was alone with my triumph for a few intoxicating minutes. To think that I had succeeded where Raffles had failed! Of all our adventures, this was the first in which I had played a commanding part; and, of them all, this was infinitely the least discreditable. It left me without a conscientious qualm; I had but robbed a robber, when all was said. And I had done it myself, single-handed—*ipse egomet!*

I pictured Raffles, his surprise, his delight. He would think a little more of me in future. And that future, it should be different. We had two thousand pounds apiece—surely enough to start afresh as honest men—and all through me!

In a glow I sprang out at Esher, and took the one belated cab that was waiting under the bridge. In a perfect fever I beheld Broom Hall, with the lower storey still lit up, and saw the front door open as I climbed the steps.

"Thought it was you," said Raffles cheerily. "It's all right. There's a bed for you. Sir Bernard's sitting up to shake your hand."

His good spirits disappointed me. But I knew the man—he was one of those who wear their brightest smile in the blackest hour. I knew him too well by this time to be deceived.

"I've got it!" I cried in his ear—"I've got it!"

"Got what?" he asked me, stepping back.

"The picture!"

"*What?*"

"The picture. He showed it me. You had to go without it; I saw that. So I determined to have it. And here it is."

"Let's see," said Raffles grimly.

I threw off my cape and unwound the canvas from about my body. While I was doing so an untidy old gentleman made his appearance in the hall, and stood looking on with raised eyebrows.

"Looks pretty fresh for an Old Master, doesn't it?" said Raffles.

His tone was strange. I could only suppose that he was jealous of my success.

"So Craggs said. I hardly looked at it myself."

"Well, look now—look closely. By Jove, I must have faked it better than I thought!"

"It's a copy!" I cried.

"It's *the* copy," he answered. It's the copy I've been tearing all over the country to procure. It's the copy I faked back and front, so that, on your own showing, it imposed upon Craggs, and might have made him happy for life. And you go and rob him of that!"

I could not speak.

"How did you manage it?" inquired Sir Bernard Debenham.

"Have you killed him?" asked Raffles sardonically.

I did not look at him; I turned to Sir Bernard Debenham, and to him I told my story, hoarsely, excitedly, for it was all that I could do to keep from breaking down. But as I spoke I became calmer, and I finished in mere bitterness, with the remark that another time Raffles might tell me what he meant to do.

"Another time!" he cried instantly. "My dear Bunny, you speak as though we were going to turn burglars for a living!"

"I trust you won't," said Sir Bernard, smiling, "for you are certainly two very daring young men. Let us hope our friend from Queensland will do as he said, and not open the case till he gets back there. He will find my cheque awaiting him, and I shall be very much surprised if he troubles any of us again."

Raffles and I did not speak till I was in the room which had been prepared for me. Nor was I anxious to do so then. But he followed me and took my hand.

"Bunny," said he, "don't you be hard on a fellow! I was in the deuce of a hurry, and didn't know that I should ever get what I wanted in time, and that's a fact. But it serves me right that you should have gone and undone one of the best things I ever did. As for *your* handiwork, old chap, you won't mind my saying that I didn't think you had it in you? In future——"

"For God's sake, don't talk about the future!" I cried. "I hate the whole thing; I'm going to give it up!"

"So shall I," said Raffles, "when I've made my pile."

ROBERT BARR

"The Mystery of the Five Hundred Diamonds" is the only story in this book to feature a detective. That is, a detective narrates it, but his every move is in response to a clever thief who remains offstage throughout. Therefore the story seems to get along just fine with its unsavory neighbors. As much as any tale in this volume, it brings to mind G. K. Chesterton's remark that the detective serves primarily as after-the-fact critic of the true artist, the criminal.

History has demoted Barr's French detective, Eugene Valmont, to ancestor status. In other Valmont stories—there are only eight—he seems a predecessor to Agatha Christie's vainglorious Hercule Poirot. But Valmont, while not as vivid as Poirot and lacking his staying power, has virtues of his own, including a glib narrative pace with just the right amount of detail. Although he isn't precisely a satirical writer, Barr has fun mocking the English, the French, and some of the already hoary traditions of the genre. Many critics rate the Valmont story "The Absent-Minded Coterie" as one of the great detective stories of the early days. The following adventure is Valmont's debut and takes place in Paris. Later he retires from the official police and moves to London, where he becomes an illustrious private detective. (In 1920, in Agatha Christie's debut novel, *The Mysterious Affair at Styles,* Poirot would settle into unofficial detection in England after retiring from the Belgian police.)

Like many of the authors in this book, Robert Barr was a nomad. He was born in Glasgow but grew up in Toronto. Early on he began writing facetious squibs under the pen name Luke Short—which he also used when he invented Sherlaw Kombs, his shot at the parody-magnet of Baker Street. One of his earliest published works was a comic account of a boating mishap on Lake Erie. After five years as reporter and columnist at the *Detroit Free Press*, which at the time provided entertainment as much as news, he moved to London in 1881 to found a British offshoot.

Eleven years later, with the popular humorist Jerome K. Jerome (famous for the comic novel *Three Men in a Boat*), he founded *The Idler*. Until it folded in 1911, this esteemed glossy monthly magazine serialized novels and ran short stories by such luminaries as Mark Twain, Rudyard Kipling, and Arthur Conan Doyle. A popular wit and socialite, Barr was friends with some of the more eminent authors in the present volume, including H. G. Wells and Arnold Bennett. Just as Conan Doyle completed Grant Allen's last novel, so did Barr finish *The O'Ruddy: A Romance* after the death of his friend Stephen Crane.

Barr's numerous novels include *Jennie Baxter, Journalist* and *The Speculations of John Steele*. Several of his short story collections, such as *The Face and the Mask*, deal with crime and detection. "The Mystery of the Five Hundred Diamonds" first appeared in the November 1904 issue of *The Windsor Magazine* and was reprinted in Barr's 1906 collection *The Triumphs of Eugene Valmont*—although, despite the title, not every case leaves the detective triumphant.

THE MYSTERY OF THE FIVE HUNDRED DIAMONDS

When I say I am called Valmont, the name will convey no impression to the reader, one way or another. My profession is that of private detective in London, and my professional name differs from that which I have just given you; but if you ask any policeman in Paris who Valmont was, he will likely be able to tell you, unless he is a recent recruit. If you ask him where Valmont is now, he may not know, yet I have a good deal to do with the Parisian police.

For a period of seven years I was chief detective to the Government of France; and if I am unable to prove myself a great crime-hunter, it is because the record of my career is in the secret archives of Paris.

I may say at the outset that I have no grievances to air. The French Government considered itself justified in dismissing me, and it did so. In this action it was quite within its right, and I should be the last to dispute that right; but, on the other hand, I consider myself justified in publishing the following account of what actually occurred, especially as so many false rumours have been put abroad concerning the case. However, as I said at the beginning, I have no grievance, because my worldly affairs are now much more prosperous than they were in Paris, my intimate knowledge of that city and the country of which it is the capital having brought to me many cases with which I have dealt more or less successfully since I established myself in London.

Without further preliminary I shall at once plunge into an account of the case which a few years ago riveted the attention of the whole world.

The year 1893 was a prosperous twelve months for France. The weather was good, the harvest excellent, and the wine of that vintage is celebrated to this day. Everyone was well-off and reasonably happy, a marked contrast to the state of things a few years later, when dissension rent the country in twain.

Newspaper readers may remember that in '93 the Government of France fell heir to an unexpected treasure which set the whole civilized world agog, especially those inhabitants of it who are interested in historical relics. This was the finding of the diamond necklace in the Château de Chaumont, where it had lain for a century in a rubbish heap of an attic. I believe it has not been questioned that this was the veritable necklace which the Court jeweller, Boehmer, hoped to sell to Marie Antoinette, although how it came to be in the Château de Chaumont, no one has been able to form even a conjecture. For a century it was supposed that the necklace had been broken up in London, and its five hundred stones, great and small, sold separately. It has always seemed strange to me that the Countess de Lamotte-Valois, who was thought to have profited by the sale of these jewels, should not have abandoned France if she possessed money to leave that country, for exposure was inevitable if she remained. Indeed, the unfortunate woman was branded and imprisoned, and afterwards was dashed to death from the third storey of a London house, when, in the direst poverty, she sought escape from the consequences of debt.

I am not superstitious in the least, yet this celebrated piece of treasure-trove seems actually to have exerted a malign influence over everyone who had the misfortune to be connected with it. Indeed, in a small way, I who write these words suffered dismissal and disgrace, though I caught but one glimpse of this dazzling scintillation of jewels. The jeweller who made it met financial ruin; the Queen for whom it was constructed was beheaded; that high-born Prince Louis René Édouard, Cardinal de Rohan, who purchased it, was flung into prison; the unfortunate Countess, who said she acted as go-between, clung for five awful minutes to a London window-sill before dropping to her death to the flags below; and now, a hundred and eight years later, up comes this devil's display of fireworks to the light again.

Droulliard, the working man who found the ancient box, seems to have prised it open and, ignorant though he was—he had probably never seen a diamond in his life before—realised that a fortune was in his grasp. The baleful light from the combination must have sent madness into his brain, working havoc therein as though they were those mysterious rays which scientists have recently discovered. He might quite easily have walked out of the main gate of the Château unsuspected and unquestioned with the diamonds concealed about his person, but instead of this he crept from the attic window on to the steep roof, slipped to the eaves, dropped and lay dead with a broken neck, while the necklace, intact, shimmered in the sunlight beside his body.

No matter where these jewels had been found, the Government had doubtless the first claim upon them; but as the Château de Chaumont was an historical monument, and the property of France, there could be no question to whom the necklace belonged. The Government at once claimed it and ordered it to be sent by a trustworthy military man to Paris. It was carried safely and delivered promptly to the authorities by a young captain of artillery, to whom its custody had been entrusted.

In spite of its fall from the tall tower, neither case nor jewels was perceptibly damaged. The lock of the box had apparently been forced by Droulliard's hatchet, or perhaps by the clasp-knife found on his body. On reaching the ground, the lid had flown open and the necklace was thrown out.

I believe there was some discussion in the Cabinet regarding the fate of this ill-omened trophy, one section wishing it to be placed in a museum, on account of its historical interest, another advocating the breaking-up of the necklace and the selling of the diamonds for what they would fetch. But a third party maintained that the method to get the most money into the coffers of the country was to sell the necklace as it stood; for as the world now contains so many rich amateurs who collected undoubted rarities regardless of expense, the historic associations of the jewelled collar would enhance the intrinsic value of the stones; and this view prevailing, it was announced that the necklace would be sold by auction a month later in the rooms of Meyer, Renault and Co., in the Boulevard des Italiens, near the Bank of the Crédit-Lyonnais.

This announcement elicited much comment from the newspapers of all countries, and it seemed that from a financial point of view, at least, the decision of the Government had been wise, for it speedily became evident that a notable coterie of wealthy buyers would be congregated in Paris on the thirteenth, when the sale was to take place. But we of the inner circle were made aware of another result somewhat more disquieting, which was that the most expert criminals in the world were also gathering like vultures upon the fair city. The honour of France was at stake. Whoever bought that necklace must be assured of a safe conduct out of the country. Whatever happened afterwards we might view with equanimity, but while he was a resident of France his life and property must not be endangered. Thus it came about that I was given full authority to insure that neither murder nor theft, nor both combined, should be committed while the purchaser of the necklace remained within our boundaries, and for this purpose the police resources of France were placed unreservedly at my disposal. If I failed, there should be no one to blame but myself; consequently, as I have remarked before, I do not complain of my dismissal by the Government.

The broken lock of the jewel-case had been very deftly repaired by an expert locksmith, who in executing his task was so unfortunate as to scratch a finger on the broken metal, whereupon blood poisoning set in, and although his life was saved, he was dismissed from the hospital with one arm gone, and his usefulness destroyed.

When the jeweller Boehmer made the necklace, he asked a hundred and sixty thousand pounds for it, but after years of disappointment he was content to sell it to Cardinal de Rohan for sixty-four thousand pounds, to be liquidated in three instalments, not one of which was ever paid. This latter amount was probably somewhere near the value of the five hundred and sixteen separate stones, one of which was of tremendous size, a very monarch of diamonds, holding its court among seventeen brilliants each as large as a filbert. This iridescent concentration of wealth was in my care, and I had to see to it that no harm came to the necklace or to its prospective owner until they had safely crossed the boundaries of France.

The four weeks previous to the thirteenth proved a busy and anxious time for me. Thousands, most of whom were actuated by mere curiosity, wished to view the diamonds. We were compelled to discriminate, and sometimes discriminated against the wrong person, which caused unpleasantness. Three distinct attempts were made to rob the safe, but luckily these were frustrated, and so we came unscathed to the eventful thirteenth of the month.

The sale was to take place at two o'clock, and on the morning of that day I took the somewhat tyrannical precaution to have the more dangerous of our own criminals, and as many of the foreigners as I could trump up charges against, laid by the heels, yet I knew very well it was not these rascals I had to fear, but the suave, well-groomed gentlemen, amply supplied with unimpeachable credentials, stopping at our fine hotels and living like princes. Many of these were foreigners against whom we could prove nothing, and whose arrest might land us into temporary international difficulties. Nevertheless, I had each of them shadowed, and on the morning of the thirteenth, if one of them had even disputed a cab fare, I should have had him in prison half an hour later, and taken the consequences; but these gentlemen are very shrewd and do not commit mistakes.

I made up a list of all the men in the world who were able or likely to purchase the necklace. Many of them would not be in person at the auction-rooms; their bidding would be done by agents. This simplified matters a good deal, for the agents kept me duly informed of their purposes, and, besides, an agent who handles treasure every week is an adept at the business, and does not need the protection which must surround an amateur who, in nine cases out of ten, has but scant idea of the dangers that threaten him, beyond knowing that if he goes down a dark street in a dangerous quarter, he is likely to be maltreated and robbed.

There were no less than sixteen clients, all told, who we learned were to attend personally on the day of the sale, any one of whom might well have made the purchase. The Marquis of Warlingham and Lord Oxtead, from England, were well-known jewel-fanciers, while at least half-a-dozen millionaires were expected from the United States, with a smattering from Germany, Austria, and Russia, and one each from Italy, Belgium, and Holland.

Admission to the auction-rooms was allowed by ticket only, to be applied for at least a week in advance, applications to be accompanied by satisfactory testimonials. It would possibly have surprised many of the rich men collected there to know that they sat cheek by jowl with some of the most noted thieves of England and America; but I allowed this for two reasons: first, I wished to keep these sharpers under my own eye until I knew who had bought the necklace; and secondly, I was desirous that they should not know they were suspected.

I had trusty men stationed outside on the Boulevard des Italiens, each of whom knew by sight most of the probable purchasers of the necklace. It was arranged that when the sale was over, I should walk out to the Boulevard alongside the man who was the new owner of the diamonds, and from that moment until he quitted France my men were not to lose sight of him if he took personal custody of the stones, instead of doing the sensible and proper thing of having them insured and forwarded to his residence by some responsible transit company, or depositing them in the bank. In fact, I took every precaution that occurred to me. All police Paris was on the *qui vive* and felt itself pitted against the scoundrelism of the world.

For one reason or another, it was nearly half-past two before the sale began. There had been considerable delay because of forged tickets, and, indeed, each order of admittance was so closely scrutinised that this in itself took a good deal more time than we anticipated. Every chair was occupied, and still a number of the visitors had to stand. I stationed myself by the swinging-doors at the entrance and of the hall, where I could command a view of the entire assemblage. Some of my men were standing with backs against the wall, whilst others were distributed amongst the chairs, all in plain clothes. During the sale, the diamonds themselves were not displayed, but the box containing them rested in front of the auctioneer, and three policemen in uniform stood guard on either side.

Very quietly the auctioneer said that there was no need for him to expatiate on the notable character of the treasure he had to offer for sale, and with this preliminary he requested them to bid. Someone said twenty thousand francs, which was received with much laughter; then the bidding went steadily on until it reached nine hundred thousand francs, which I knew to be less than half the reserve the Government had put upon the necklace. The contest advanced more slowly until the million and a half was touched, and there it hung fire for a time, while the auctioneer remarked that this sum did not equal that which the maker of the necklace had finally been forced to accept for it. After another pause, he said that as the reserve was not exceeded, the necklace would be withdrawn, and probably never again offered for sale. He therefore urged those who were holding back to make their bid. At this the contest livened until the sum of two million three hundred thousand francs had been offered, and now I knew the necklace would be sold. Nearing the three million mark the competition thinned down to a few dealers from Hamburg and the Marquis of Warlingham, from England, when a voice that had not yet been heard in the auction-room said, in a tone of some impatience—

"One million dollars."

There was an instant hush, then the scribbling of pencils, as each person there reduced the sum to its equivalent in his own currency: pounds for the English, francs for the French, marks for the German, and so on. The aggressive tone and the clear-cut face of the bidder proclaimed him an American, not less than the financial denomination he had used. In a moment it was realised that his bid was a clear leap of more than two million francs, and a sigh went up from the audience as if this settled it, and the great sale was done. Nevertheless, the auctioneer's hammer hovered over the lid of his desk, and he looked up and down the long line of faces turned towards him. He seemed reluctant to tap the board, but there was no further price bid against this tremendous sum, and with a sharp click the mallet fell.

"What name?" he asked, bending over towards the customer.

"Cash," replied the American. "Here's the cheque for the amount. I'll take the diamonds with me."

"Your request is somewhat unusual," protested the auctioneer mildly.

"I know what you mean," interrupted the American—"you think the cheque may not be cashed. You will notice it is drawn on the Crédit-Lyonnais, which is practically next door. I must have the jewels with me. Send round your messenger with the cheque: it will take only a few minutes to find out whether or not the money is there to meet it. The necklace is mine, and I insist on having it."

The auctioneer with some demur handed the cheque to the representative of the French Government who was present, and this official himself went to the bank. There were some other things to be sold, and the auctioneer endeavoured to go on through the list, but no one paid the slightest attention to him.

Meanwhile I was studying the countenance of the man who had made the astounding bid, when I should instead have adjusted my preparations to meet the new conditions confronting me. Here was a man about whom we knew nothing whatever. I had come to the instant conclusion that he was a prince of criminals, and that some design, not at that moment fathomed by me, was on foot to get possession of the jewels. The handing up of the cheque was clearly a trick of some sort, and I fully expected the official to return and say the draft was good. I determined to prevent this man from getting the case until I knew more of his game. Quietly I removed from my place near the door to the auctioneer's desk, having two objects in view: first, to warn the auctioneer not to part with the treasure too easily; and secondly, to study the suspected man at closer range. Of all evil-doers, the American is most to be feared; he uses more ingenuity in the planning of his projects, and will take greater risks in carrying them out, than any other malefactor on earth.

From my new station I saw I had two to deal with. The bidder had a keen, intellectual face, and refined, ladylike hands, clean and white, showing they had long been divorced from manual labour, if, indeed, they had ever done any useful work. Coolness and imperturbability were his beyond a doubt. The companion who sat at his right was of an entirely different stamp. His hands were hairy and sun-tanned; his face bore the stamp of grim determination and unflinching bravery. I knew that these two types usually hunted in couples—the one to scheme, the other to execute, and they always formed a combination dangerous to encounter and difficult to circumvent.

There was a buzz of conversation up and down the hall, and these two men talked together in low tones. I knew now that I was face to face with the most hazardous problem of my life.

I whispered to the auctioneer, who bent his head to listen. He knew very well who I was, of course.

"You must not give up the necklace," I said.

He shrugged his shoulders.

"I am under the orders of the officials of the Ministry of the Interior. You must speak to him."

"I shall not fail to do so," I replied. "Nevertheless, do not give up the box too readily."

"I am helpless," he said with another shrug. "I obey the orders of the Government."

Seeing it was useless to parley further with the auctioneer, I set my wits to work to meet the new emergency. I felt convinced that the cheque would prove to be genuine, and that the fraud, wherever it lay, would be disclosed too late to be of service to the authorities. My duty, therefore, was to make sure we lost sight neither of the buyer nor the thing bought. Of course, I could not arrest him merely on suspicion; besides, it would make the Government the laughing-stock of the world if they were to sell a case of jewels and immediately arrest the buyer when they themselves had handed his purchase over to him; and ridicule kills in France. A breath of laughter will blow a Government out of existence in Paris much more effectually than a whiff of cannon-smoke. My duty, then, was to give the Government full warning, and never lose sight of my man until he was clear of France; then my responsibility was ended.

I took aside one of my own men in plain clothes and said to him—

"You have seen the American who has bought the necklace?"

"Yes, sir."

"Very well. Go outside quietly and station yourself there. He is likely to emerge presently with the casket in his possession. You are not to lose sight of either the man or the jewels. I shall follow him and be close behind him as he emerges, and you are to shadow us. If he parts with the case, you must be ready at a sign from me to follow either the man or the jewels. Do you understand?"

"Yes, sir," he answered, and left the room.

It is ever the unforseen that baffles us: it is easy to be wise after the event. I should have sent two men, and I have often thought since how wise is the regulation of the Italian Government, which sends out its policemen in pairs. Or I should have given my man power to call for help; but even as it was, he did only half as well as I had a right to expect of him, and the blunder he committed by a moment's dull-witted hesitation. Ah, well! there is no use in scolding. After all, the result might have been the same.

Just as my man disappeared through the two folding-doors, the official from the Ministry of the Interior entered. I intercepted him about half-way between the door and the auctioneer.

"Possibly the cheque appears to be genuine," I whispered to him.

"Certainly," he replied pompously. He was a man greatly impressed with his own importance—a kind of character with whom it is always difficult to deal. Afterwards the Government claimed that this official had warned me, and the utterances of an empty-headed ass, "dressed in a little brief authority," as the English poet says, were looked upon as the epitome of wisdom.

"I advise you strongly not to hand over the necklace as has been requested," I went on.

"Why?" he asked.

"Because I am convinced the bidder is a criminal."

"If you have proof of that, arrest him."

"I have no proofs at the present moment, but I request you to delay the delivery of the goods."

"That is absurd!" he cried impatiently. "The necklace is his, not ours. The money has already been transferred to the account of the Government. We cannot retain the five million francs and refuse to hand over to him what he has bought with them"; and so the official left me standing there, nonplussed and anxious. The eyes of everyone in the room had been turned on us during our brief conversation, and now the official proceeded ostentatiously up the room with a grand air of importance; then, with a bow and a flourish of the hand, he said dramatically—

"The jewels belong to Monsieur."

The two Americans rose simultaneously, the taller holding out his hand while the auctioneer passed to him the case he had apparently paid so highly for. The American nonchalantly opened the box, and for the first time the electric radiance of the jewels burst upon that audience, each member of which craned his neck to behold it. It seemed to me a most reckless thing to do. He examined the jewels minutely for a few moments, then snapped the lid shut again and calmly put the box in his outside pocket; and I could not help noticing now that the light overcoat he wore had pockets made extraordinarily large, as if on purpose for this very case. And now this amazing man walked serenely down the room past miscreants who would have joyfully cut his throat for even the smallest diamond in that conglomeration; yet he did not take the trouble to put his hand on the pocket which contained the case, or in any way attempt to protect it. The assemblage seemed stricken dumb at his audacity. His friend followed closely at his heels, and the tall man disappeared through the folding-doors. Not so the other, however. He turned quickly and whipped two revolvers out of his pocket, which he presented at the astonished crowd. There had been a movement on the part of everyone to leave the room, but the sight of these deadly weapons confronting them made each one shrink into his place again.

The man with his back to the door spoke in a loud and domineering voice, asking the auctioneer to translate what he had to say into French and German. He spoke in English.

"These here shiners are valuable; they belong to my friend who has just gone out. Casting no reflections on the generality of people in this room, there are, nevertheless, half-a-dozen 'crooks' among us whom my friend wishes to avoid. Now, no honest man here will object to giving the buyer of that there trinket five clear minutes in which to get away. It's only the 'crooks' that can kick. I ask these five minutes as a favour, but if they are not granted, I am going to take them as a right. Any man who moves will get shot."

"I am an honest man," I cried, "and I object. I am chief detective of the Government. Stand aside; the police will protect your friend."

"Hold on, my son," warned the American, turning one weapon directly upon me, while the other held a sort of roving commission, pointing all over the room. "My friend is from New York, and he distrusts the police as much as he does the grafters. You may be twenty detectives, but if you move before that clock stikes three, I'll bring you down—and don't you forget it."

It is one thing to face death in a fierce struggle, but quite another to advance coldly upon it towards the muzzle of a pistol held so steadily that there could be no chance of escape. The gleam of determination in the man's eye convinced me he meant what he said. I did not consider then, nor have I considered since, that the next five minutes, precious as they were, would be worth paying my life for. Apparently everyone else was of my opinion, for none moved hand or foot until the clock slowly struck three.

"Thank you, gentlemen," said the American, as he vanished between the spring-doors. When I say vanished, I mean that word and no other, because my men outside saw nothing of this individual then or later. He vanished as if he had never existed, and it was some hours before we found how this had been accomplished.

I rushed out almost on his heels, as one might say, and hurriedly questioned my waiting men. They had all seen the tall

American come out with the greatest leisureness and stroll towards the west. As he was not the man any of them were looking for, they paid no further attention to him, as, indeed, is the custom with our Parisian force. They have eyes for nothing but what they are sent to look for, and this trait has its drawbacks for their superiors.

I ran up the Boulevard, my whole thought intent on the diamonds and their bidder. I knew my subordinate in command of the men inside the hall would look after the scoundrel with the pistols. A short distance up I found the stupid fellow I had sent out, standing in a dazed manner at the corner of the Rue Michodière, gazing alternately towards the Place de l'Opéra and down the short street at whose corner he stood. The very fact that he was there was proof that he had failed.

"Where is that American?" I cried.

"He went down this street, sir."

"And why are you standing there like a fool?"

"I followed him this far, then a man came up the Rue Michodière, and without a word the American handed him the jewel-box, turning instantly down the street up which the other had come. The other jumped into a cab and drove towards the Place de l'Opéra."

"And what did you do? Stood here like a post, I suppose?"

"I didn't know what to do, sir. It all happened in a moment."

"Why didn't you follow the cab?"

"I didn't know which to follow, sir, and the cab was gone instantly while I watched the American."

"What was its number?"

"I don't know, sir."

"You clod! Why didn't you call one of our men, whoever was nearest, and leave him to follow the American while you followed the cab?"

"I did shout to the nearest man, sir, but he said you told him to stay there and watch the English lord; and even before he had said that, both American and cabman had disappeared."

"Was the man to whom he gave the box an American, too?"

"No, sir, he was French."

"How do you know?"

"By his appearance and the words he spoke."

"I thought you said he didn't speak?"

"He did not speak to the American, sir, but he said to the cabman: 'Drive to the Madeline as quickly as you can.'"

"Describe the man."

"He was a head shorter than the American, wore a black beard and moustache rather neatly trimmed, and seemed to be a superior sort of artisan."

"You did not take the number of the cab. Should you know the cabman if you saw him again?"

"Yes, sir, I should."

Taking this fellow with me, I returned to the now empty auction-room and there gathered all my men about me. Each in his notebook took down descriptions of the cabman and his passenger from the lips of my incompetent spy; then I dictated a full description of the two Americans, and scattered my men to the various railway stations of the lines leading out of Paris, with orders to make inquiries of the police on duty there, and to arrest one or more of the four persons described, should they be so fortunate as to find any of them, which I much doubted.

I now learned how the man with the pistols vanished so completely as he did. My subordinate in the auction-room had speedily solved the mystery. To the left of the main entrance of the auction-room was a door that gave access to the premises in the rear. As the attendant in charge confessed when questioned, he had been bribed by the American earlier in the day to leave this side-door open and to allow the man to escape by the goods-entrance. Thus the ruffian had not appeared on the Boulevard at all, and so had not been observed by any of my men.

Taking my spy with me, I returned to my own office and sent an order throughout the city that every cabman who had been in the Boulevard des Italiens between half-past two and half-past three that afternoon was to report to me. The examination of these men proved a very tedious business indeed; but whatever other countries may say of us, we French are patient, and if the haystack is searched long enough, the needle will be found. I did not discover the needle I was looking for, but I came upon one quite as important, if not more so.

It was nearly ten o'clock at night when a cabman answered my oft-repeated question in the affirmative.

"Did you take up a passenger a few minutes past three o'clock on the Boulevard des Italiens, near the Crédit-Lyonnais? Had he a short, black beard? Did he carry a small box in his hand and order you to drive to the Madeline?"

The cabman seemed puzzled.

"He had a short, black beard when he got out of the cab," he replied.

"What do you mean by that?"

"I drive a closed cab, sir. When he got in, he was a smooth-faced gentleman; when he got out, he wore a short, black beard."

"Was he a Frenchman?"

"No, sir, he was a foreigner—either English or American."

"Did he carry a box?"

"No, sir; he had in his hand a small handbag."

"Where did he tell you to drive?"

"He told me to follow the cab in front, which had just driven off very rapidly towards the Madeline. In fact, I heard the man such as you describe order the other cabman to drive to the Madeline. I had come up to the kerb when this man held up his hand for a cab, but the open cab cut in ahead of me. Just then my passenger stepped up and said in French, but with a foreign accent: 'Follow that cab wherever it goes.'"

I turned with some indignation to my spy.

"You told me," I said, "that the American had gone down a side street. Yet he evidently met a second man, obtained from him the handbag, turned back, and got into the closed cab directly behind you."

"Well, sir," stammered the man, "I could not look in two directons at the same time. The American certainly went down the side street, but of course I watched the cab which contained the jewels."

"And you saw nothing of the closed cab right at your elbow?"

"The Boulevard was full of cabs, sir, and the pavement crowded with passers-by, as it always is at that hour of the day; and I have only two eyes in my head."

"I am glad to know you had that many, for I was beginning to think you were blind."

Although I said this, I knew in my heart it was useless to censure the poor wretch, for the fault was entirely my own in not sending two men, and in failing to guess the possibility of the jewels and their owner being separated. Besides, here was a clue to my hand at last, and no time must be lost in following it up. So I continued my interrogation of the cabman.

"The other cab was an open vehicle, you say?"

"Yes, sir."

"You succeeded in following it?"

"Oh, yes, sir. At the Madeline the man in front re-directed the coachman, who turned to the left and drove to the Place de la Concorde, then up the Champs Élysées to the Arch, and so down the Avenue de la Grand Armée and the Avenue de Neuilly, where it came to a standstill. My fare got out, and I saw he wore a short, black beard, which he had evidently put on inside the cab. He gave me a ten-franc piece, which was very satisfactory."

"And the fare you were following? What did he do?"

"He got out, paid the cabman, went down the bank of the river, and on board a steam launch that seemed to be waiting for him."

"Did he look behind or appear to know that he was being followed?"

"No, sir."

"And your fare?"

"He ran after the first man and also went aboard the steam launch, which instantly started down the river."

"And that was the last you saw of them?"

"Yes, sir."

"At what time did you reach the Pont de Nenilly?"

"I do not know, sir; I had to drive rather fast, but the distance is seven or eight kilometres."

"You would do it under the hour?"

"Yes, certainly under the hour."

"Then you must have reached there about four o'clock?"

"It is very likely, sir."

The plan of the tall American was now perfectly clear to me, and it comprised nothing that was contrary to law. He had evidently placed his luggage on board the steam launch in the morning. The handbag had contained various materials which would enable him to disguise himself, and this bag he had probably left in some shop down the side street, or else someone was waiting with it for him. The giving of the treasure to another man was not so risky as it had at first appeared, because he instantly followed that man, who was probably his confidential servant. Despite the windings of the river, there was ample time for the launch to reach Havre before the American steamer sailed on Saturday morning. I surmised it was his intention to come alongside of the steamer before she left her berth in Havre harbour, and thus transfer himself and his belongings unperceived by anyone on watch at the land side of the liner. All this, of course, was perfectly justifiable, and was, in truth, a well-laid scheme for escaping observation. His only danger of being tracked was when he got into the cab. Once away from the neighbourhood of the Boulevard des Italiens, he was reasonably sure to evade pursuit, and the five minutes which his friend with the pistols had won for him gave him just about the time he needed to get as far as the Place Madeline, and after that everything was easy. Yet if it had not been for this five minutes secured by coercion, I should not have had the slightest excuse for arresting him. But he was accessory after the act in that piece of illegality—in fact, it was absolutely certain that he had been accessory before the act, and guilty of conspiracy with the man who had presented firearms to the auctioneer's audience, and who had interfered with an officer in the discharge of his duty by threatening me and my men. So I was now legally in the right if I arrested every person on board that steam launch.

With a map of the river before me, I proceeded to make some calculations. It was now nearly ten o'clock at night. The launch had had six hours to go at its utmost speed. It was doubtful if so small a vessel could make ten miles an hour, even with the current in its favour, which is rather sluggish because of the locks and the level country.

Sixty miles would place her beyond Meulan, which is fifty-eight miles from the Pont Royal, and, or course, a lesser distance from the Pont de Neuilly. But the navigation of the river is difficult at all times, and almost impossible after dark. There were chances of the boat running aground, and then there was the inevitable delay at the locks. So I estimated that the launch could not yet have reached Meulan, which was less than twenty-five miles from Paris by rail. Looking up the time-table, I saw there were still two trains to Meulan—the next at 10.25, which reached Meulan at 11.40. I had time to reach St. Lazarus station and there do some telegraphing before the train left.

With three of my assistants, I got into a cab and drove to the station, sending one of my men to hold the train while I went into the telegraph-office, cleared the wires, and got into communication with the lock-master at Meulan. He replied that no steam-launch had passed down since an hour before sunset. I then instructed him to allow the yacht to enter the lock, close the upper gate, let half of the water out, and hold the vessel there until I came. I also ordered the local Meulan police to send enough men to the lock to enforce this command. Lastly, I sent messages all along the river asking the police to report to me on the train passage of the steam-launch.

The 10.25 is a slow train, stopping at every station. However, every drawback has its compensations, and these stoppages enabled me to receive and to send telegraphic messages. I was quite well aware that I might be on a fool's errand in going to Meulan. The yacht might turn before it had steamed a mile, and come back into Paris. There had been no time to learn whether this were so or not, if I was to catch the 10.25. Also it might have landed its passengers anywhere along the river. I may say at once that neither of these two things happened, and my calculations as to her movements were accurate to the letter. But a trap most carefully set may be prematurely sprung by inadvertence, or more often by the over-zeal of some stupid ass who fails to understand his instructions, or oversteps them if they are understood. I received a most annoying telegram from Denouval, a lock about thirteen miles above that of Meulan. The local policeman, arriving at the lock, found that

the yacht had just cleared. The fool shouted to the captain to
return, threatening him with all the pains and penalties of
the law if he refused. The captain did refuse, rang on "Full
speed ahead!" and disappeared in the darkness. Through this
well-meant blunder of an understrapper, those on board the
launch had received warning that we were on their track. I
telegraphed to the lock-keeper at Denouval to allow no craft to
pass towards Paris until further orders. We had the launch
trapped in a thirteen-mile stretch of water, but the night was
pitch dark, and passengers might be landed on either bank,
with all France before them.

It was midnight when I reached the lock at Meulan, and, as
I expected, nothing had been seen or heard of the launch. It
gave me some satisfaction to telegraph to that dunderhead at
Denouval to walk along the river-bank to Meulan and report if
he learnt the launch's whereabouts. We took up our quarters in
the lock-keeper's house and waited. There was little sense in
sending men to scour the country at this time of night, for the
pursued were on the alert and were not likely to allow themselves to be caught if they did go ashore. On the other hand,
there was every chance that the captain would refuse to let
them land, because he must know his vessel was in a trap from
which he could not escape; and although the demand of the policeman at Denouval was quite unauthorised, nevertheless the
captain must be well aware of his danger in refusing to obey
that command. Even if he got away for the moment, he must
know that arrest was certain and that his punishment would be
severe. His only plea could be that he had not heard and understood the order to return. But this plea would be invalidated if
he aided in the escape of two men who, he must now know,
were wanted by the police. I was, therefore, very confident that
if the men demanded to be set ashore, the captain would refuse
when he had had time to think about his own danger. My estimate proved accurate, for towards one o'clock the lock-keeper
came in and said the green and red lights of an approaching
craft were visible, and as he spoke, the yacht whistled for the
opening of the lock. I stood by the lock-keeper while he opened
the gates; my men and the local police were concealed on each

side of the lock. The launch came slowly in, and as soon as it had done so, I asked the captain to step ashore, which he did.

"I wish a word with you," I said. "Follow me."

I took him to the lock-keeper's house and closed the door.

"Where are you going?"

"To Havre."

"Where did you come from?"

"Paris."

"From what quay?"

"From the Pont de Neuilly."

"When did you leave there?"

"At five minutes to four o'clock this afternoon."

"Yesterday afternoon, you mean?"

"Yesterday afternoon."

"Who engaged you to make this voyage!"

"An American—I do not know his name."

"He paid you well, I suppose?"

"He paid me what I asked."

"Have you received the money?"

"Yes, sir."

"I may inform you, captain, that I am chief detective of the French Government, and that all the police of France at this moment are under my control. I ask you, therefore, to be careful of your answers. You were ordered by a policeman at Denouval to return. Why did you not do so?"

"The lock-keeper ordered me to return, but as he had no right to order me, I went on."

"You know very well it was the police who ordered you, and you ignored the command. Again I ask you why you did so."

"I did not know it was the police."

"I thought you would say that. You knew very well, but were paid to take the risk, and it is likely to cost you dear. You had two passengers aboard?"

"Yes, sir."

"Did you put them ashore between here and Denouval?"

"No, sir, but one of them went overboard, and we couldn't find him again."

"Which one?"

"The short man."

"Then the American is still aboard?"

"What American, sir?"

"Captain, you must not trifle with me. The man who engaged you is still aboard."

"Oh, no, sir—he has never been aboard."

"Do you mean to tell me that the second man who came on your launch at the Pont de Neuilly is not the American who engaged you?"

"Oh, no; the American was a smooth-faced man, this man has a black beard."

"Yes, a false beard."

"I did not know that, sir. I understood from the American that I was to take but one passenger. One came aboard with a small box in his hand, the other with a small bag. Each claimed to be the passenger in question. I did not know what to do, so I left with both of them on board."

"Then the tall man with the beard is still with you?"

"Yes, sir."

"Well, captain, is there anything else you have to tell me? I think you will find it better in the end to make a clean breast of it."

The captain hesitated, turning his cap about in his hands for a few moments, then he said—

"I am not sure that the first passenger went overboard of his own accord. When the police hailed us at Denouval——"

"Ah! you knew it was the police, then?"

"I was afraid after I left it might have been. You see, when the bargain was made with me, the American said that if I reached Havre at a certain time, a thousand francs extra would be paid to me, so I was anxious to get along as quickly as I could. I told him it was dangerous to navigate the Seine at night, but he paid me well for attempting it. After the policeman called to us at Denouval, the man with the small box became very much excited and asked me to put him ashore, which I refused to do. The tall man appeared to be watching him, never letting him get far away. When I heard the splash in the water, I ran aft, and I saw the tall man putting the box which the other had held into his handbag, although I said nothing of it at the time. We cruised back and forward about the spot where the other man had gone overboard, but saw nothing more of him. Then I came on to Meulan, intending to give information about what I had seen. That is all I know of the matter, sir."

"Was the man who had the jewels a Frenchman?"

"What jewels, sir?"

"The man with the small box."

"Oh, yes, sir, he was French."

"You hinted that the foreigner threw him overboard. What grounds have you for such a belief if you did not see the struggle?"

"The night is very dark, sir, and I did not see what happened. I was at the wheel in the forward part of the launch, with my back turned to these two. I heard a scream, then a splash. If the man had jumped overboard as the other said, he would not have screamed. Besides, as I told you, when I ran aft, I saw the foreigner put the little box in his handbag, which he shut up quickly, as if he did not wish me to notice."

"Very good, captain. If you have told the truth, it will go easier with you in the investigation that is to follow."

I now turned the captain over to one of my men and ordered in the foreigner with his bag and bogus black whiskers. Before questioning him, I ordered him to open the handbag, which he did with evident reluctance. It was filled with false whiskers, false moustaches, and various bottles, but on top of them all lay the jewel-case. I raised the lid and displayed that accursed necklace. I looked up at the man, who stood there calmly enough, saying nothing in spite of the overwhelming evidence against him.

"Will you oblige me by removing those false whiskers?"

He did so at once, throwing them into the open bag. I knew the moment I saw him that he was not the American, and thus my theory had broken down—in one very important part, at least. Informing him who I was, and cautioning him to speak the truth, I asked how he came into possession of the jewels.

"Am I under arrest?" he asked.

"Certainly," I replied.

"Of what am I accused?"

"You are accused in the first place of having in your possession property which does not belong to you."

"I plead guilty to that. What in the second place?"

"In the second place, you may find yourself accused of murder."

"I am innocent of the second charge. The man jumped overboard."

"If that is true, why did he scream as he went over?"

"Because, too late to recover his balance, I seized this box and held it."

"He was in the rightful possession of the box; the owner gave it to him."

"I admit that; I saw the owner give it to him."

"Then why should he jump overboard?"

"I do not know. He seemed to become panic-stricken when the police at the last lock ordered us to return. He implored the captain to put him ashore, and from that moment I watched him keenly, expecting that if we drew near to the land, he would attempt to escape, as the captain had refused to beach the launch. He remained quiet for about half an hour, seated on a camp-chair by the rail, with his eyes turned towards the shore, trying, as I imagined, to penetrate the darkness and estimate the distance. Then suddenly he sprang up and made his dash. I was prepared, and instantly caught the box in his hand. He gave a half-turn, trying either to save himself or to retain the box, then with a scream went down shoulders first into the water. It all happened within a second after he leaped from his chair."

"You admit yourself, then, indirectly responsible for his drowning, at least?"

"I see no reason to suppose that the man was drowned. If able to swim, he could easily have reached the river-bank. If unable to swim, why should he attempt it encumbered by the box?"

"You believed he escaped, then?"

"I think so."

"It will be lucky for you should that prove to be the case."

"Certainly."

"How did you come to be in the yacht at all?"

"I shall give you a full account of the affair, concealing nothing. I am a private detective, with an office in London. I was certain that some attempt would be made by probably the most expert criminals at large to rob the possessor of this necklace. I came over to Paris, anticipating trouble, determined to keep an eye upon the jewel-case, if this proved possible. If the jewels were stolen, the crime was bound to be one of the most celebrated in legal annals. I was present during the sale and saw the buyer of the necklace. I followed the official who went to the Bank, and thus learned that the money was behind the cheque. I then stopped outside and waited for the buyer to appear. He had the case in his hand."

"In his pocket, you mean?"

"He had it in his hand when I saw him. Then the man who afterwards jumped overboard approached him, took the case without a word, held up his hand for a cab, and when an open vehicle approached the kerb, he stepped in, saying 'The Madeline.' I hailed a closed cab, instructed the cabman to follow the first, disguising myself with whiskers as near like those of the man in front as I had in my collection."

"Why did you do that?"

"As a detective, you should know why I did it. I wished as nearly as possible to resemble the man in front, so that if necessity arose I could pretend that I was the person commissioned to carry the jewel case. As a matter of fact, the crisis arose when we came to the end of our cab journey. The captain did not know which was his true passenger, and so let us both aboard the launch. And now you have the whole story."

"An extremely improbable one, sir. Even by your own account, you had no right to interfere in this business at all."

"I quite agree with you there," he replied with great nonchalance, taking a card from his pocket-book, which he handed to me.

"That is my London address; you may make inquiries, and you will find I am exactly what I represent myself to be."

The first train for Paris left Meulan at eleven minutes past four in the morning. It was now a quarter after two. I left the captain, crew, and launch in charge of two of my men, with orders to proceed to Paris as soon as it was daylight. I, supported by the third man, waiting at the station with our English prisoner, and reached Paris at half past five in the morning.

The English prisoner, though severely interrogated by the judge, stood by his story. Inquiry by the police in London proved that what he said of himself was true. His case, however, began to look very serious when two of the men from the launch asserted that they had seen him push the Frenchman overboard, and their statement could not be shaken. All our energies were bent for the next two weeks on trying to find something of the identity of the missing man, or to get any trace of the two Americans. If the tall American were alive, it seemed incredible that he should not have made application for his missing property. All attempts to trace him by means of the Crédit-Lyonnais proved futile.

We made inquiries about every missing man in Paris, but also without result.

The case had excited much attention throughout the world, and doubtless was published in full in the American papers. The Englishman had been in custody three weeks when the Chief of Police of Paris received the following letter:—

"DEAR SIR,—On my arrival in New York by the English steamer *Lucania,* I was much amused to read in the papers accounts of the exploits of detectives, French and English. I am sorry that only one of them seems to be in prison; I think his French *confrère* ought to be there also. I regret exceedingly, however, that there is the rumour of the death, by drowning, of my friend, Eugène Dubois, of 375, Rue aux Juifs, Rouen. If this is indeed the case, he has met his death through the blunders of the police. Nevertheless, I wish you would communicate with his family at the address I have given, and assure them that I will make arrangements for their future support.

"I may say that I am a manufacturer of imitation diamonds, and, through extensive advertising, have accumulated a fortune of many millions. I was in Europe when the necklace was found, and had in my posssession over a thousand imitation diamonds of my own manufacture. It occurred to me that here was the opportunity of the most magnificent advertisement in the world. I saw the necklace, received its measurements, and also obtained photographs of it taken by the French Government. Then I set my expert friend, Eugène Dubois, at work, and he made an imitation necklace so closely resembling the original that you apparently do not know it is the unreal you have in your possession. I was not nearly so much afraid of the villainy of the crooks as of the blundering of the police, who would have protected me with brass-band vehemence if I could not elude them. I knew that the detectives would overlook the obvious, but would at once follow a clue if I provided one for them. Consequently I laid my plans, just as you have discovered, and got Eugène Dubois up from Rouen to carry the case I gave him down to Havre. I had had another box prepared in brown paper with my address in New York written thereon. The moment I emerged from the auction-room, while my friend the cowboy was holding up the audience, I turned my face to the door, took out the genuine diamonds from the case, and slipped it into the box I had prepared for mailing. Into the genuine case I put the bogus diamonds. After handing the box to Dubois, I turned down a side street, and then into another whose name I do not know, and there in a shop, with sealing-wax and string, did up my packet for posting. I labelled the package 'Books,' went to the nearest post-office, paid letter postage, and handed it over unregistered, as if it were of no particular value. After this I went to my rooms in the Grand Hotel, where I had been staying under my own name for more than a month. Next morning I took train for London, and the day after sailed from Liverpool on the *Lucania*. I arrived before the *Gascoigne*, which sailed from Havre on Saturday, met my box at the Customs-house, paid duty, and it now reposes in my safe. I intend to construct an imitation necklace which will be so like the genuine one that nobody can tell the two apart; then I shall come to Europe and exhibit the pair, for the publication of the truth of this matter will give me the greatest advertisement that ever was.

                                    "Yours truly,
                                        "JOHN P. HAZARD."

I at once communicated with Rouen and found Eugène Dubois all right. His first words were—

"I swear I did not steal the jewels."

He had swum ashore, tramped to Rouen, and kept quiet in great fear as to what would happen.

It took Mr. Hazard longer to make his imitation necklace than he supposed, and several years later he took passage with the two necklaces on the ill-fated steamer *Burgoyne,* and now rests beside them at the bottom of the Atlantic. As the English poet says—

> Full many a gem of purest ray serene,
> The dark, unfathom'd caves of ocean bear.

ARNOLD BENNETT

Arnold Bennett is the first of two prominent mainstream novelists—the other being Sinclair Lewis—whose little-known crime stories enliven this volume. Bennett's father was a pawnbroker-turned-solicitor who urged young Arnold to follow in his footsteps. After failing an important law exam, however, the future novelist had to settle for clerking for a solicitor in London. In 1893 he joined the popular new magazine *Woman* and eventually wound up as its editor. Around the turn of the century, halfway through his life, he committed to writing as a career.

Bennett is remembered as the author of fiction about the industrial Midlands of England, the central belt of the island that includes Staffordshire, where he was born, and such busy cities as Birmingham. His many novels include *Anna of the Five Towns*, *Clayhanger*, and *Riceyman Steps*. Virginia Woolf fans recall him from her essay "Mr. Bennett and Mrs. Brown," in which she complains that writers such as Bennett capture the external details of everyday life but overlook the unique and invisible psyche lurking within. Now and then the workaday Mr. Bennett took a holiday from realism and wrote a crime story as a lark.

Like Simon Carne, Cecil Thorold is a gentleman of leisure—elegant, well dressed, at ease among those who would now be called the glitterati. Bored with his predictable moneyed world, he gets involved in crime for amusement and, on occasion, to benefit others. "What was I to do?" asks Thorold in reply to the question of why he turned to crime. "I was rich. I was bored. I had no great attainments. I was interested in life and in the arts, but not desperately, not vitally. . . . So finally I took to these rather original 'schemes,' as you call them. They had the advantage of being exciting and sometimes dangerous, and though they were often profitable, they were not too profitable. In short, they amused me and gave me joy." Clearly, writing the stories had the same effect on Bennett. He keeps the pace lively and the banter amusing.

Each story takes place in a different exotic port. Set in Belgium, "A Comedy on the Gold Coast" first appeared in *The Windsor Magazine* in July 1905. It was one of six stories under the serial title "The Loot of Cities: The Adventures of a Millionaire in Search of Joy." A few months later, this became the title of the collected Cecil Thorold stories, with the addition of two more words that indicate Bennett's lighthearted vacation from his realistic books: *A Fantasia*.

Incidentally, the Miss Fincastle who appears late in the story makes Thorold blush because she has witnessed his illegal diversions in the past.

A COMEDY ON THE
GOLD COAST

It was five o'clock on an afternoon in mid-September, and a couple of American millionaires (they abounded that year, did millionaires) sat chatting together on the wide terrace which separates the entrance to the Kursaal from the promenade. Some yards away, against the balustrade of the terrace, in the natural, unconsidered attitude of one to whom short frocks are a matter of history, certainly, but very recent history, stood a charming and imperious girl; you could see that she was eating chocolate while meditating upon the riddle of life. The elder millionaire glanced at every pretty woman within view, excepting only the girl; but his companion seemed to be intent on counting the chocolates.

The immense crystal dome of the Kursaal dominated the gold coast, and on either side of the great building were stretched out in a straight line the hotels, the restaurants, the *cafés,* the shops, the theatres, the concert-halls, and the pawnbrokers of the City of Pleasure—Ostend. At one extremity of that long array of ornate white architecture (which resembled the icing on a bride-cake more than the roofs of men) was the palace of a king; at the other were the lighthouse and the railway signals which guided into the city the continuously arriving cargoes of wealth, beauty, and desire. In front, the ocean, grey and lethargic, idly beat up a little genteel foam under the promenade for the wetting of pink feet and stylish bathing-costumes. And after a hard day's work, the sun, by arrangement with the authorities during August and September, was setting over the sea exactly opposite the superb portals of the Kursaal.

The younger of the millionaires was Cecil Thorold. The other, a man fifty-five or so, was Simeon Rainshore, father of the girl at the balustrade, and president of the famous Dry Goods Trust, of exciting memory. The contrast between the two men, alike only in extreme riches, was remarkable: Cecil still youthful, slim, dark, languid of movement, with delicate features, eyes almost Spanish, and an accent of purest English; and Rainshore with his nasal twang, his stout frame, his rounded, bluish-red chin, his little eyes, and that demeanour of false briskness by means of which ageing men seek to prove to themselves that they are as young as ever they were. Simeon had been a friend and opponent of Cecil's father; in former days those twain had victimised each other for colossal sums. Consequently Simeon had been glad to meet the son of his dead antagonist, and, in less than a week of Ostend repose, despite a fundamental disparity of temperament, the formidable president and the Europeanised wanderer had achieved a sort of intimacy, an intimacy which was about to be intensified.

"The difference between you and me is this," Cecil was saying. "You exhaust yourself by making money among men who are all bent on making money, in a place specially set apart for the purpose. I amuse myself by making money among men who, having made or inherited money, are bent on spending it, in places specially set apart for the purpose. I take people off their guard. They don't precisely see me coming. I don't rent an office and put up a sign which is equivalent to announcing that the rest of the world had better look out for itself. Our codes are the same, but is not my way more original and more diverting? Look at this place. Half the wealth of Europe is collected here; the other half is at Trouville. The entire coast reeks of money; the sands are golden with it. You've only to put out your hand—so!"

"So?" ejaculated Rainshore, quizzical. "How? Show me?"

"Ah! That would be telling."

"I guess you wouldn't get much out of Simeon—not as much as your father did."

"Do you imagine I should try?" said Cecil gravely. "My amusements are always discreet."

"But you confess you are often bored. Now, on Wall Street we are never bored."

"Yes," Cecil admitted. "I embarked on these—these enter-prises mainly to escape boredom."

"You ought to marry," said Rainshore pointedly. "You ought to marry, my friend."

"I have my yacht."

"No doubt. And she's a beauty, and feminine too; but not feminine enough. You ought to marry. Now, I'll——"

Mr. Rainshore paused. His daughter had suddenly ceased to eat chocolates and was leaning over the balustrade in order to converse with a tall, young man whose fair, tanned face and white hat overtopped the carved masonry and were thus visible to the millionaires. The latter glanced at one another and then glanced away, each slightly self-conscious.

"I thought Mr. Vaux-Lowry had left?" said Cecil.

"He came back last night," Rainshore replied curtly. "And he leaves again to-night."

"Then—then it's a match after all!" Cecil ventured.

"Who says that?" was Simeon's sharp inquiry.

"The birds of the air whisper it. One heard it at every corner three days ago."

Rainshore turned his chair a little towards Cecil's. "You'll al-low I ought to know something about it," he said. "Well, I tell you it's a lie."

"I'm sorry I mentioned it," Cecil apologised.

"Not at all," said Simeon, stroking his chin. "I'm glad you did. Because now you can just tell all the birds of the air direct from me that in this particular case there isn't going to be the usual alliance between the beauty and dollars of America and the aristocratic blood of Great Britain. Listen right here," he con-tinued confidentially, like a man whose secret feelings have been inconveniencing him for several hours. "This young spark—mind, I've nothing against him!—asks me to consent to his en-gagement with Geraldine. I tell him that I intend to settle half a million dollars on my daughter, and that the man she marries must cover that half-million with another. He says he has a thousand a year of his own, pounds—just nice for Geraldine's

gloves and candy!—and that he is the heir of his uncle, Lord
Lowry; and that there is an entail; and that Lord Lowry is very
rich, very old, and very unmarried; but that, being also very peculiar, he won't come down with any money. It occurs to me to
remark: 'Suppose Lord Lowry marries and develops into the
father of a man-child, where do *you* come in, Mr. Vaux-Lowry?'
'Oho! Lord Lowry marry! Impossible! Laughable!' Then
Geraldine begins to worry at me, and her mother too. And so I
kind of issue an ultimatum—namely, I will consent to an en-
gagement without a settlement if, on the marriage, Lord Lowry
will give a note of hand for half a million dollars to Geraldine,
payable on *his* marriage. See? My lord's nephew goes off to
persuade my lord, and returns with my lord's answer in an envelope sealed with the great seal. I open it and I read—this is
what I read: 'To Mr. S. Rainshore, American draper. Sir—as a
humorist you rank high. Accept the admiration of Your obedient servant, Lowry.'"

The millionaire laughed.

"Oh! It's clever enough!" said Rainshore. "It's very English
and grand. Dashed if I don't admire it! All the same, I've requested Mr. Vaux-Lowry, under the circumstances, to quit this
town. I didn't show him the letter—no. I spared his delicate
feelings. I merely told him Lord Lowry had refused, and that I
would be ready to consider his application favourably any time
when he happened to have half a million dollars in his pocket."

"And Miss Geraldine?"

"She's flying the red flag, but she knows when my back's
against the wall. She knows her father. She'll recover. Great
Scott! She's eighteen, he's twenty-one; the whole affair is a high
farce. And, moreover, I guess I want Geraldine to marry an
American, after all."

"And if she elopes?" Cecil murmured as if to himself, gazing at the set features of the girl, who was now alone once
more.

"*Elopes?*"

Rainshore's face reddened as his mood shifted suddenly from
indulgent cynicism to profound anger. Cecil was amazed at the

transformation, until he remembered to have heard long ago that Simeon himself had eloped.

"It was just a fancy that flashed into my mind," Cecil smiled diplomatically.

"I should let it flash out again if I were you," said Rainshore, with a certain grimness. And Cecil perceived the truth of the maxim that a parent can never forgive his own fault in his child.

II

"You've come to sympathise with me," said Geraldine Rainshore calmly, as Cecil, leaving the father for a few moments, strolled across the terrace towards the daughter.

"It's my honest, kindly face that gives me away," he responded lightly. "But what am I to sympathise with you about?"

"You know what," the girl said briefly.

They stood together near the balustrade, looking out over the sea into the crimson eye of the sun; and all the afternoon activities of Ostend were surging round them—the muffled sound of musical instruments from within the Kursaal, the shrill cries of late bathers from the shore, the toot of a tramway-horn to the left, the roar of a siren to the right, and everywhere the ceaseless hum of an existence at once gay, feverish, and futile; but Cecil was conscious of nothing but the individuality by his side. Some women, he reflected, are older at eighteen than they are at thirty-eight, and Geraldine was one of those. She happened to be very young and very old at the same time. She might be immature, crude, even gawky in her girlishness; but she was just then in the first flush of mentally realising the absolute independence of the human spirit. She had force, and she had also the enterprise to act on it.

As Cecil glanced at her intelligent, expressive face, he thought of her playing with life as a child plays with a razor.

"You mean——?" he inquired.

"I mean that father has been talking about me to you. I could tell by his eyes. Well?"

"Your directness unnerves me," he smiled.

"Pull yourself together, then, Mr. Thorold. Be a man."

"Will you let me treat you as a friend?"

"Why, yes," she said, "if you'll promise not to tell me I'm only eighteen."

"I am incapable of such rudeness," Cecil replied. "A woman is as old as she feels. You feel at least thirty; therefore you are at least thirty. This being understood, I am going to suggest, as a friend, that if you and Mr. Vaux-Lowry are—perhaps pardonably—contemplating any extreme step——"

"Extreme step, Mr. Thorold?"

"Anything rash."

"And suppose we are?" Geraldine demanded, raising her chin scornfully and defiantly and dangling her parasol.

"I should respectfully and confidentially advise you to refrain. Be content to wait, my dear middle-aged woman. Your father may relent. And also, I have a notion that I may be able to—to——"

"Help us?"

"Possibly."

"You are real good," said Geraldine coldly. "But what gave you the idea that Harry and I were meaning to——?"

"Something in your eyes—your fine, daring eyes. I read you as you read your father, you see?"

"Well, then, Mr. Thorold, there's something wrong with my fine, daring eyes. I'm just the last girl in all America to do anything—rash. Why! if I did anything rash, I'm sure I should feel ever afterwards as if I wanted to be excused off the very face of the earth. I'm that sort of girl. Do you think I don't know that father will give way? I guess he's just got to. With time and hammering, you can knock sense into the head of any parent."

"I apologise," said Cecil, both startled and convinced. "And I congratulate Mr. Vaux-Lowry."

"Say. You like Harry, don't you?"

"Very much. He's the ideal type of Englishman."

Geraldine nodded sweetly. "And so obedient! He does everything I tell him. He is leaving for England to-night, not because father asked him to, but because I did. I'm going to take mother to Brussels for a few days' shopping—lace, you know. That will give father an opportunity to meditate in solitude on his own greatness. Tell me, Mr. Thorold, do you consider that Harry and I would be justified in corresponding secretly?"

Cecil assumed a pose of judicial gravity.

"I think you would," he decided. "But don't tell anyone I said so."

"Not even Harry?"

She ran off into the Kursaal, saying she must seek her mother. But instead of seeking her mother, Geraldine passed straight through the concert-hall, where a thousand and one wondrously attired women were doing fancy needlework to the accompaniment of a band of music, into the maze of corridors beyond, and so to the rear entrance of the Kursaal on the Boulevard van Isoghem. Here she met Mr. Harry Vaux-Lowry, who was most obviously waiting for her. They crossed the road to the empty tramway waiting-room and entered it and sat down; and by the mere act of looking into each other's eyes, these two—the stiff, simple, honest-faced young Englishman with "Oxford" written all over him, and the charming child of a civilisation equally proud, but with fewer conventions, suddenly transformed the little bureau into a Cupid's bower.

"It's just as I thought, you darling boy," Geraldine began to talk rapidly. "Father's the least bit in the world scared; and when he's scared, he's bound to confide in someone; and he's confided in that sweet Mr. Thorold. And Mr. Thorold has been requested to reason with me and advise me to be a good girl and wait. I know what *that* means. It means that father thinks we shall soon forget each other, my poor Harry. And I do believe it means that father wants me to marry Mr. Thorold."

"What did you say to him, dear?" the lover demanded, pale.

"Trust me to fool him, Harry. I simply walked round him. He thinks we are going to be very good and wait patiently. As if father ever *would* give way until he was forced!"

She laughed disdainfully. "So we're perfectly safe so long as we act with discretion. Now let's clearly understand. To-day's Monday. You return to England to-night."

"Yes. And I'll arrange about the licence and things."

"Your cousin Mary is just as important as the licence, Harry," said Geraldine primly.

"She will come. You may rely on her being at Ostend with me on Thursday."

"Very well. In the meantime, I behave as if life were a blank. Brussels will put them off the scent. Mother and I will return from there on Thursday afternoon. That night there is a *soirée dansante* at the Kursaal. Mother will say she is too tired to go to it, but she will have to go all the same. I will dance before all men till a quarter to ten—I will even dance with Mr. Thorold. What a pity I can't dance before father, but he's certain to be in the gambling-rooms then, winning money; he always is at that hour! At a quarter to ten I will slip out, and you'll be here at this back door with a carriage. We drive to the quay and just catch the 11.5 steamer, and I meet your cousin Mary. On Friday morning we are married; and then, then we shall be in a position to talk to father. He'll pretend to be furious, but he can't say much, because he eloped himself. Didn't you know?"

"I didn't," said Harry, with a certain dryness.

"Oh, yes! It's in the family! But you needn't look so starched, my English lord." He took her hand. "You're sure your uncle won't disinherit you, or anything horrid of that kind?"

"He can't," said Harry.

"What a perfectly lovely country England is!" Geraldine exclaimed. "Fancy the poor old thing not being *able* to disinherit you! Why, it's just too delicious for words!"

And for some reason or other he kissed her violently.

Then an official entered the bureau and asked them if they wanted to go to Blankenburghe; because, if so, the tram was awaiting their distinguished pleasure. They looked at each other foolishly and sidled out, and the bureau ceased to be Cupid's bower.

III

By Simeon's request, Cecil dined with the Rainshores that night at the Continental. After dinner they all sat out on the balcony and sustained themselves with coffee while watching the gay traffic of the Digue, the brilliant illumination of the Kursaal, and the distant lights on the invisible but murmuring sea. Geraldine was in one of her moods of philosophic pessimism, and would persist in dwelling on the uncertainty of riches and the vicissitudes of millionaires. She found a text in the famous Bowring case, of which the newspaper contained many interesting details.

"I wonder if he'll be caught?" she remarked.

"I wonder," said Cecil.

"What do you think, father?"

"I think you had better go to bed," Simeon replied.

The chit rose and kissed him duteously.

"Good night," she said. "Aren't you glad the sea keeps so calm?"

"Why?"

"Can you ask? Mr. Vaux-Lowry crosses to-night, and he's a dreadfully bad sailor. Come along, mother. Mr. Thorold, when mother and I return from Brussels, we shall expect to be taken for a cruise in the *Claribel*."

Simeon sighed with relief upon the departure of his family and began a fresh cigar. On the whole, his day had been rather too domestic. He was quite pleased when Cecil, having apparently by accident broached the subject of the Dry Goods Trust, proceeded to exhibit a minute curiosity concerning the past, the present, and the future of the greatest of all the Rainshore enterprises.

"Are you thinking of coming in?" Simeon demanded at length, pricking up his ears.

"No," said Cecil, "I'm thinking of going out. The fact is, I haven't mentioned it before, but I'm ready to sell a very large block of shares."

"The deuce you are!" Simeon exclaimed. "And what do you call a very large block?"

"Well," said Cecil, "it would cost me nearly half a million to take them up now."

"Dollars?"

"Pounds sterling. Twenty-five thousand shares at 95⅜."

Rainshore whistled two bars of "Follow me!" from "The Belle of New York."

"Is this how you amuse yourself at Ostend?" he inquired.

Cecil smiled: "This is quite an exceptional transaction. And not too profitable, either."

"But you can't dump that lot on the market," Simeon protested.

"Yes, I can," said Cecil. "I must, and I will. There are reasons. You yourself wouldn't care to handle it, I suppose?"

The president of the Trust pondered.

"I'd handle it at 93⅜," he answered quietly.

"Oh, come! That's dropping two points!" said Cecil, shocked. "A minute ago you were prophesying a further rise."

Rainshore's face gleamed out momentarily in the darkness as he puffed at his cigar.

"If you must unload," he remarked, as if addressing the red end of the cigar, "I'm your man at 93⅜."

Cecil argued: but Simeon Rainshore never argued—it was not his method. In a quarter of an hour the younger man had contracted to sell twenty-five thousand shares of a hundred dollars each in the United States Dry Goods Trust at two points below the current market quotation, and six and five-eighths points below par.

The hoot of an outgoing steamer sounded across the city.

"I must go," said Cecil.

"You're in a mighty hurry," Simeon complained.

IV

Five minutes later Cecil was in his own rooms at the Hôtel de la Plage. Soon there was a discreet knock at the door.

"Come in, Lecky," he said.

It was his servant who entered, the small, thin man with very mobile eyes and of no particular age, who, in various capacities and incarnations—now as liftman, now as financial agent, now as no matter what—assisted Cecil in his diversions.

"Mr. Vaux-Lowry really did go by the boat, sir."

"Good. And you have given directions about the yacht?"

"The affair is in order."

"And you've procured one of Mr. Rainshore's Homburg hats?"

"It is in your dressing-room. There was no mark of identification on it. So, in order to smooth the difficulties of the police when they find it on the beach, I have taken the liberty of writing Mr. Rainshore's name on the lining."

"A kindly thought," said Cecil. "You'll watch the special G.S.N. steamer direct for London at 1 a.m. That will get you into town before two o'clock to-morrow afternoon. Things have turned out as I expected, and I've nothing else to say to you; but, before leaving me, perhaps you had better repeat your instructions."

"With pleasure, sir," said Lecky. "Tuesday afternoon—I call at Cloak Lane and intimate that we want to sell Dry Goods shares. I ineffectually try to conceal a secret cause for alarm, and I gradually disclose the fact that we are very anxious indeed to sell really a lot of Dry Goods shares, in a hurry. I permit myself to be pumped, and the information is wormed out of me that Mr. Simeon Rainshore has disappeared, has possibly committed suicide; but that, at present, no one is aware of this except ourselves. I express doubts as to the soundness of the Trust, and I remark on the unfortunateness of this disappearance so soon after the lamentable panic connected with the lately vanished Bruce Bowring and his companies. I send our friends on 'Change with orders to see what they can do and to report. I then go to Birchin Lane and repeat the performance there without variation. Then I call at the City office of the *Evening Messenger* and talk privily in a despondent vein with the financial editor concerning the Trust, but I breathe not a word as to Mr. Rainshore's disappearance. Wednesday morning.—The rot in Dry Goods has set in sharply, but I am now, very foolishly, disposed to haggle about the selling price. Our friends urge me to accept what I can get, and I leave them, saying that I must telegraph to you. Wednesday afternoon.—I see a reporter of the *Morning Journal* and let out that Simeon Rainshore has disappeared. The *Journal* will wire to Ostend for confirmation, which confirmation it will receive. Thursday morning.—The bottom is knocked out of the price of Dry Goods shares. Then I am to call on our other friends in Throgmorton Street and tell them to buy, buy, buy, in London, New York, Paris, everywhere."

"Go in peace," said Cecil. "If we are lucky, the price will drop to seventy."

V

"I see, Mr. Thorold," said Geraldine Rainshore, "that you are about to ask me for the next dance. It is yours."

"You are the queen of diviners," Cecil replied, bowing.

It was precisely half-past nine on Thursday evening, and they had met in a corner of the pillared and balconied *salle de danse*, in the Kursaal behind the concert-hall. The slippery, glittering floor was crowded with dancers—the men in ordinary evening dress, the women very variously attired, save that nearly all wore picture-hats. Geraldine was in a white frock, high at the neck, with a large hat of black velvet; and amidst that brilliant, multicoloured, light-hearted throng, lit by the blaze of the electric chandeliers and swayed by the irresistible melody of the "Doctrinen" waltz, the young girl, simply dressed as she was, easily held her own.

"So you've come back from Brussels?" Cecil said, taking her arm and waist.

"Yes. We arrived just on time for dinner. But what have you been doing with father? We've seen nothing of him."

"Ah!" said Cecil mysteriously. "We've been on a little voyage, and, like you, we've only just returned."

"In the *Claribel?*"

He nodded.

"You might have waited," she pouted.

"Perhaps you wouldn't have liked it. Things happened, you know."

"Why, what? Do tell me."

"Well, you left your poor father alone, and he was moping all day on Tuesday. So on Tuesday night I had the happy idea of going out in the yacht to witness a sham night attack by the French Channel Squadron on Calais. I caught your honoured parent just as he was retiring to bed, and we went. He was only too glad. But we hadn't left the harbour much more than an hour and a half when our engines broke down."

"What fun! And at night, too!"

"Yes. Wasn't it? The shaft was broken. So we didn't see much of any night attack on Calais. Fortunately the weather was all that the weather ought to be when a ship's engines break down. Still, it took us over forty hours to repair—over forty hours! I'm proud we were able to do the thing without being ignominiously towed into port. But I fear your father may have grown a little impatient, though we had excellent views of Ostend and Dunkirk, and the passing vessels were a constant diversion."

"Was there plenty to eat?" Geraldine asked simply.

"Ample."

"Then father wouldn't really mind. When did you land?"

"About an hour ago. Your father did not expect you to-night, I fancy. He dressed and went straight to the tables. He has to make up for a night lost, you see."

They danced in silence for a few moments, and then suddenly Geraldine said—

"Will you excuse me? I feel tired. Good night."

The clock under the orchestra showed seventeen minutes to ten.

"Instantly?" Cecil queried.

"Instantly." And the girl added, with a hint of mischief in her voice, as she shook hands: "I look on you as quite a friend since our last little talk; so you will excuse this abruptness, won't you?"

He was about to answer when a sort of commotion arose near behind them. Still holding her hand he turned to look.

"Why!" she said. "It's your mother! She must be unwell!"

Mrs. Rainshore, stout, and robed, as always, in tight, sumptuous black, sat among a little bevy of chaperons. She held a newspaper in trembling hands, and she was uttering a succession of staccato "Oh-oh's," while everyone in the vicinity gazed at her with alarm. Then she dropped the paper, and, murmuring, "Simeon's dead!" sank gently to the polished floor just as Cecil and Geraldine approached.

Geraldine's first instinctive move was to seize the newspaper, which was that day's Paris edition of the *New York Herald*. She read the headlines in a flash: "Strange disappearance of Simeon Rainshore. Suicide feared. Takes advantage of his family's absence. Heavy drop in Dry Goods. Shares at 72 and still falling."

VI

"My good Rebecca, I assure you that I am alive."

This was Mr. Rainshore's attempt to calm the hysteric sobbing of his wife, who had recovered from her short swoon in the little retreat of the person who sold Tauchnitzes, picture-postcards, and French novels, between the main corridor and the reading-rooms. Geraldine and Cecil were also in the tiny chamber.

"As for this," Simeon continued, kicking the newspaper, "it's a singular thing that a man can't take a couple of days off without upsetting the entire universe. What should you do in my place, Thorold? This is the fault of your shaft."

"I should buy Dry Goods shares," said Cecil.

"And I will."

There was an imperative knock at the door. An official of police entered.

"Monsieur Ryneshor?"

"The same."

"We have received telegraphs from New York and Londres to demand if you are dead."

"I am not. I still live."

"But Monsieur's hat has been found on the beach."

"My hat?"

"It carries Monsieur's name."

"Then it isn't mine, sir."

"*Mais comment donc——?*"

"I tell you it isn't mine, sir."

"Don't be angry, Simeon," his wife pleaded between her sobs.

The exit of the official was immediately followed by another summons for admission, even more imperative. A lady entered and handed to Simeon a card: "Miss Eve Fincastle. *The Morning Journal.*"

"My paper——" she began.

"You wish to know if I exist, madam!" said Simeon.

"I——" Miss Fincastle caught sight of Cecil Thorold, paused, and bowed stiffly. Cecil bowed; he also blushed.

"I continue to exist, madam," Simeon proceeded. "I have not killed myself. But homicide of some sort is not improbable if—— In short, madam, good night!"

Miss Fincastle, with a long, searching, silent look at Cecil, departed.

"Bolt that door," said Simeon to his daughter.

Then there was a third knock, followed by a hammering.

"Go away!" Simeon commanded.

"Open the door!" pleaded a muffled voice.

"It's Harry!" Geraldine whispered solemnly in Cecil's ear. "Please go and calm him. Tell him I say it's too late tonight."

Cecil went, astounded.

"What's happened to Geraldine?" cried the boy, extremely excited, in the corridor. "There all sorts of rumours. Is she ill?"

Cecil gave an explanation, and in his turn asked for another one. "You look unnerved," he said. "What are you doing here? What is it? Come and have a drink. And tell me all, my young friend." And when, over cognac, he had learnt the details of a scheme which had no connection with his own, he exclaimed, with the utmost sincerity: "The minx! The minx!"

"What do you mean?" inquired Harry Vaux-Lowry.

"I mean that you and the minx have had the nearest possible shave of ruining your united careers. Listen to me. Give it up, my boy. I'll try to arrange things. You delivered a letter to the father-in-law of your desire a few days ago. I'll give you another one to deliver, and I fancy the result will be different."

The letter which Cecil wrote ran thus:—

"DEAR RAINSHORE,—I enclose cheque for £100,000. It represents parts of the gold that can be picked up on the gold coast by putting out one's hand—so! You will observe that it is dated the day after the next settling-day of the London Stock Exchange. I contracted on Monday last to sell you 25,000 shares of a certain Trust at 93⅜. I did not possess the shares then, but my agents have to-day bought them for me at an average price of 72. I stand to realise, therefore, rather more than half a million dollars. The round half-million Mr. Vaux-Lowry happens to bring you in his pocket; you will not forget your promise to him that when he did so you would consider his application favourably. I wish to make no profit out of the little transaction, but I will venture to keep the balance for out-of-pocket expenses, such as mending the *Claribel*'s shaft. (How convenient it is to have a yacht that will break down when required!) The shares will doubtless recover in due course, and I hope the reputation of the Trust may not suffer, and that for the sake of old times with my father you will regard the episode in its proper light and bear me no ill-will.—Yours sincerely,

"C. Thorold."

The next day the engagement of Mr. Harry Nigel Selincourt Vaux-Lowry and Miss Geraldine Rainshore was announced to two continents.

WILLIAM LE QUEUX

William Le Queux was outrageously, shamelessly prolific. His bibliography takes up more space than the life history of many writers. After traveling Europe, he worked as a journalist and wound up foreign editor of the London *Globe*. Le Queux's many intriguing titles include *Strange Tales of a Nihilist, If Sinners Entice Thee,* and *The Money Spider: A Mystery of the Arctic.* One of his chief preoccupations, and the topic most associated with him, was espionage and the international dangers that faced Britain. Scholar Kevin Radaker calls Le Queux "the writer who set the guidelines for all subsequent British spy fiction until the advent of Eric Ambler." Fortunately for readers nowadays, he traveled widely and left behind vivid snapshots of the European haunts of the rich and titled in the early years of the twentieth century.

His best-known work during his lifetime was the 1906 cautionary novel *The Invasion of 1910, with a Full Account of the Siege of London.* For all his foresight and genuine concern for his homeland, Le Queux was imitating an earlier success, *The Great War in England in 1897,* which he published in 1894. Apparently he genuinely had experience as an agent of the secret service, but most commentators take with a grain of salt his grand claims of intimate knowledge of behind-the-scenes machinations in high places.

Le Queux loved to entice readers with the words *secret* and *mystery,* including them in numerous story and book titles. "The Story of a Secret" was the third installment of a 1906 series in *Cassell's Magazine* entitled "The Count's Chauffeur: Being the Confessions of George Ewart, Chauffeur to Count Bindo di

Ferraris." A few months later, with more adventures added, the series became a book with the same title. Undoubtedly the count's name, like Colonel Clay and Arsène Lupin, is fictitious even within the story. In the first adventure, Ewart narrates his unwitting involvement in the alleged count's many nefarious schemes. By the time of this story, Ewart is caught up in the entertaining and profitable game of impersonation, as he gets assigned more and more tasks beyond chauffeuring the count's gleaming roadster.

THE STORY OF A SECRET

The story of the secret was not without its humorous side.

Before entering Paris, after our quick run up from Marseilles after the affair of the jeweller's shop, we had stopped at Melun, beyond Fontainebleau. There, a well-known carriage-builder had been ordered to repaint the car pale blue, with a dead white band. Upon the panels, my employer, the impudent Bindo, had ordered a count's coronet, with the cipher "G. B." beneath, all to be done in the best style and regardless of expense. Then, that same evening, we took the express to the Gare de Lyon, and put up, as before, at the Ritz.

For three weeks, without the car, we had a pleasant time. Usually Count Bindo di Ferraris spent his time with his gay friends, lounging in the evening at Maxim's, or giving costly suppers at the Americain. One lady with whom I often saw him walking in the streets, or sitting in cafés, was, I discovered, known as "Valentine of the Beautiful Eyes," for I recognised her one night on the stage of a music-hall in the Boulevard de Clichy, where she was evidently a great favourite. She was young—not more than twenty, I think—with wonderful big coal-black eyes, a wealth of dark hair worn with a *bandeau*, and a face that was perfectly charming.

She seemed known to Blythe, too, for one evening I saw her sitting with him in the Brasserie Universelle, in the Avenue de l'Opéra—that place where one dines so well and cheaply. She was laughing, and had a *demi-blonde* raised to her lips. So essentially a Parisienne, she was also something of a mystery, for though she often frequented cafés, and went to the Folies Bergères and Olympia, sang at the Marigny, and mixed with a

Bohemian crowd of champagne-drinkers, she seemed nevertheless a most decorous little lady. In fact, though I had not spoken to her, she had won my admiration. She was very beautiful,
and I—well, I was only a man, and human.

One bright morning, when the car came to Paris, I called for
her, at Bindo's orders, at her flat in the Avenue Kléber, where
she lived, it appeared, with a prim, sharp-nosed old aunt, of an-
gular appearance, peculiarly French. She soon appeared, dressed
in the very latest motor clothes, with her veil properly fixed, in
a manner which showed me instantly that she was a motorist.
Besides, she would not enter the car, but got up beside me,
wrapped a rug about her skirts in a business-like manner, and
gave me the order to move.

"Where to, Mademoiselle?" I asked.

"Did not the Count give you instructions?" she asked in her
pretty broken English, turning her great dark eyes upon me in
surprise. "Why, to Brussels, of course."

"To Brussels!" I ejaculated, for I thought the run was to be
only about Paris—to meet Bindo, perhaps.

"Yes. Are you surprised?" she laughed. "It is not far—two
hundred kilometres, or so. Surely that is nothing for you?"

"Not at all. Only the Count is at the Ritz. Shall we not call
there first?"

"The Count left for Belgium by the seven-fifty train this morning," was her reply. "He has taken our baggage with his, and
you will take me by road alone."

I was, of course, nothing loth to spend a few hours with such
a charming companion as La Valentine; therefore in the Avenue
des Champs Elysées I pulled up, and consulting my road-book,
decided to go by way of Arras, Douai, St. Amand, and Ath.
Quickly we ran out beyond the fortifications; while, driving in
silence, I wondered what this latest manœuvre was to be. This
sudden flight from Paris was more than mysterious. It caused
me considerable apprehension, for when I had seen the Count
in his room at midnight he had made no mention of his intention to leave so early.

At last, out upon the straight high road that ran between

lines of high bare poplars, I put on speed, and quickly the cloud of white dust rose behind us. The northerly wind that grey day was biting, and threatened snow; therefore my pretty companion very soon began to feel the cold. I saw her turning up the collar of her cloth motor-coat, and guessed that she had no leather beneath. To do a day's journey in comfort in such weather one must be wind-proof.

"You are cold, Mademoiselle," I remarked. "Will you not put on my leather jacket? You'll feel the benefit of it, even though it may not appear very smart." And I pulled up.

With a light merry laugh she consented, and I got out the garment in question, helped her into it over her coat, and though a trifle tight across the chest, she at once declared that it was a most excellent idea. She was, indeed, a merry child of Paris, and allowed me to button the coat, smiling the while at my masculine clumsiness.

Then we continued on our way, and a few moments later were going for all we were worth over the dry, well-kept, level road eastward, towards the Belgian frontier. She laughed and chatted as the hours went by. She had been in London last spring, she told me, and had stayed at the Savoy. The English were so droll, and lacked *cachet,* though the hotel was smart—especially at supper.

"We pass Douai," she remarked presently, after we had run rapidly through many villages and small towns. "I must call for a telegram." And then, somehow, she settled down into a thoughtful silence.

At Arras I pulled up, and got her a glass of hot milk. Then on again, for she declared that she was not hungry, and preferred to get to Brussels than to linger on the road. On the broad highway to Douai we went at the greatest speed that I could get out of the fine six-cylinder, the engines beating beautiful time, and the car running as smoothly as a watch. The clouds of whirling dust became very bad, however, and I was compelled to goggle, while the tall-fronted veil adequately protected my sweet-faced travelling companion.

At Douai she descended and entered the post-office herself,

returning with a telegram and a letter. The latter she handed to me, and I found it was addressed in my name, and had been sent to the Posterestante.

Tearing it open in surprise I read the hastily pencilled lines it contained—instructions in the Count's handwriting which were extremely puzzling, not to say disconcerting. The words I read were:—

"After crossing the frontier you will assume the name of Count de Bourbriac, and Valentine will pass as the Countess. A suitable suite of rooms have been taken for you at the Grand Hotel, Brussels, where you will find your luggage on your arrival. Mademoiselle will supply you with funds. I shall be in Brussels, but shall not approach you.—B. di F."

The pretty Valentine who was to be my *pseudo*-wife crushed the blue telegram into her coat-pocket, mounted into her seat, wrapped her rug around her, and ordered me to proceed.

I glanced at her, but she was to all appearances quite unconscious of the extraordinary contents of the Count's letter.

We had run fully twenty miles in silence when at last, on ascending a steep hill, I turned to her and said:

"The Count has sent me some very extraordinary instructions, Mademoiselle. I am, after passing the frontier, to become Count de Bourbriac, and you are to pass as the Countess!"

"Well?" she asked, arching her well-marked eyebrows. "Is that so very difficult, m'sieur? Are you disinclined to allow me to pass as your wife?"

"Not at all," I replied smiling. "Only—well—it is somewhat—er—unconventional, is it not?"

"Rather an amusing adventure than otherwise," she laughed. "I shall call you *mon cher* Gaston, and you—well, you will call me your *petite* Liane—Liane de Bourbriac will sound well, will it not?"

"Yes. But why this masquerade?" I inquired. "I confess, Mademoiselle, I don't understand it at all."

"Dear Bindo does. Ask him." Then, after a brief pause, she

added: "This is really a rather novel experience," and she laughed gleefully, as though thoroughly enjoying the adventure.

Without slackening speed I drove on through the short winter afternoon. The faint yellow sunset slowly disappeared behind us, and darkness crept on. With the fading day the cold became intense, and when I stopped to light the head-lamps I got out my cashmere muffler and wrapped it around her throat.

At last we reached the small frontier village, where we pulled up before the Belgian Custom House, paid the deposit upon the car, and obtained the leaden seal. Then, after a liqueur-glass of cognac each at a little café in the vicinity, we set out again upon that long wide road that leads through Ath to Brussels.

A puncture at a place called Leuze caused us a little delay, but the *pseudo* Countess descended and assisted me, even helping me to blow up the new tube, declaring that the exercise would warm her.

For what reason the pretty Valentine was to pass as my wife was, to me, entirely mysterious. That Bindo was engaged in some fresh scheme of fraud was certain, but what it was I racked my brains in vain to discover.

Near Enghien we had several other tyre troubles, for the road had been newly metalled for miles. As every motorist knows, misfortunes never come singly, and in consequence it was already seven o'clock next morning before we entered Brussels by the Porte de Hal, and ran along the fine Boulevard d'Anspach, to the Grand Hotel.

The gilt-laced hall-porter, who was evidently awaiting us, rushed out cap in hand, and I, quickly assuming my *rôle* as Count, helped out the "Countess" and gave the car over to one of the employés of the hotel garage.

By the manager we were ushered into a fine suite of six rooms on the first floor, overlooking the Boulevard, and treated with all the deference due to persons of highest standing.

At that moment Valentine showed her cleverness by remarking that she had not brought Elise, her maid, as she was to follow by train, and that I would employ the services of one of the hotel valets for the time being. Indeed, so cleverly did she assume the part that she might really have been one of the ancient nobility of France.

I spoke in English. On the Continent just now it is considered rather smart to talk English. One often hears two German or Italian women speaking atrocious English together, in order to air their superior knowledge before strangers. Therefore that I spoke English was not remarked by the manager, who explained that our courier had given him all instructions, and had brought the baggage in advance. The courier was, I could only suppose, the audacious Bindo himself.

That day passed quite merrily. We lunched together, took a drive in the pretty Bois de la Cambre, and after dining, went to the Monnaie to see *Madame Butterfly*. On our return to the hotel I found a note from Bindo, and saying good-night to Valentine I went forth again to keep the appointment he had made in a café in the quiet Chausée de Charleroi, on the opposite side of the city.

When I entered the little place I found the Count seated at a table with Blythe and Henderson. The two latter were dressed shabbily, while the Count himself was in dark grey, with a soft felt hat—the perfect counterfeit of the foreign courier.

With enthusiasm I was welcomed into the corner.

"Well?" asked Bindo with a laugh, "And how do you like your new wife, Ewart?" and the others smiled.

"Charming," I replied. "But I don't see exactly where the joke comes in."

"I don't suppose you do, just yet."

"It's a risky proceeding, isn't it?" I queried.

"Risky! What risk is there in gulling hotel people?" he asked. "If you don't intend to pay the bill it would be quite another matter."

"But why is the lady to pass as my wife? Why am I the Count de Bourbriac? Why, indeed, are we here at all?"

"That's our business, my dear Ewart. Leave matters to us. All you've got to do is to just play your part well. Appear to be very devoted to La Comtesse, and it'll be several hundreds into your pocket—perhaps a level thou'—who knows?"

"A thou' each—quite," declared Blythe, a cool, audacious international swindler of the most refined and cunning type.

"But what risk is there?" I inquired, for my companions seemed to be angling after big fish this time, whoever they were.

"None—as far as you are concerned. Be advised by Valentine. She's as clever a girl as there is in all Europe. She has her eyes and ears open all the time. A lover will come on the scene before long, and you must be jealous—devilish jealous—you understand?"

"A lover? Who? I don't understand."

"You'll see, soon enough. Go back to the hotel—or stay with us to-night, if you prefer it. Only don't worry yourself over risks. We never take any. Only fools do that. Whatever we do is always a dead certainty before we embark upon the job."

"Then I'm to understand that some fellow is making love to Valentine—eh?"

"Exactly. To-morrow night you are both invited to a ball at the Belle Vue, in aid of the Hospital St. Jean. You will go, and there the lover will appear. You will withdraw, and allow the little flirtation to proceed. Valentine herself will give you further instructions as the occasion warrants."

"I confess I don't half like it. I'm working too much in the dark," I protested.

"That's just what we intend. If you knew too much you might betray yourself, for the people we've got to deal with have eyes in the backs of their heads," declared Bindo.

It was five o'clock next morning before I returned to the Grand, but during the hours we smoked together, at various obscure cafés, the trio told me nothing further, though they chaffed me regarding the beauty of the girl who had consented to act the part of my wife, and who, I could only suppose, "stood in" with us.

At noon, surely enough, came a special invitation to the "Comte et Comtesse de Bourbriac" for the great ball that evening at the Hotel Belle Vue, and at ten o'clock that night Valentine entered our private salon splendidly dressed in a low-cut gown of smoke-grey chiffon covered with sequins. Her hair had been dressed by a maid of the first order, and as she stood pulling on her long gloves she looked superb.

"How do you find me, my dear M'sieur Ewart? Do I look like a Comtesse?" she asked laughing.

"You look perfectly charming, Mademoiselle."

"Liane, if you please," she said reprovingly, holding up her slim forefinger. "Liane, Comtesse de Bourbriac, Château de Bourbriac, Côtes du Nord!" and her pretty lips parted, showing her even pearly teeth.

When, half an hour later, we entered the ball-room we found all smart Brussels assembled around a royal prince and his wife who had given their patronage in the cause of charity. The affair was, I saw at a glance, a distinctly society function, for many men from the Ministries were present, and several of the Ambassadors in uniform, together with their staffs, who, wearing their crosses and ribbons, made a brave show, as they do in every ball-room.

We had not been there ten minutes before a tall good-looking young man in a German cavalry uniform strode up in recognition, and bowing low over Valentine's outstretched hand, said in French:

"My dear Countess! How very delighted we are to have you here with us to-night. You will spare me a dance, will you not? May I be introduced to the Count?"

"My husband—Captain von Stolberg, of the German Embassy."

And we shook hands. Was this fellow the lover, I wondered?

"I met the Countess at Vichy last autumn," explained the Captain in very good English. "She spoke very often of you. You were away in Scotland, shooting the grouse," he said.

"Yes—yes." I replied for want of something better to say.

We both chatted with the young attaché for a few minutes, and then, as a waltz struck up, he begged a dance of my "wife," and they both whirled down the room. Valentine was a splendid dancer, and as I watched them I wondered what could be the nature of the plot in progress.

I did not come across my pretty fellow-traveller for half-an-hour, and then I found that the captain had half filled her programme. Therefore I "laid low," danced once or twice with uninteresting Belgian matrons, and spent the remainder of the night in the *fumoir*, until I found my "wife" ready to return to the Grand.

When we were back in the salon at the hotel she asked:

"How do you like the Captain, M'sieur Ewart? Is he not—what you call in English—a duck?"

"An overdressed, swaggering young idiot, I call him," was my prompt reply.

"And there you are right—quite right, my dear M'sieur Ewart. But you see we all have an eye to business in this affair. He will call to-morrow because he is extremely fond of me. Oh! If you had heard all his pretty love phrases! I suppose he has learnt them out of a book. They couldn't be his own. Germans are not romantic—how can they be? But he—ah! he is Adonis in the flesh—with corsets!" And we laughed merrily together.

"He thinks you are fond of him—eh?"

"Why, of course. He made violent love to me at Vichy. But he was not attaché then."

"And how am I to treat him when he calls to-morrow?"

"As your bosom friend. Give him confidence—the most perfect confidence. Don't play the jealous husband yet. "That will come afterwards. *Bon soir, m'sieur,*" and when I had bowed over her soft little hand she turned, and swept out of the room with a loud *frou-frou* of her silken train.

That night I sat before the fire smoking for a long time. My companions were evidently playing some deep game upon this young German, a game in which neither trouble nor expense was being spared—a game in which the prize was a level thousand pounds apiece all round. I quite appreciated that I had now become an adventurer, but I had done so out of pure love of adventure.

About four o'clock next afternoon the Captain came to take "fif-o'-clock," as he called it. He clicked his heels together as he bowed over Valentine's hand, and she smiled upon him even more sweetly than she had smiled at me when I had helped her into my leather motor-coat. She wore a beautiful toilette, one of the latest of Doeillet's she had explained to me, and really presented a delightfully dainty figure as she sat there pouring out tea, and chatting with the infatuated Captain of Cuirassiers.

I saw quickly that I was not wanted; therefore I excused myself, and went for a stroll along to the Café Métropole, afterwards taking a turn up the Montagne de la Cour. All day I had been on the look-out to see either Bindo or his companions, but they were evidently in hiding.

When I returned, just in time to dress for dinner, I asked Valentine what progress her lover was making, but she merely replied:

"Slow—very slow. But in things of this magnitude one must have patience. We are invited to the Embassy ball in honour of the Crown Prince of Saxony to-morrow night. It will be amusing."

Next night she dressed in a gown of pale rose chiffon, and we went to the Embassy, where one of the most brilliant balls of the season was in progress, King Leopold himself being present to honour the young Crown Prince. Captain Stolberg soon discovered the woman who held him beneath her spell, and I found myself dancing attendance upon the snub-nosed little daughter of a Burgomaster, with whom I waltzed the greater part of the evening.

On our return my "wife" told me with a laugh that matters were progressing well. "Otto," she added, "is such a fool. Men in love will believe any fiction a woman tells them. Isn't it really extraordinary?"

"Perhaps I'm one of those men, Mademoiselle," I said looking straight into her beautiful eyes, for I own she had in a measure fascinated me, even though I knew her to be an adventuress.

She burst out laughing in my face.

"Don't be absurd, M'sieur Ewart," she cried. "Fancy you! But you certainly wouldn't fall in love with me. We are only friends—in the same swim, as I believe you term it in English."

I was a fool. I admit it. But when one is thrown into the society of a pretty woman even a chauffeur may make speeches he regrets.

So the subject dropped, and with a mock curtsey, and a saucy wave of the hand, she went to her room.

On the following day she went out alone at eleven, not returning until six. She offered no explanation of where she had been, and of course it was not for me to question her. As we sat at dinner in our private salle-à-manger an hour later she laughed at me across the table, and declared that I was sitting as soberly as though I really were her dutiful husband. And next day she was absent again the whole day, while I amused myself in visiting the Law Courts, the picture galleries, and the general sights of the little capital of which Messieurs the brave Belgians are so proud. On her return she seemed thoughtful, even *triste*. She had been on an excursion somewhere with Otto, but she did not enlighten me regarding its details. I wondered that I had had no word from Bindo. Yet he had told me to obey Valentine's instructions, and I was now doing so. At dinner she once clenched her little hand involuntarily, and drew a deep breath, showing me that she was indignant at something.

The following morning, as she mentioned that she should be absent all day, I took a run on the car as far as the quaint little town of Dinant, up the Meuse, getting back to dinner.

In the salon she met me, already in her dinner-gown, and told me that she had invited Otto to dine.

"To-night you must show your jealousy. You must leave us together here, in the salon, after dinner, and then a quarter of an hour later return suddenly. I will compromise him. Then you will quarrel violently, order him to leave the hotel, and thus part bad friends."

I hardly liked to be a party to such a trick, yet the whole plot interested me. I could not see to what material end all this tended.

Well, the gay Captain duly arrived, and we dined together merrily. His eyes were fixed admiringly upon Valentine the whole time and his conversation was mainly reminiscent of the days at Vichy. The meal over, we passed into the salon, and there I left them. But on reentering shortly afterwards I found him standing behind the couch, bending over and kissing her. She had her arms clasped around his neck so tightly he could not disengage himself.

In pretended fury I dashed across to the pair with my fists clenched in jealous anger. What I said I scarcely remember. All I know is that I let forth a torrent of reproaches and condemnations, and ended by practically kicking the fellow out of the room, while my "wife" sank upon her knees and implored my forgiveness which I flatly refused.

The Captain took his kicking in silence, but in his glance was murder, as he turned once and faced me ere he left the room.

"Well, Valentine," I asked, when he was safely out of hearing, and when she raised herself from her knees laughing. "And what now?"

"The whole affair is now plain sailing. To-morrow you will take the car to Liège, and there await me outside the cathedral at midnight on the following night. You will easily find the place. Wait until two o'clock, and if I am not there go on to Cologne, and put up at the Hotel du Nord."

"Without baggage?"

"Without baggage. Don't trouble about anything. Simply go there and wait."

At midday on the following day the pretty Valentine dressed herself carefully, and went out. Then, an hour later, pretending that I was only going for a short run, I mounted into the car and set out for Liège, wondering what was now to happen.

Next day I idled away, and at a quarter to twelve that night, after a run around town, I pulled up in the shadow before the cathedral and stopped the engines. The old square was quite quiet, for the good Liègois retire early, and the only sound was the musical carillon of the bells.

In impatience I waited. The silent night was clear, bright, and frosty, with a myriad shining stars above. Time after time the great clock above me chimed the quarters, until just before two o'clock, there came a dark female figure round the corner, walking quickly. In an instant I recognised Valentine, who was dressed in a long travelling coat with fur collar, and a sealskin toque. She was carrying something beneath her coat.

"Quick!" she said breathlessly. "Let us get away. Get ready. Count Bindo is following me!" And ere I could start the engines, my employer, in a long dark overcoat and felt hat, hurriedly approached us, saying:

"Come, let's be off, Ewart. We've a long journey to-night to

Cassel. We must go through Aix, and pick up Blythe, and then on by way of Cologne, Arnsburg, and the Hoppeke-Tal."

Quickly they both put on the extra wraps from the car, entered, and wrapped the rugs about them, while two minutes later, with our big head-lamps shedding a broad white light before us, we turned out upon the wide high road to Verviers.

"It's all right!" cried Bindo, leaning over to me when we had covered about five miles or so. "Everything went off perfectly."

"And M'sieur made a most model 'husband,' I assure you," declared the pretty Valentine, with a musical laugh.

"But what have you done?" I inquired half turning, but afraid to take my eyes from the road.

"Be patient. We'll explain everything when we get to Cassel," responded Valentine. And with that I had to be content.

At the station at Aix we found Blythe awaiting us, and when he had taken the seat beside me we set out by way of Duren to Cologne, and on to Cassel, a long and bitterly cold journey.

It was not until we were dining together late the following night in the comfortable old König von Preussen, at Cassel, that Valentine revealed the truth to me.

"When I met the German at Vichy I was passing as Countess de Bourbriac, and pretending that my husband was in Scotland. At first I avoided him," she said. "But later on I was told, in confidence, that he was a spy in the service of the War Office in Berlin. Then I wrote to Count Bindo, and he advised me to pretend to reciprocate the fellow's affections, and to keep a watchful eye for the main chance. I have done so—that's all."

"But what was this 'main chance'?" I asked.

"Why, don't you see, Ewart," exclaimed the Count, who was standing by, smoking a cigarette. "The fact that he was in the Intelligence Department in Berlin, and that he had been suddenly appointed military attaché at Brussels, made it plain that he was carrying out some important secret-service work in Belgium. On making inquiries I heard that he was constantly travelling in the country, and, speaking French so well, he was passing himself off as a Belgian. Blythe, in the guise of an English tourist, met him in Boxtel two months ago, and satisfied himself as to the character of the task he had undertaken, a risky but most important one. Then we all agreed that, when completed, the secrets he had possessed himself of should become ours, for the Intelligence Department of either France or England would be certain to purchase them for almost any sum we liked to name, so important were they. About two months we waited for the unsuspecting Otto to complete his work, and then suddenly the Countess reappears, accompanied by her husband. And—well, Valentine, you can best tell Ewart the remainder of the story," added the audacious scoundrel, replacing his cigarette in his mouth.

"As M'sieur Ewart knows, Captain Stolberg was in love with me, and I pretended to be infatuated with him. The other night he kissed me, and my dear 'Gaston' saw it, and in just indignation and jealousy promptly kicked him out. Next day I met him, told him that my husband was a perfect hog, and urged him to take me from him. At first he would not sacrifice his official position as attaché, for he was a poor man. Then we talked money matters, and I suggested that he surely possessed something which he could turn into money sufficient to keep us for a year or two, as I had a small income though not absolutely sufficient for our wants. In fact, I offered, now that he had compromised me in the eyes of my husband, to elope with him. We walked in the Bois de la Cambre for two solid hours that afternoon, until I was footsore, and yet he did not catch on. Then I played another game, declaring that he did not love me sufficiently to make such a sacrifice, and at last taking a dramatic farewell of him. He allowed me to get almost to the gates of the Bois, then he suddenly ran after me, and told me that he had a packet of documents for which he could obtain a large sum abroad. He would take them, and myself, to Berlin by that night's mail, and then we would go on to St. Petersburg, where he could easily dispose of the mysterious papers. So we met at the station at midnight, and by the same train travelled Bindo and M'sieurs Blythe and Henderson. In the carriage he told me where the precious papers were—in a small leathern hand-bag—and this fact I whispered to Blythe when he brushed past me in the corridor. At Pepinster, the junction for

Spa, we both descended to obtain some refreshment, and when we returned to our carriage the Captain glanced reassuringly at his bag. Bindo passed along the corridor, and I knew the truth. Then on arrival at Liège I left the Captain smoking, and strolled to the back end of the carriage, waiting for the train to move off. Just as it did so I sprang out upon the platform, and had the satisfaction of seeing, a moment later, the red tail-lights of the Berlin express disappear. I fancy I saw the Captain's head out of the window and heard him shout, but next instant he was lost in the darkness."

"As soon as you had both got out at Pepinster Blythe slipped into the compartment, broke the lock of the bag with a special tool we call 'the snipper,' and had the papers in a moment. These he passed on to me, and travelled past Liège on to Aix."

"Here are the precious plans," remarked the Count, producing a voluminous packet in a big blue envelope, the seal of which had been broken.

And on opening this he displayed to me a quantity of carefully drawn plans of the whole canal system, and secret defences between the Rhine and the Meuse, the waterway, he explained, which one day Germany, in time of war with England, will require to use in order to get her troops through the port of Antwerp, and the Belgian coast—the first complete and reliable plans ever obtained of the chain of formidable defences that Belgium keeps a profound secret.

What sum was paid to the pretty Valentine by the French Intelligence Department for them I am not aware. I only know that she one day sent me a beautiful gold cigarette-case inscribed with the words "From Liane de Bourbriac," and inside it was a draft on the London Branch of the Crédit Lyonnais for eight hundred and fifty pounds.

Captain Otto Stolberg has, I hear, been transferred as attaché to another European capital. No doubt his first thoughts were of revenge, but on mature consideration he deemed it best to keep his mouth closed or he would have betrayed himself as a spy. The Count had, no doubt, foreseen that. As for Valentine, she actually declares that, after all, she merely rendered a service to her country!

O. HENRY

William Sidney Porter was born in Greensboro, North Carolina in 1862 and, less than half a century later, died in New York City, internationally famous under the pen name O. Henry. In between, he lived in Austin and Pittsburgh, traveled the Caribbean and South America with outlaws, spent time in prison for embezzlement, and wrote hundreds of stories. Apparently he proved memorable in every place he visited. Greensboro has an O. Henry Boulevard, Austin an O. Henry Middle School, and New York City will always be nicknamed Bagdad-on-the-Hudson after O. Henry's phrase.

Since 1919 there has been an annual short-story award named after O. Henry, but probably he couldn't win it himself. Nowadays we consider surprise endings unnecessarily contrived; they have all but disappeared from serious fiction. But contrivance—outwitting the reader, reeling your own variations on the conjuror's patter—is of course a staple of crime fiction. Caper stories, in fact, almost demand surprise endings.

O. Henry's best known story is probably "The Gift of the Magi," but most of us also remember "The Ransom of Red Chief" and a few others. Undoubtedly his most famous crime story is "A Retrieved Reformation," the sentimental safecracker tale that begat the 1928 movie *Alias Jimmy Valentine*. The story that follows is not sentimental. "The Chair of Philanthromathematics" first appeared in *McClure's* in 1908 and later the same year in O. Henry's collection *The Gentle Grafter*. This volume is required reading for any fan of the genre. The primary con man is Jeff Peters, who tortures language but never hurts human beings, and his colleagues include Buckingham Skinner and Andy Tucker.

A century after O. Henry's death, none of his work holds up better than these chronicles of itinerant con men. For one thing, the stories don't taste artificially sweetened, unlike many of his tales of ill-starred lovers and good-hearted bums. And the dialect, which would be harder to find in the real world than a speaker of Sinclair Lewisese, is irresistible. Incidentally, fans of the genre need to know that O. Henry also wrote a couple of the most amusing parodies of Sherlock Holmes, "The Adventures of Shamrock Jolnes" and "The Sleuths," as well as inventing the great detective Tictocq to parody both real and fictional French tales.

THE CHAIR OF PHILANTHROMATHEMATICS

"I see that the cause of Education has received the princely gift of more than fifty millions of dollars," said I.

I was gleaning the stray items from the evening papers while Jeff Peters packed his briar pipe with plug cut.

"Which same," said Jeff, "calls for a new deck, and a recitation by the entire class in philanthromathematics."

"Is that an allusion?" I asked.

"It is," said Jeff. "I never told you about the time when me and Andy Tucker was philanthropists, did I? It was eight years ago in Arizona. Andy and me was out in the Gila mountains with a two-horse wagon prospecting for silver. We struck it, and sold out to parties in Tucson for $25,000. They paid our check at the bank in silver—a thousand dollars in a sack. We loaded it in our wagon and drove east a hundred miles before we recovered our presence of intellect. Twenty-five thousand dollars don't sound like so much when you're reading the annual report of the Pennsylvania Railroad or listening to an actor talking about his salary; but when you can raise up a wagon sheet and kick around your bootheel and hear every one of 'em ring against another it makes you feel like you was a night-and-day bank with the clock striking twelve.

"The third day out we drove into one of the most specious and tidy little towns that Nature or Rand and McNally ever turned out. It was in the foothills, and mitigated with trees and flowers and about 2,000 head of cordial and dilatory inhabitants. The town seemed to be called Floresville, and Nature had not contaminated it with many railroads, fleas or Eastern tourists.

"Me and Andy deposited our money to the credit of Peters and Tucker in the Esperanza Savings Bank, and got rooms at the Skyview Hotel. After supper we lit up, and sat out on the gallery and smoked. Then was when the philanthropy idea struck me. I suppose every grafter gets it sometime.

"When a man swindles the public out of a certain amount he begins to get scared and wants to return part of it. And if you'll watch close and notice the way his charity runs you'll see that he tries to restore it to the same people he got it from. As a hydrostatical case, take, let's say, A. A made his millions selling oil to poor students who sit up nights studying political economy and methods for regulating the trusts. So, back to the universities and colleges goes his conscience dollars.

"There's B got his from the common laboring man that works with his hands and tools. How's he to get some of the remorse fund back into their overalls?

" 'Aha!' says B, "I'll do it in the name of Education. I've skinned the laboring man,' says he to himself, 'but, according to the old proverb, "Charity covers a multitude of skins." '

"So he puts up eighty million dollars' worth of libraries; and the boys with the dinner pail that builds 'em gets the benefit.

" 'Where's the books?' asks the reading public?

" 'I dinna ken,' says B. 'I offered ye libraries; and there they are. I suppose if I'd given ye preferred steel trust stock instead ye'd have wanted the water in it set out in cut glass decanters. Hoot, for ye!'

"But, as I said, the owning of so much money was beginning to give me philanthropitis. It was the first time me and Andy had ever made a pile big enough to make us stop and think how we got it.

" 'Andy,' says I, 'we're wealthy—not beyond the dreams of average; but in our humble way we are comparatively as rich as Greasers. I feel as if I'd like to do something for as well as to humanity.'

" 'I was thinking the same thing, Jeff,' says he. 'We've been gouging the public for a long time with all kinds of little schemes from selling self-igniting celluloid collars to flooding Georgia with Hoke Smith presidential campaign buttons. I'd like, myself, to hedge a bet or two in the graft game if I could do it without actually banging the cymbalines in the Salvation Army or teaching a bible class by the Bertillon system.'

" 'What'll we do?' says Andy. 'Give free grub to the poor or send a couple of thousand to George Cortelyou?'

" 'Neither,' says I. 'We've got too much money to be implicated in plain charity; and we haven't got enough to make restitution. So, we'll look about for something that's about half way between the two.'

"The next day in walking around Floresville we see on a hill a big red brick building that appears to be disinhabited. The citizens speak up and tell us that it was begun for a residence several years before by a mine owner. After running up the house he finds he only had $2.80 left to furnish it with, so he invests that in whiskey and jumps off the roof on a spot where he now requiescats in pieces.

"As soon as me and Andy saw that building the same idea struck both of us. We would fix it up with lights and pen wipers and professors, and put an iron dog and statues of Hercules and Father John to the lawn, and start one of the finest free educational institutions in the world right there.

"So we talks it over to the prominent citizens of Floresville, who falls in fine with the idea. They give a banquet in the engine house to us, and we make our bow for the first time as benefactors to the cause of progress and enlightenment. Andy makes an hour-and-a-half speech on the subject of irrigation in Lower Egypt, and we have a moral tune on the phonograph and pineapple sherbet.

"Andy and me didn't lose any time in philanthropping. We put every man in town that could tell a hammer from a step ladder to work on the building, dividing it up into class rooms and lecture halls. We wire to Frisco for a car load of desks, footballs, arithmetics, penholders, dictionaries, chairs for the professors, slates, skeletons, sponges, twenty-seven cravenetted gowns and caps for the senior class, and an open order for all the truck that goes with a first-class university. I took it on myself to put a campus and a curriculum on the list; but the telegraph operator must have got the words wrong, being an ignorant man, for when the goods come we found a can of peas and a curry-comb among 'em.

"While the weekly papers was having chalk-plate cuts of me and Andy we wired an employment agency in Chicago to express us f. o. b., six professors immediately—one English literature, one up-to-date dead languages, one chemistry, one political economy—democrat preferred—one logic, and one wise to painting, Italian and music, with union card. The Esperanza bank guaranteed salaries, which was to run between $800 and $800.50.

"Well, sir, we finally got in shape. Over the front door was carved the words: 'The World's University; Peters & Tucker, Patrons and Proprietors.' And when September the first got a cross-mark on the calendar, the come-ons begun to roll in. First the faculty got off the tri-weekly express from Tucson. They was mostly young, spectacled and red-headed, with sentiments divided between ambition and food. Andy and me got 'em billeted on the Floresvillians and then laid for the students.

"They came in bunches. We had advertised the University in all the state papers, and it did us good to see how quick the country responded. Two hundred and nineteen husky lads aging along from 18 up to chin whiskers answered the clarion call of free education. They ripped open that town, sponged the seams, turned it, lined it with new mohair; and you couldn't have told it from Harvard or Goldfields at the March term of court.

"They marched up and down the streets waving flags with the World's University colors—ultramarine and blue—and they certainly made a lively place of Floresville. Andy made them a speech from the balcony of the Skyview Hotel, and the whole town was out celebrating.

"In about two weeks the professors got the students disarmed and herded into classes. I don't believe there's any pleasure equal to being a philanthropist. Me and Andy bought high silk hats and pretended to dodge the two reporters of the Floresville Gazette. The paper had a man to kodak us whenever we appeared on the street, and ran our pictures every week over the column headed 'Educational Notes.' Andy lectured twice a week at the University; and afterward I would rise and tell a humorous story. Once the Gazette printed my pictures with Abe Lincoln on one side and Marshall P. Wilder on the other.

"Andy was as interested in philanthropy as I was. We used to wake up of nights and tell each other new ideas for booming the University.

"'Andy,' says I to him one day, 'there's something we overlooked. The boys ought to have dromedaries.'

"'What's that?' Andy asks.

"'Why, something to sleep in, of course,' says I. 'All colleges have 'em.'

"'Oh, you mean pajamas,' says Andy.

"'I do not,' says I. 'I mean dromedaries.' But I never could make Andy understand; so we never ordered 'em. Of course, I meant them long bedrooms in colleges where the scholars sleep in a row.

"Well, sir, the World's University was a success. We had scholars from five States and territories, and Floresville had a boom. A new shooting gallery and a pawn shop and two more saloons started; and the boys got up a college yell that went this way:

"'Raw, raw, raw,
   Done, done, done,
 Peters, Tucker
   Lots of fun.
 Bow-wow-wow,
   Haw-hee-haw,
 World University,
   Hip, hurrah!'

"The scholars was a fine lot of young men, and me and Andy was as proud of 'em as if they belonged to our own family.

"But one day about the last of October Andy come to me and asks if I have any idea how much money we had left in the bank. I guesses about sixteen thousand. 'Our balance,' says Andy, 'is $821.62.'

"'What!' says I, with a kind of a yell. 'Do you mean to tell me that them infernal clod-hopping, dough-headed, pup-faced, goose-brained, gate-stealing, rabbit-eared sons of horse thieves have soaked us for that much?'

" 'No less,' says Andy.

" 'Then, to Helvetia with philanthropy,' says I.

" 'Not necessarily,' says Andy. 'Philanthropy,' says he, 'when run on a good business basis is one of the best grafts going. I'll look into the matter and see if it can't be straightened out.'

"The next week I am looking over the payroll of our faculty when I run across a new name—Professor James Darnley Mc-Corkle, chair of mathematics; salary $100 per week. I yells so loud that Andy runs in quick.

" 'What's this,' says I. 'A professor of mathematics at more than $5,000 a year? How did this happen? Did he get in through the window and appoint himself?'

" 'I wired to Frisco for him a week ago,' says Andy. 'In ordering the faculty we seemed to have overlooked the chair of mathematics.'

" 'A good thing we did,' says I. 'We can pay his salary two weeks, and then our philanthropy will look like the ninth hole on the Skibo golf links.'

" 'Wait a while,' says Andy, 'and see how things turn out. We have taken up too noble a cause to draw out now. Besides, the further I gaze into the retail philanthropy business the better it looks to me. I never thought about investigating it before. Come to think of it now,' goes on Andy, 'all the philanthropists I ever knew had plenty of money. I ought to have looked into that matter long ago, and located which was the cause and which was the effect.'

"I had confidence in Andy's chicanery in financial affairs, so I left the whole thing in his hands. The University was flourishing fine, and me and Andy kept our silk hats shined up, and Floresville kept on heaping honors on us like we was millionaires instead of almost busted philanthropists.

"The students kept the town lively and prosperous. Some stranger came to town and started a faro bank over the Red Front livery stable, and began to amass money in quantities.

Me and Andy strolled up one night and piked a dollar or two for sociability. There were about fifty of our students there drinking rum punches and shoving high stacks of blues and reds about the table as the dealer turned the cards up.

" 'Why, dang it, Andy,' says I, 'these free-school-hunting, gander-headed, silk-socked little sons of sapsuckers have got more money than you and me ever had. Look at the rolls they're pulling out of their pistol pockets?'

" 'Yes,' says Andy, 'a good many of them are sons of wealthy miners and stockmen. It's very sad to see 'em wasting their opportunities this way.'

"At Christmas all the students went home to spend the holidays. We had a farewell blowout at the University, and Andy lectured on 'Modern Music and Prehistoric Literature of the Archipelagos.' Each one of the faculty answered to toasts, and compared me and Andy to Rockefeller and the Emperor Marcus Autolycus. I pounded on the table and yelled for Professor McCorkle; but it seems he wasn't present on the occasion. I wanted a look at the man that Andy thought could earn $100 a week in philanthropy that was on the point of making an assignment.

"The students all left on the night train; and the town sounded as quiet as the campus of a correspondence school at midnight. When I went to the hotel I saw a light in Andy's room, and I opened the door and walked in.

"There sat Andy and the faro dealer at a table dividing a two-foot high stack of currency in thousand-dollar packages.

" 'Correct,' says Andy. 'Thirty-one thousand apiece. Come in, Jeff,' says he. 'This is our share of the profits of the first half of the scholastic term of the World's University, incorporated and philanthropated. Are you convinced now,' says Andy, 'that philanthropy when practiced in a business way is an art that blesses him who gives as well as him who receives?'

" 'Great!' says I, feeling fine. 'I'll admit you are the doctor this time.'

" 'We'll be leaving on the morning train,' says Andy. 'You'd better get your collars and cuffs and press clippings together.'

"'Great!' says I. 'I'll be ready. But, Andy,' says I, 'I wish I could have met that Professor James Darnley McCorkle before we went. I had a curiosity to know that man.'

"'That'll be easy,' says Andy, turning around to the faro dealer.

"'Jim,' says Andy, 'shake hands with Mr. Peters.'"

GEORGE RANDOLPH CHESTER

The American writer George Randolph Chester worked as a journalist, dramatist, and scriptwriter, but he was most successful as the author of several books about J. Rufus Wallingford, a con man whose chief talent lies in beating American businessmen at their own game. He can walk into a boardroom in an expensive suit, with nary a dime in his pocket, and walk out as president of an imaginary company. In the early decades of the twentieth century, Get-Rich-Quick Wallingford became a household name, thanks partly to a popular stage adaptation.

The first series of stories began appearing in the *Saturday Evening Post* on October 5, 1907, with "Getting Rich Quick," and appeared in book form in early 1908 as *Get-Rich-Quick Wallingford*. When the series in the *Post* proved popular, George M. Cohan quickly snapped up the stage rights. In his usual "Cohanizing," as he called the process himself, he transformed Chester's tall, stout businessman Wallingford into a diminutive faux patriot. Silent films and then talkies followed. Chester wrote three volumes of sequels between 1910 and 1913. By 1915 a *New York Times* profile of him was headlined AMERICANS LIKE TO BE FOOLED.

Chester had fun with his book titles, which include *Five Thousand an Hour: How Johnny Gamble Won the Heiress* and *The Early Bird: A Business Man's Love Story.* He subtitled the first Wallingford collection *A Cheerful Account of the Rise and Fall of an American Business Buccaneer* and even added a sly dedication that seems a masterpiece of target marketing: "To the live businessmen of America—those who have been 'stung' and those who have yet to undergo that painful experience—this little tale is sympathetically dedicated."

Chester himself said of Wallingford, "I gave him the power of seeming hospitable, generous and unselfish because the assumption of these virtues is one of the chief weapons of the confidence man." After all, *con* is short for "confidence," and the profession depends upon earning the mark's trust. In one sequel, the entertaining *Young Wallingford*, Chester takes us back in time to the master's beginnings as an ambitious rube, but it doesn't equal this first volume, in which Wallingford is at his cheerful, despicable best—or worst. The following selection from *Get-Rich-Quick Wallingford*, comprising the book's first two chapters, demonstrates perfectly how a con artist orchestrates the illusions, lays the trap, and builds toward the goal—a transfer of funds.

GET-RICH-QUICK
WALLINGFORD

The mud was black and oily where it spread thinly at the edges of the asphalt, and wherever it touched it left a stain; it was upon the leather of every pedestrian, even the most fastidious, and it bordered with almost laughable conspicuousness the higher marking of yellow clay upon the heavy shoes of David Jasper, where he stood at the curb in front of the big hotel with his young friend, Edward Lamb. Absorbed in "lodge" talk, neither of the oddly assorted cronies cared much for drizzle overhead or mire underfoot; but a splash of black mud in the face must necessarily command some attention. This surprise came suddenly to both from the circumstance of a cab having dashed up just beside them. Their resentment, bubbling hot for a moment, was quickly chilled, however, as the cab door opened and out of it stepped one of those impressive beings for whom the best things of this world have been especially made and provided. He was a large gentleman, a suave gentleman, a gentleman whose clothes not merely fit him but distinguished him, a gentleman of rare good living, even though one of the sort whose faces turn red when they eat; and the dignity of his worldly prosperousness surrounded him like a blessed aura. Without a glance at the two plain citizens who stood mopping the mud from their faces, he strode majestically into the hotel, leaving Mr. David Jasper and Mr. Edward Lamb out in the rain.

The clerk kowtowed to the signature, though he had never seen nor heard of it before—"J. Rufus Wallingford, Boston." His eyes, however, had noted a few things: traveling suit, scarf

pin, watch guard, ring, hatbox, suit case, bag, all expensive and
of the finest grade.

"Sitting room and bedroom; outside!" directed Mr. Wallingford. "And the bathroom must have a large tub."

The clerk ventured a comprehending smile as he noted the
bulk before him.

"Certainly, Mr. Wallingford. Boy, key for 44-A. Anything
else, Mr. Wallingford?"

"Send up a waiter and a valet."

Once more the clerk permitted himself a slight smile, but this
time it was as his large guest turned away. He had not the
slightest doubt that Mr. Wallingford's bill would be princely, he
was positive that it would be paid; but a vague wonder had
crossed his mind as to who would regrettingly pay it. His pen-
etration was excellent, for at this very moment the new arrival's
entire capitalized worth was represented by the less than one
hundred dollars he carried in his pocket, nor had Mr. Wallingford the slightest idea of where he was to get more. This latter
circumstance did not distress him, however; he knew that there
was still plenty of money in the world and that none of it was
soldered on, and a reflection of this comfortable philosophy
was in his whole bearing. As he strode in pomp across the
lobby, a score of bellboys, with a carefully trained scent for
tips, envied the cheerfully grinning servitor who followed him
to the elevator with his luggage.

Just as the bellboy was inserting the key in the lock of 44-A,
a tall, slightly built man in a glove-fitting black frock suit, a
quite ministerial-looking man, indeed, had it not been for the
startling effect of his extravagantly curled black mustache and
his piercing black eyes, came down the hallway, so abstracted
that he had almost passed Mr. Wallingford. The latter, however, had eyes for everything.

"What's the hurry, Blackie?" he inquired affably.

The other wheeled instantly, with the snappy alertness of a
man who has grown of habit to hold himself in readiness
against sudden surprises from any quarter.

"Hello, J. Rufus!" he exclaimed, and shook hands. "Boston
squeezed dry?"

Mr. Wallingford chuckled with a cumbrous heaving of his shoulders.

"Just threw the rind away," he confessed. "Come in."

Mr. Daw, known as "Blackie" to a small but select circle of gentlemen who make it their business to rescue and put carefully hoarded money back into rapid circulation, dropped moodily into a chair and sat considering his well-manicured finger-nails in glum silence, while his masterful host disposed of the bellboy and the valet.

"Had your dinner?" inquired Mr. Wallingford as he donned the last few garments of a fresh suit.

"Not yet," growled the other. "I've got such a grouch against myself I won't even feed right, for fear I'd enjoy it. On the cheaps for the last day, too."

Mr. Wallingford laughed and shook his head.

"I'm clean myself," he hastened to inform his friend. "If I have a hundred I'm a millionaire, but I'm coming and you're going, and we don't look at that settle-up ceremony the same way. What's the matter?"

"I'm the goat!" responded Blackie moodily. "The original goat! Came clear out here to trim a sucker that looked good by mail, and have swallowed so much of the citric fruit that if I scrape myself my skin spurts lemon juice. Say, do I look like a come-on?"

"If you only had the shaving-brush goatee, Blackie, I'd try to make you bet on the location of the little pea," gravely responded his friend.

"That's right; rub it in!" exclaimed the disgruntled one. "Massage me with it! Jimmy, if I could take off my legs, I'd kick myself with them from here to Boston and never lose a stroke. And me wise!"

"But where's the fire?" asked J. Rufus, bringing the end of his collar to place with a dexterous jerk.

"This lamb I came out to shear—rot him and burn him and scatter his ashes! Before I went dippy over two letter-heads and a nice round signature, I ordered an extra safety-deposit vault back home and came on to take his bank roll and house and lot, and make him a present of his clothes if he behaved. But

not so! *Not*—so! Jimmy, this whole town blew right over from
out of the middle of Missouri in the last cyclone. You've got to
show everybody, and then turn it over and let 'em see the other
side, and I haven't met the man yet that you could separate
from a dollar without chloroform and an ax. Let me tell you
what to do with that hundred, J. Rufe. Just get on the train and
give it to the conductor, and tell him to take you as far ay-way
from here as the money will reach!"

Mr. Wallingford settled his cravat tastefully and smiled at
himself in the glass.

"I like the place," he observed. "They have tall buildings
here, and I smell soft money. This town will listen to a legitimate business proposition. What?"

"Like the milk-stopper industry?" inquired Mr. Daw, grinning appreciatively. "How is your Boston corporation coming
on, anyhow?"

"It has even quit holding the bag," responded the other, "because there isn't anything left of the bag. The last I saw of them,
the thin and feeble stockholders were chasing themselves
around in circles, so I faded away."

"You're a wonder," complimented the black-haired man with
genuine admiration. "You never take a chance, yet get away
with everything in sight, and you never leave 'em an opening to
put the funny clothes on you."

"I deal in nothing but straight commercial propositions that
are strictly within the pale of the law," said J. Rufus without a
wink; "and even at that they can't say I took anything away
from Boston."

"Don't blame Boston. You never cleaned up a cent less than
five thousand a month while you were there, and if you spent
it, that was your lookout."

"I had to live."

"So do the suckers," sagely observed Mr. Daw, "but they
manage it on four cents' worth of prunes a day, and save up
their money for good people. How is Mrs. Wallingford?"

"All others are base imitations," boasted the large man,
pausing to critically consider the flavor of his champagne. "Just
now, Fanny's in New York, eating up her diamonds. She was

swallowing the last of the brooch when I left her, and this morning she was to begin on the necklace. That ought to last her quite some days, and by that time J. Rufus expects to be on earth again."

A waiter came to the door with a menu card, and Mr. Wallingford ordered, to be ready to serve in three quarters of an hour, at a choice table near the music, a dinner for two that would gladden the heart of any tip-hunter.

"How soon are you going back to Boston, Blackie?"

"To-night!" snapped the other. "I was going to take a train that makes it in nineteen hours, but I found there is one that makes it in eighteen and a half, so I'm going to take that; and when I get back where the police are satisfied with half, I'm not going out after the emerald paper any more. I'm going to make them bring it to me. It's always the best way. I never went after money yet that they didn't ask me why I wanted it."

The large man laughed with his eyes closed.

"Honestly, Blackie, you ought to go into legitimate business enterprises. That's the only game. You can get anybody to buy stock when you make them print it themselves, if you'll only bait up with some little staple article that people use and throw away every day, like ice-cream pails, or corks, or cigar bands, or—or—or carpet tacks." Having sought about the room for this last illustration, Mr. Wallingford became suddenly inspired, and, arising, went over to the edge of the carpet, where he gazed down meditatively for a moment. "Now, look at this, for instance!" he said with final enthusiasm. "See this swell red carpet fastened down with rusty tacks? There's the chance. Suppose those tacks were covered with red cloth to match the carpet. Blackie, that's my next invention."

"Maybe there are covered carpet tacks," observed his friend, with but languid interest.

"What do I care?" rejoined Mr. Wallingford. "A man can always get a patent, and that's all I need, even if it's one you can throw a cat through. The company can fight the patent after I'm out of it. You wouldn't expect me to fasten myself down to the grease-covered details of an actual manufacturing business, would you?"

"Not any!" rejoined the dark one emphatically. "You're all right, J. Rufus. I'd go into your business myself if I wasn't honest. But on the level, what do you expect to do here?"

"Organize the Universal Covered Carpet Tack Company. I'll begin to-morrow morning. Give me the list you couldn't use."

"Don't get in bad from the start," warned Mr. Daw. "Tackle fresh ones. The particular piece of Roquefort, though, that fooled me into a Pullman compartment and kept me grinning like a drunken hyena all the way here, was a pinhead by the name of Edward Lamb. When Eddy fell for an inquiry about Billion Strike gold stock, he wrote on the firm's stationery, all printed in seventeen colors and embossed so it made holes in the envelopes when the cancellation stamp came down. From the tone of Eddy's letter I thought he was about ready to mortgage father's business to buy Billion Strike, and I came on to help him do it. Honest, J. Rufus, wouldn't it strike you that Lamb was a good name? Couldn't you hear it bleat?"

Mr. Wallingford shook silently, the more so that there was no answering gleam of mirth in Mr. Daw's savage visage.

"Say, do you know what I found when I got here?" went on Blackie still more ferociously. "I found he was a piker bookkeeper, but with five thousand dollars that he'd wrenched out of his own pay envelope, a pinch at a clip; and every time he takes a dollar out of his pocket his fingers creak. His whole push is like him, too, but I never got any further than Eddy. He's not merely Johnny Wise—he's the whole Wise family, and it's only due to my Christian bringing up that I didn't swat him with a brick during our last little chatter when I saw it all fade away. Do you know what he wanted me to do? He wanted me to prove to him that there actually was a Billion Strike mine, and that gold had been found in it!"

Mr. Wallingford had ceased to laugh. He was soberly contemplating.

"Your Lamb is my mutton," he finally concluded, pressing his finger tips together. "He'll listen to a legitimate business proposition."

"Don't make me fuss with you, J. Rufus," admonished Mr. Daw. "Remember, I'm going away to-night," and he arose.

Mr. Wallingford arose with him. "By the way, of course I'll want to refer to you; how many addresses have you besides the Billion Strike? A mention of that would probably get me arrested."

"Four: the Mexican and Rio Grande Rubber Company, Tremont Building; the St. John's Blood Orange Plantation Company, 643 Third Street; the Los Pocos Lead Development Company, 868 Schuttle Avenue, and the Sierra Cinnabar Grant, Schuttle Square, all of which addresses will reach me at my little old desk-room corner in 1126 Tremont Building, Third and Schuttle Avenues; and I'll answer letters of inquiry on four different letter-heads. If you need more I'll post Billy Riggs over in the Cloud Block and fix it for another four or five."

"I'll write Billy a letter myself," observed J. Rufus. "I'll need all the references I can get when I come to organize the Universal Covered Carpet Tack Company."

"Quit kidding," retorted Mr. Daw.

"It's on the level," insisted J. Rufus seriously. "Let's go down to dinner."

There were twenty-four applicants for the position before Edward Lamb appeared, the second day after the initial insertion of the advertisement which had been designed to meet his eye alone. David Jasper, who read his paper advertisements and all, in order to get the full worth of his money out of it, telephoned to his friend Edward about the glittering chance.

Yes, Mr. Wallingford was in his suite. Would the gentleman give his name? Mr. Lamb produced a card, printed in careful imitation of engraving, and it gained him admission to the august presence, where he created some surprise by a sudden burst of laughter.

"Ex-cuse me!" he exclaimed. "But you're the man that splashed mud on me the other night!"

When the circumstance was related, Mr. Wallingford laughed with great gusto and shook hands for the second time with his visitor. The incident helped them to get upon a most cordial footing at once. It did not occur to either of them, at the time, how appropriate it was that Mr. Wallingford should splash mud upon Mr. Lamb at their very first meeting.

"What can I do for you, Mr. Lamb?" inquired the large man.

"You advertised——" began the caller.

"Oh, you came about that position," deprecated Mr. Wallingford, with a nicely shaded tone of courteous disappointment in his voice. "I am afraid that I am already fairly well suited, although I have made no final choice as yet. What are your qualifications?"

"There will be no trouble about that," returned Mr. Lamb, straightening visibly. "I can satisfy anybody." And Mr. Wallingford had the keynote for which he was seeking.

He knew at once that Mr. Lamb prided himself upon his independence, upon his local standing, upon his efficiency, upon his business astuteness. The observer had also the experience of Mr. Daw to guide him, and, moreover, better than all, here was Mr. Lamb himself. He was a broad-shouldered young man, who stood well upon his two feet; he dressed with a proper and decent pride in his prosperity, and wore looped upon his vest a watch chain that by its very weight bespoke the wearer's solid worth. The young man was an open book, whereof the pages were embossed in large type.

"Now you're talking like the right man," said the prospective employer. "Sit down. You'll understand, Mr. Lamb, that my question was only a natural one, for I am quite particular about this position, which is the most important one I have to fill. Our business is to be a large one. We are to conduct an immense plant in this city, and I want the office work organized with a thorough system from the beginning. The duties, consequently, would begin at once. The man who would become secretary of the Universal Covered Carpet Tack Company, would need to know all about the concern from its very inception, and until I have secured that exact man I shall take no steps toward organization."

Word by word, Mr. Wallingford watched the face of Edward Lamb and could see that he was succumbing to the mental chloroform. However, a man who at thirty has accumulated five thousand is not apt to be numbed without struggling.

"Before we go any further," interposed the patient, with deep, deep shrewdness, "it must be understood that I have no money to invest."

"Exactly," agreed Mr. Wallingford. "I stated that in my advertisement. To become secretary it will be necessary to hold one share of stock, but that share I shall give to the right applicant. I do not care for him to have any investment in the company. What I want is the services of the best man in the city, and to that end I advertised for one who had been an expert bookkeeper and who knew all the office routine of conducting a large business, agreeing to start such a man with a salary of two hundred dollars a month. That advertisement stated in full all that I expect from the one who secures this position—his expert services. I may say that you are only the second candidate who has had the outward appearance of being able to fulfill the requirements. Actual efficiency would naturally have to be shown."

Mr. Wallingford was now quite coldly insistent. The proper sleep had been induced.

"For fifteen years," Mr. Lamb now hastened to advise him, "I have been employed by the A. J. Dorman Manufacturing Company, and can refer you to them for everything you wish to know. I can give you other references as to reliability if you like."

Mr. Wallingford was instant warmth.

"The A. J. Dorman Company, indeed!" he exclaimed, though he had never heard of that concern. "The name itself is guarantee enough, at least to defer such matters for a bit while I show you the industry that is to be built in your city." From his dresser Mr. Wallingford produced a handful of tacks, the head of each one covered with a bit of different-colored bright cloth. "You have only to look at these," he continued, holding them forth, and with the thumb and forefinger of the other hand turning one red-topped tack about in front of Mr. Lamb's eyes, "to appreciate to the full what a wonderful business certainty I am preparing to launch. Just hold these tacks a moment," and he turned the handful into Mr. Lamb's outstretched palm. "Now come over to the edge of this carpet. I have selected here a tack which matches this floor covering. You see those rusty heads? Imagine the difference if they were replaced by this!"

Mr. Lamb looked and saw, but it was necessary to display his business acumen.

"Looks like a good thing," he commented; "but the cost?"

"The cost is comparatively nothing over the old steel tack, although we can easily get ten cents a paper as against five for the common ones, leaving us a much wider margin of profit than the manufacturers of the straight tack obtain. There is no family so poor that will use the old, rusty tinned or bronze tack when these are made known to the trade, and you can easily compute for yourself how many millions of packages are used every year. Why, the Eureka Tack Company, which practically has a monopoly of the carpet-tack business, operates a manufacturing plant covering twenty solid acres, and a loaded freight car leaves its warehouse doors on an average of every seven minutes! You cannot buy a share of stock in the Eureka Carpet Tack Company at any price. It yields sixteen per cent. a year dividends, with over eighteen million dollars of undivided surplus—and that business was built on carpet tacks alone! Why, sir, if we wished to do so, within two months after we had started our factory wheels rolling we could sell out to the Eureka Company for two million dollars; or a profit of more than one thousand per cent. on the investment that we are to make."

For once Mr. Lamb was overwhelmed. Only three days before he had been beset by Mr. Daw, but that gentleman had grown hoarsely eloquent over vast possessions that were beyond thousands of miles of circumambient space, across vast barren reaches where desert sands sent up constant streams of superheated atmosphere, with the "hot air" distinctly to be traced throughout the conversation; but here was something to be seen and felt. The points of the very tacks that he held pricked his palm, and his eyes were still glued upon the red-topped one which Mr. Wallingford held hypnotically before him.

"Who composes your company?" he managed to ask.

"So far, I do," replied Mr. Wallingford with quiet pride. "I have not organized the company. That is a minor detail. When

I go searching for capital I shall know where to secure it. I have chosen this city on account of its manufacturing facilities, and for its splendid geographical position as a distributing center."

"The stock is not yet placed, then," mused aloud Mr. Lamb, upon whose vision there already glowed a pleasing picture of immense profits.

Why, the thing was startling in the magnificence of its opportunity! Simple little trick, millions and millions used, better than anything of its kind ever put upon the market, cheaply manufactured, it was marked for success from the first!

"Stock placed? Not at all," stated Mr. Wallingford. "My plans only contemplate incorporating for a quarter of a million, and I mean to avoid small stockholders. I shall try to divide the stock into, say, about ten holdings of twenty-five thousand each."

Mr. Lamb was visibly disappointed.

"It looks like a fine thing," he declared with a note of regret.

"Fine? My boy, I'm not much older than you are, but I have been connected with several large enterprises in Boston and elsewhere—if any one were to care to inquire about me they might drop a line to the Mexican and Rio Grande Rubber Company, the St. John's Blood Orange Plantation Company, the Los Pocos Lead Development Company, the Sierra Cinnabar Grant, and a number of others, the addresses of which I could supply—and I never have seen anything so good as this. I am staking my entire business judgment upon it, and, of course, I shall retain the majority of stock myself, inasmuch as the article is my invention."

This being the psychological moment, Mr. Wallingford put forth his hand and had Mr. Lamb dump the tacks back into the large palm that had at first held them. He left them open to view, however, and presently Mr. Lamb picked out one of them for examination. This particular tack was of an exquisite apple-green color, the covering for which had been clipped from one of Mr. Wallingford's own expensive ties, glued to its place and carefully trimmed by Mr. Wallingford's own hands. Mr. Lamb took it to the window for closer admiration, and the promoter, left to himself for a moment, stood before the glass to mop his face and head and neck. He had been working until he had perspired; but, looking into the glass at Mr. Lamb's rigid back, he perceived that the work was well done. Mr. Lamb was profoundly convinced that the Universal Covered Carpet Tack Company was an entity to be respected; nay, to be revered! Mr. Lamb could already see the smoke belching from the tall chimneys of its factory, the bright lights gleaming out from its myriad windows where it was working overtime, the thousands of workmen streaming in at its broad gates, the loaded freight cars leaving every seven minutes!

"You're not going home to dinner, are you, Mr. Lamb?" asked Mr. Wallingford suddenly. "I owe you one for the splash, you know."

"Why—I'm expected home."

"Telephone them you're not coming."

"We—we haven't a telephone in the house."

"Telephone to the nearest drug store and send a messenger over."

Mr. Lamb looked down at himself. He was always neatly dressed, but he did not feel equal to the glitter of the big dining room downstairs.

"I am not—cleaned up," he objected.

"Nonsense! However, as far as that goes, we'll have 'em bring a table right here." And, taking the matter into his own hands, Mr. Wallingford telephoned for a waiter.

From that moment Mr. Lamb strove not to show his wonder at the heights to which human comfort and luxury can attain, but it was a vain attempt; for from the time the two uniformed attendants brought in the table with its snowy cloth and began to place upon it the shining silver and cut-glass service, with the centerpiece of red carnations, he began to grasp at a new world—and it was about this time that he wished he had on his best black suit. In the bathroom Mr. Wallingford came upon him as he held his collar ruefully in his hand, and needed no explanation.

"I say, old man, we can't keep 'em clean, can we? We'll fix that."

The bellboys were anxious to answer summons from 44-A

by this time. Mr. Wallingford never used money in a hotel except for tips. It was scarcely a minute until a boy had that collar, with instructions to get another just like it.

"How are the cuffs? Attached, old man? All right. What size shirt do you wear?"

Mr. Lamb gave up. He was now past the point of protest. He told Mr. Wallingford the number of his shirt. In five minutes more he was completely outfitted with clean linen, and when, washed and refreshed and spotless as to high lights, he stepped forth into what was now a perfectly appointed private dining room, he felt himself gradually rising to Mr. Wallingford's own height and able to be supercilious to the waiters, under whose gaze, while his collar was soiled, he had quailed.

It was said by those who made a business of dining that Mr. Wallingford could order a dinner worth while, except for the one trifling fault of over-plenty; but then, Mr. Wallingford himself was a large man, and it took much food and drink to sustain that largeness. Whatever other critics might have said, Mr. Lamb could have but one opinion as they sipped their champagne, toward the end of the meal, and this opinion was that Mr. Wallingford was a genius, a prince of entertainers, a master of finance, a gentleman to be imitated in every particular, and that a man should especially blush to question his financial standing or integrity.

They went to the theater after dinner—box seats—and after the theater they had a little cold snack, amounting to about eleven dollars, including wine and cigars. Moreover, Mr. Lamb had gratefully accepted the secretaryship of the Universal Covered Carpet Tack Company.

FREDERICK IRVING ANDERSON

Frederick Irving Anderson was a journalist and a prolific author of clever, discursive short stories. His is not the gum-chewing, wisecracking tone that would soon show up in hard-boiled mysteries. He takes his time and he has fun.

Anderson spent ten years as a reporter with the *New York World* and eventually became a regular contributor to the *Saturday Evening Post* and other major magazines. Besides the Infallible Godahl, whom you will meet in "Blind Man's Buff," Anderson created several other recurring characters. He liked to weave his favorite characters in and out of each other's stories. In fact, one character, mystery writer Oliver Armiston, is occasionally presented as the creator of Godahl. One of Anderson's best ideas is that Armiston is too clever for his own good. Criminals read and copy his ingenious crime stories, so he has to quit writing and become a special consultant to the New York City police. Perhaps best known among Anderson's characters was Deputy Parr, who is a successful detective in his own stories but fails against Godahl and Anderson's other series thief, Sophie Lang. Unfortunately the charming Lang came along late enough to fall, like a couple of other great female rogues, outside our anthology's purview. Hollywood had a great time with her until censors declared that the wily young woman shouldn't be profiting from crimes up on a movie screen for all of America's impressionable youth to learn from.

The Infallible Godahl, who seems to have supplied himself with this grand moniker, is a man of many talents, as he demonstrates in "Blind Man's Buff." The story appeared first in the May 24, 1913, issue of the *Saturday Evening Post*. The next year

Anderson included it in a collection of stories about his unpredictable thief, *The Infallible Godahl*. This was one of only three volumes of fiction that Anderson published. The great majority of his nonseries magazine stories, and even some of those in a series, have never been reprinted.

BLIND MAN'S BUFF

"Godahl, attend!" said that adept in smart crime to himself as he paused at the curb. "You think you are clever; but there goes your better."

He had to step into the street to make way for the crowd that overflowed the pavement—men and women, newsboys, even unhorsed actors leaving their pillars for the time for the passing sensation, the beginning of the homing matinée crowds—all elbowing for a place about a tall, slender man in black who, as he advanced, gently tapped a cane-point before him. What attracted the vortex, however, was not so much the man himself as the fact that he wore a black mask. The mask was impenetrable. People said he had no eyes. It was Malvino the Magician, born to eternal darkness. From a child, so the story went, his fingers had been schooled with the same cruel science they ply in Russia to educate the toes of their ballet dancers—until his fingers saw for him.

Head erect, shoulders squared, body poised with the precision of a skater—his handsome, clear-cut features, almost ghastly in contrast to the band of silk ribbon that covered the sockets where sight should have been—he advanced with military step in the cleared circle that ever revolved about him, his slender cane shooting out now and again with the flash of a rapier to tap-tap-tap on the flags. Why pay for an orchestra chair to witness his feats of legerdemain? Peopling silk hats with fecund families of rabbits, or even discovering a hogshead of boiling water in an innocent bystander's vest pocket, was as nothing to this theatric negotiation of Broadway in the rush hour of late

Saturday afternoon. Malvino the Magician seemed oblivious to everything save the subtle impulses of that wand of a cane.

He stopped, suddenly alert to some immediate impression. The vague features relaxed; the teeth shone.

"Ah! Godahl, my friend!" he cried. He turned and advanced deliberately through the crowd that opened a path in front of him. Those wonderful hands reached out and touched Godahl on the arm, without hesitation as to direction.

Godahl could not repress a smile. Such a trick was worth a thousand dollars a week to the front of the house; and nobody knew better than the great Malvino the value of advertising. That was why he walked Broadway unattended twice a day.

When he spoke it was in French. "I am sickened of them all," he said, sweeping his cane in a circle to indicate the gaping crowd straining to catch his words. "See! We have at hand a public chauffeur with nothing better to do than to follow in the wake of the Great Malvino. Godahl, my friend, you are at leisure? Then we will enter."

And Godahl, playing his cards with enjoyment and admiration as well, permitted the blind man to open the door and help him—Godahl, possessing five senses—into the cab; pleased doubly, indeed, to note that the magician had managed to steal his wallet in the brief contact. "To the park!" ordered Malvino, showing his teeth to the crowd as he shut the door.

Godahl had known Malvino first in Rome. The great of the earth gravitate toward each other. No one knew how great Godahl was except himself. He knew that he had never failed. No one knew how great Malvino was except Godahl. Once he had attempted to imitate Malvino and had almost failed. The functions of the third finger of his left hand lacked the wonderful coördination possessed by the magician. Malvino knew Godahl as an entertaining cosmopolitan, of which the world possesses far too few.

"I would exercise my Eng-lish," said the mask, "if you will be so good, my friend. Tell me—you know the lake shore in that city of Chicago?"

"As a book," said Godahl. "You are about to parade there—eh?"

"I am about to parade there," replied Malvino, imitating the accents of the other. "Therefore I would know it—as a book. Read it to me—slowly—page by page, my friend. I walk there shortly."

Godahl possessed, first of all, a marvelous faculty of visualizing. It was most necessary, almost as much so in fact for him in his profession as for Malvino in his—Malvino without eyes. In a matter-of-fact manner, like a mariner charting some dangerous channel, he plotted the great thoroughfare from the boulevard entrance to the Auditorium. The other listened attentively, recording every word. He had made use of Godahl in this way before and knew the value of that man's observations. Then suddenly, impatiently:

"One moment; there is another thing—of immediate need. The Pegasus Club? We are passing it at this moment—eh? You are one of the—what is it they say?—ah, yes, the fifty little millionaires—ha-ha!—yes?"

Godahl looked out of the window. Indeed, they were passing the club now. They had been proceeding slowly, turning this way and that, halted now and again or hurried on by traffic policemen, until now they were merely a helpless unit in the faltering tide of Fifth Avenue; it was past five in the evening and all uptown New York was on the move, afoot and awheel.

It was said of Malvino that he would suffer himself to be whirled round twenty times on being set down in some remote neighborhood of a strange city, and with the aid of his cane find his way back to his hotel with the surety of a pigeon. But even that faculty did not explain how he knew they were passing a certain building, the Pegasus Club, at this moment. Unless, thought Godahl—who was better pleased to study the other's methods than to ask questions—unless the sly fox had it recorded in his strange brain-map that carriage wheels rattled over car-tracks a hundred yards below this point. Godahl smiled. It was simple after all.

"I perform for your club Tuesday night. One thousand dollars they will pay me—the monkey who sees without eyes! My friend, it is good to be a monkey, even for such as these, who—but——" He paused and laid his hand on his companion's arm.

"If I could but see the color that is called blue once! They tell me it is cool. They cannot make me feel how cool it is. You will go to sea with me next summer and tell me about it—eh? Will you not, my friend? But three of these—what you call the fifty little millionaires—you will tell me why they are called that— three of these came to me in my hotel and would grasp my hand. And why not? I would grasp the hand of the devil himself if he but offered it. They are surprised. They would blind-fold my poor eyes—my poor eyes, Godahl!—blindfold them again, and again offer me their hands—thinking Malvino a charlatan. Ha-ha! Again I must shake hands with them! One wears a ring, with a great greasy stone. See! I have it here with me. It is bottleglass. Yet would this barbarian wear it until I in pity took it from him."

Godahl burst into a laugh. So this was the thief! Colwell, one of the so-called fifty little millionaires who gave the Pegasus Club its savor—who exhibited their silk hats and ample boot-soles in the plate-glass windows every Sunday afternoon—had been crying over the loss of a ringstone—a garish green affair for which he had paid hugely abroad.

"I am a marvelous man—eh, friend Godahl?"

"Indeed yes!" agreed the other, smiling.

"Malvino the Magician sought Godahl, his friend, this after-noon. Petroff—my manager—he walks ten steps behind me, in the crowd. He taps three times with his stick. Three steps to the right. Ha!—There is Godahl! The *canaille* applaud; even Go-dahl must smile. My friend, Tuesday night Petroff is too clumsy. You will be my manager; but you must be somewhere else."

"Indeed not!" cried Godahl warmly; and to himself: "What does he drive at?"

"Indeed yes!" said the blind man, laying his hand again on the other's arm. "I ask it of you. You will be in other places. If you but say yes you will take me to sea in June and tell me what is the color blue. Listen! First, Malvino will play the monkey. Then I am to be locked in a room for five minutes. At the end of five minutes, if I am gone, that which I have is mine—even to their fat wallets—fat wallets like this one of yours, which I now return intact."

Godahl accepted the return of his wallet absentmindedly. "It is what Mr. Colwell calls a sporting proposition. See! I have it in writing. It is in addition to the one thousand dollars. That I already possess. Now these fifty little millionaires, friend Godahl—are they all like the three who come to me in my hotel? The one with the slippery stone in his ring—the stone that I have—that one had eight thousand dollars—forty thousand francs—in one wallet—in one-thousand-dollar notes. Does the American nation make new money especially for such as these? The notes were new, the imprint still crisp, like the face of my watch. Forty thousand francs in one wallet! I know, because I had the wallet as he talked. No, my friend. I have it not now. I put it back. Ha-ha! What? And there are fifty of them like that. I am to carry away what I can find! Godahl, it is told that the very servants of the club own rows of brick houses and buy consols at correct times. But fifty little millionaires! And Malvino is to be locked in a room, alone! I have it in writing."

A passing street lamp looked in and caught Godahl in the act of blinking.

"Godahl, my friend, if you will tell me what I must know, then I will teach you what you wish to know. You wish to know many things—eh? I can tell, for I always feel your eyes when you are by. Tell me now, every inch of the way—play it is the lake front in that city of Chicago."

Godahl chuckled. He did not love the fifty little millionaires. Those marvelous fingers! Malvino was playing with them in the air now in his earnestness. They could rob a poor-box! Godahl, smiling grimly, began to draw the map his friend desired. Three steps up from the street, then the first glass door. Inside, two vestibules. Past them, on the right, the smoking-room and lounge, a log fire at each end. On the left the street parlor, a great table in the center, and heavy chairs, all upholstered— none far from the walls. Between the rooms, on the left wall, the electric-switch panel. Would he play with light and darkness? It would be as well to hold the secret of this panel. On the floors, deep carpets——

"Deep carpets!" repeated the magician. "It is well I know. I do not like deep carpets. And this room, where I shall be left alone behind locked doors——"

"It would have to be the cloak-room, on the left of the main entrance," said Godahl. Yes, that would be the only available room for such a test. No other rooms off the street parlor could be locked, as there were no doors. In this cloak-room there were two doors—one on the main corridor and one on the first vestibule. There was a small window, but it was not to be thought of for one of Malvino's girth. The doors were massive, of oak; and the locks—Godahl remembered the locks well, having had need to examine them on a recent occasion—were tumblerlocks. It would be rare business to see a man, even a magician, leave the cloak-room without help. And that, too, was in the bond—this sporting proposition.

"The locks have five tumblers," laughed Godahl, more and more amused.

"Let there be fifty!" whispered the other contemptuously. "Tell me, my observing friend—who counts the tumblers of a lock from the outside—do these doors open in or out?"

"In," said Godahl—and the long fingers closed on his wrist in a twinkling.

"In, you say?"

"In!" repeated Godahl; and he made a mental note to study the peculiar characteristics of doors that open in.

Malvino buried himself in his furs. The car sped on through the winding thoroughfares of the park, and Godahl fell to counting the revolving flashes of the gas-lamps as they rushed by.

"This is the one place in your great city where I find joy," said the blind man at length. "There are no staring crowds; I can pick my thoughts; and the pavements are glass. Outside of these walls your city is a rack that would torture me. Tell me, why is blue so cool? June will be too late for the Mediter-ranean. We will start before. If you will but tell me, friend Go-dahl, so that I can feel it, I will give you the half—— No! I will not. What is money to you? Are you quite sure about the doors opening in? Yes? That is good. Godahl, if I could see I think I would be like you—looking on and laughing. Let me tell you something of doors that open in—— What! We are traveling at an unlawful speed! Mistair Offiçaire—indeed, yes, the Great Malvino! Pity his poor eyes! Here is money falling from your hair! You are not a frugal man—so careless!"

The park policeman who had stopped them to warn them against speed stood staring at the crisp bill the blind man had plucked from his hair, as the taxicab sped forward again. Malvino directed the driver to his hotel through the speaking tube, and a few minutes later they were set down there. Godahl declined dinner with his queer friend.

"I have here your wallet once more, friend Godahl!" laughed the blind magician. "The fifty little millionaires! Ha-ha! You promise? You will not be there when I am there?"

"You have my stickpin," said Godahl. "I believe you are collecting bogus stones. That one is bogus, but it was thought to be a fine gift by a friend who is now dead."

The other, with evident disappointment, returned the pilfered stickpin. "You promise! You will not be there when I am there, my friend?"

Godahl held the blue-white hand in his own for a moment as they parted. "No; I promise you," he said; and he watched his queer friend away—Malvino erect, smiling, unfaltering in his fine stride, conscious to the last dregs of the interest he excited on all sides. He shunned the elevator and started up the broad marble stairs, his slender cane tap-tap-tapping, lighting the way for his confident tread.

Godahl dined at his club—looking on and laughing, as Malvino had said with a directness that rather startled the easy rogue into wakefulness. Godahl's career had defied innuendo; his was not an art, but a science, precise, infallible. But several times that afternoon in the somber shadows of their cab he had felt, with a strange thrill, that black impenetrable mask turn on him as though an inner vision lighted those darkened orbs.

Frankly he avoided afflicted persons in the pursuit of his trade, not because of compunctions, which troubled him not at all, but because a person lacking in any of the five senses was apt to be uncannily alert in some one of the remaining four. He was intensely a materialist, a gambler who pinned his faith to marked cards, never to superstition. He believed intuition largely a foolish fetish, except as actuated by the purely physical cravings; yet he recognized a strange clarity in the mental outlook of the afflicted that seemed unexplainable by any other means.

Malvino, too, played with marked cards. After all, magic is but the clever arrangement of properties. But why had Malvino picked him? Why had Malvino confided in him at all? There were a dozen other members of the Pegasus Club who would have served as well, so far as furnishing the business of the affair; who would have entered the game as a huge joke. To hold up the fifty little millionaires in their upholstered wallow would surely set the whole town by the ears. Something of the sort was needed to bring the ribald crew back to earth. But—thought Godahl—if the task were to be done he would much prefer to do it himself, not look on as a supernumerary.

Malvino, of course, was a thief. The only reason he did not practice his profession was that he found the business of playing the monkey paid better. Then, too, as a thief he must bury his talents; and there is nothing so sweet to the Latin as applause. Malvino could not keep his fingers quiet. Godahl had permitted himself to be stripped in their ride through sheer enjoyment of observation. There is nothing too small to be learned and learned well. Nevertheless it had irritated him to think that this master had whispered in his ear familiarly. It smacked too much of kinship. Godahl knew no kin!

As he swept the magnificent dining-room with his eyes, however, he could not repress a chuckle of sheer delight. It would be a hundred-day jest. They all conformed pretty well to type—a type against which the finer sensibilities of Godahl revolted. In the beginning the Pegasus had been the coming together of a few kindred souls—modest, comfortable, homelike; a meeting-place of intellectual men who took their chiefest pleasure in the friction of ideas. In this way the organization had come to have a name, even among the many clubs of the city.

Godahl had adopted it as his home; and—he cynically paraphrased it—he might be without honor in his own country, but never in his own home. He had always been pleased to think that when he entered here he left the undesirable something outside, like the dust of his shoes on the doormat—not that he lacked the lust of the game or a conscious pride in that slick infallibility which had made him a prince for whom other men went poor. There are times and places for all things. And this had been home.

Until, one by one, this tribe had crept in, overturned traditions—substituted the brass of vulgar display for the gold of the fine communion they did not profess to understand, much less to practice. A newspaper wag had finally dubbed them the Club of the Fifty Little Millionaires, and the name had stuck. It happened that a handful of them had been brooded in the same coop, that of a copper king who had begun at the slagpile and ended in philanthropy. As the newcomers gained ascendency the old sect of friends gradually drifted away. The pace was too fast for them.

There was truth in what Malvino had said of the servants; and there is nothing quite so unappetizing as the contempt of those who serve one meat and drink. But Godahl, looking on and laughing, still preserved the habit of picking his meals here with discriminating taste—though now he was less particular about wiping his feet on the doormat than formerly. He even indulged in play occasionally, and while he played he listened to the talk about things worth knowing.

Tonight the talk was all Malvino—at the particular rubber where he chose to play. It was to be a rare occasion. True, they were to pay the magician roundly for the séance and had offered him, besides, a sporting proposition in the shape of a written permission to carry off all his fingers could lift, but they chose to interpret sport according to their own lights. Two centuries ago it was sport in merry England to tie a gamecock to a stump and shy brickbats at it. The game was conducted according to rules carefully worked out, and was popular with all concerned—except the gamecock.

Godahl at length, getting his fill, rose in disgust and passed out. At the corner the street lamp winked at him in its knowing way; and Godahl, forgetting the gorge that had risen in him, returned the wink, smiling.

Colwell, the master of ceremonies, was venturing to a chosen few that a certain faker would be ineligible for dates on a kerosene circuit in Arkansas before the evening was over, when the telephone boy brought him a message from the Victoria. Malvino had started, and was driving to avoid the inevitable crowd that dogged his steps.

The committee was giving a last touch to its properties—a camera and flashlight apparatus arranged behind a screen—when there came the familiar tap-tap-tapping of the cane on the marble steps. If the lilt of his gait were any criterion the mask was in fine fettle.

"So"—he was whispering—"three steps up from the street— two vestibules—and deep carpets. Deep carpets are bad!"

As he passed through the first vestibule this strange, impassive figure in dead black ran his fingers along the wall. There was the door, indeed, by which he would escape.

"Malvino the Magician!" cried a flunkey in gold lace as the inner doors swung open. Colwell was there, with extended hand. The hand of the other closed on it without hesitation, holding it for a moment.

"You speak no French? No? It is—most unfortunate. I speak things—and I am most awkward in your tongue. Is there the color blue here? I would touch it before I play."

He waved his cane toward the entrance. "The corridor? It is empty—yes? It is so in the bond. Thus," he cried, his teeth glowing at the circle of faces before him—"Thus am I to take away that which is mine—is it not?"

Colwell elevated a knowing eyebrow at his companions. Colwell had not been a plumber's assistant for nothing in the days of his youth. He had plugged the keyslots with molten lead. Once closed it would require the aid of a carpenter, not a locksmith—not even a magical locksmith—to negotiate the doors of the cloakroom. Colwell did not begrudge his walletful of small change at auction bridge, but he was decidedly averse to letting it fall into the hands of this blind beggar.

They helped him out of his coat. "My cane too!" he said as he handed the cane to Colwell. It was of ebony, as thin as a baton and without ornament of any kind, save a platinum top. "It is—my faithful Achates! It is—a little brother to my poor senses. It is wonderful——" He swayed slightly and put out a hand to steady himself against Colwell. "But tonight, gentlemen, in your honor Malvino disarms himself, for the—how is it?—the fifty little millionaires—ha-ha!—who are so good as to receive me."

"Am I," he continued, "to have the honor of shaking the hands of the gentlemen? I do not know." He paused as though embarrassed, shrugged his shoulders deprecatingly; and then, smiling: "Myself, as a person, is not present if you so desire—only my talents, which you buy and pay for. Ah, I am awkward in your tongue. Sometimes, gentlemen, I am the guest—sometimes I am only the monkey, with his tricks. You understand? I thank you, sir. Saunders, of Texas Union? Ah, of the landed gentry of this great country! I am indeed pleasured."

A smile went the rounds. Saunders, of Texas Union, who was shaking the hand of the mask with one hand and discreetly feeling the muscles under the black-sleeved arm with the other, had been a puddler at Homestead until his talents for ragtime rescued him from oblivion and gave him Texas Union as a pocket-piece. He brought forward Jones, of Pacific Cascade; Welton, of Tonopah Magnet; Smithers, of Excelsior Common; Jamieson, of Alleghany Western—and so on down the line. The guest, in his naïveté, seemed under the impression that the handles to the names referred to ancestral acres. These men had been named in the daily papers so often in connection with their pet manipulations in the market that they themselves had come to accept the nomenclature, using it much as an Englishman would say Kitchener, of Khartum; or Marlborough, of Blenheim.

So the mask was passed round the room. He was well worth seeing at close range. He accepted each hand with a steely grip; concentrated the vague blackness of his mask on each face, and spoke briefly and in halting phrases. In laying aside his cane he seemed to have lost something of the poise that distinguished the great Malvino on the street or on the stage; and he leaned heavily on a shoulder here, on an arm there, as he was passed from one to another. There was a tremor of excitement in the room. A diversion had been promised; but what it was to be the honorable gentlemen of the committee had kept to themselves and their confederates. Colwell, Saunders and Mason—of Independent Guano—whispered together for a moment; and when the circle of introductions was complete the guest was led to the center of the room. He took his place at the head of the big table, exploring it nervously with his fingers while he waited for the company to be seated.

What followed was somewhat tame, and they expressed themselves to that effect occasionally behind their hands. They had seen the same thing before; a two-dollar bill gave the veriest street loafer the same privilege every afternoon and evening at the Victoria—except for a few parlor pieces the Magician reserved for private entertainments. But even the makings of these were to be had for a few pennies in any one of the numerous shops in Sixth Avenue devoted to the properties of magic. It was merely quickness of hand against slowness of eye. It is said that the persistency of vision amounts to one-hundredth of a second. These fingers found ample room to work in that slit of time. Yet the circle looked on languidly, like an audience at a championship fistfight tolerating the preliminaries.

The performer had borrowed a pack of cards bearing the unbroken seal of the club, and was playing a solitary game at whist, cards faced—a trick of Malvino's, by the way, which has never been satisfactorily explained—when suddenly the barons of Tonopah, Alleghany—and so forth—sat up with a thrill of anticipation. It was evident to all, except perhaps the performer himself, that the apex of the evening was at hand. Masons softly opened the electric-switch cabinet; Colwell and Saunders moved carelessly toward the table, taking up positions on each hand of the mask, as though for a better view of the game.

Then came blank, overwhelming darkness! There was the scuffle of feet; the snapping impact of body against body; a gasp; a half-uttered cry of pain; then:

"Confound him!" It was the voice of Colwell, breathing hard. "He's like a bull—— Gad! Can't you——"

Then another voice—that of Saunders:

"Steady—I've got him? Ready?"

The unseen struggle ceased suddenly. There were several in that thrilled circle that grew sick. It seemed evident that the honorable gentlemen of the committee had overpowered the Magician, were about to strip him of his mask—to show him up as the charlatan who had too long duped a city. They wanted their money's worth. Colwell was laughing, short, sharp; he had the mask now—they could hear the silken ribbon rip as it came away.

"Now! Mason, let him have it!"

The words ended in a roar of mingled rage and pain; there came a sharp snap-snap—as of bones coming away from their sockets; and simultaneously the muffled explosion and the blinding glare of the camera flashlight. And in the one-hundredth of a second of incandescence there was indelibly imprinted on the vision of the audience the figure of the Magician holding two men at arm's length, each by the wrist, their features hideously contorted. Then dead darkness fell, in the midst of which hung the imprinted scene in silhouette against a phosphorescent pall.

Some one thought of the lights. It was the Magician himself. This curious circumstance was not noted until later. The switch clicked and the chandeliers sprang into being again. Colwell held the torn mask in his hand. Every eye, still straining for sight after the shock of the flashlight, sought the blind face of the performer. It was horribly blind now, stripped of its silk ribbon. Covering the eyesockets like plasters were great black disks larger than silver dollars. He stumbled across the room—almost fell against the table; his uncertain hand sought Colwell's arm, traveled down its length and took from the fingers the torn mask and replaced it. The master of ceremonies gazed at the cadaverous face, fascinated. The room was deathly silent. The Magician flashed his teeth in a poor attempt at a smile. His voice, when he spoke, was in whispers as crisp as leaves:

"Ah—my poor eyes! I do not sell—— Gentlemen, I am clumsy with your words. Let me not offend those who are my friends among you when I say I do not sell you my private self—it is only the monkey in me you can buy."

Colwell and Saunders were making efforts to soothe their arms, which were suffering exquisitely. Several men pushed forward, ashamed, to bridge the embarrassment with their apologies to the Magician, who stared at them imperturbably with the mask. Things gradually came to rights, except for the honorable gentlemen of the committee, who took the first chance to retire with their troubles. The hands of the mask were like steel and when he wrenched the bones in their sockets he had not dealt lightly.

"We proceed," said the Magician with a deprecating wave of his hand. "The room! I am to be your prisoner. It is so written."

The few members who knew of Colwell's precautions of plugging the keyslots with lead thought wryly of the fact now. If this thing went any further the Pegasus Club would be the butt of the town!

"We will forget that," said Welton, of Tonopah Magnet, assuming leadership in a movement to make amends. "Besides," he added with a laugh, "we haven't given you a chance to go through our pockets yet. You would have to escape empty-handed."

"Your pardon!" said the mask with a grand bow. "I have already taken the opportunity."

So saying he displayed the contents of his capacious pockets. He had at least a score of wallets and several rolls of banknotes. The room exploded in a cry of amazement. Then the truth flashed upon them. When they passed the guest from hand to hand his nimble fingers had been busy substituting wads of paper for wallets.

"The hour is late," he continued, feeling the face of his watch. "I must be gone in five minutes. The room—if you will."

Welton, of Tonopah Magnet, roaring with laughter, took the Magician—they admitted now he was at least that—and led him to the door of the cloakroom.

"One favor!" said the mask at the threshold. "My coat—my hat—my faithful cane. Ah! I thank you. I bid you good night!"

The naïveté of the words was masterly. Welton, of Tonopah Magnet, drew the door shut with a slam and the lock clicked. He faced the others and turned his trousers pockets inside out comically. He was not worrying about the safety of his cash, but he did admire the deftness of those fingers.

"I am glad to say he left my watch," he said; and he put his watch on the table. It was lacking five minutes of midnight. "What gets me," he continued, turning toward the closed door, "is how we are going to get the poor devil out without a battering ram. Colwell has most certainly earned everlasting fame by his brilliant entertainment this evening."

The keys were useless now that the spring locks had snapped on the prisoner. Some one suggested sending for the engineer; but one and all agreed that the game must be played out in common decency. They all retired to the lounging-room to give the blind beggar five minutes to find out the trick that had been played on him.

At the end of five minutes they sent for the engineer, and that grimy individual appeared, loaded down with tools; he expressed it as his reverend opinion a damned fine door was about to be turned into scrap. There was one chance—that a gasoline torch might blow the lead from the keyslot. But, no—the molten metal only completed the upsetting of the fine mechanism. There was nothing to do but to cut round the lock with a compass saw.

"Cheer up, Malvino!" said Welton through the door. "We will be with you in another minute."

Just then Godahl ran in from the street. He threw his hat and coat to an attendant.

"Ha! The devil to pay—eh?" he cried excitedly. "I just this minute heard of it; and I rushed here."

"What?" said a number of voices at once.

The usually exquisite Godahl was somewhat disheveled and his eyes were red.

"Malvino!" cried he, staring at them as though perplexed at their blandness. "Do you mean to say you don't know why he didn't show up this evening?"

"Didn't show up! What do you mean?"

"You really don't know?" cried Godahl, his eyes blazing.

"No! What? Tell us the answer!" said some one with a laugh.

"The police found him bound and gagged in a deserted cab in Central Park. They've got him in Bellevue Hospital now, raving. By Gad! if I——"

The room laughed. Even the grimy engineer boring a hole to start his compass saw looked over his shoulder and grinned at Godahl.

"Don't excite yourself, Godahl," said Welton, of Tonopah Magnet. "Somebody's been stringing you. We've got Malvino here now. Gad, I wish we didn't have him! You're just in time to help us out of a devil of a mess. That humorist Colwell has plugged the locks with lead; and we can't get the blind beggar out without sawing the door down. He's sweating blood in there now."

"In there?" cried Godahl, pushing his way through the ring round the engineer.

"In there!" repeated Welton. "The kleptomaniac has got a cool ten thousand of mine."

"No!"

"Yes!" said Welton, mimicking Godahl's tone. "You didn't know there was that much money in the world, eh?"

"Let me get this straight," said Godahl, laying a hand on the engineer's arm to stop his work. "You think you have Malvino locked in there with your wallets? I tell you Malvino hasn't been within a mile of this place tonight!"

"I lay you a thousand on it!" cried Welton.

"Tut! tut! Believe me, you are betting on the wrong card." Godahl's eyes danced.

"I lay you a thousand on it!" reiterated the Tonopah magnate. "We'll have to let Malvino hold my stake until we get him out. Gad, he went through me so clean I couldn't swear at this minute that I've got on socks!"

"You are betting on a sure thing?"

"I'm taking candy from a child," retorted Welton.

"I take you!" cried Godahl, his eyes twinkling. "Anybody else want any candy? I warn you!"

There were several. It wasn't every day in the week that they could get Godahl on the hip.

"I warn you again," said Godahl as he accepted the markers, "that Malvino is not in that room. If anybody is there, it is an imposter. You can prove it in a minute by telephoning Bellevue."

The biting saw completed its half circle about the lock; the door swung open. The room was empty!

Several volunteers ran to the rear door. Their sharp chorus of amazement started the crowd tumbling after them. The rear door was off its hinges! It stood propped against the jamb. A child could see what had happened. The prisoner, laden with the cash of the fifty little millionaires, had simply drawn the bolts of the two hinges and lifted the door out of its frame. On the floor was a wad of handbills like those the rogue had left in his dupes' pockets in place of their wallets. They read: "Malvino! He Has No Eyes! Watch His Fingers!"

The fifty little millionaires gazed at each other dumfounded, feeling their pockets the while. The infallible Godahl fell into a chair roaring with laughter. He threw back his head, kicked out his heels, buried his hands wrist-deep in the crisp bills that lined his pockets—all in cold, hard cash! On the whole, he had never spent a more profitable evening.

As for Malvino the Magician, that charlatan could be mighty thankful that it was not he whom the honorable gentlemen of the committee had subjected to manhandling. For Malvino had the eyes of a hawk. So much Godahl had ascertained earlier in the evening when he, in the guise of a murderous cabby, was subjecting the Italian to the indignity of a gag.

WILLIAM HOPE HODGSON

William Hope Hodgson was born in the quiet countryside of Essex, on the English coast northeast of London. Perhaps he found life as the son of a clergyman too claustrophobic, because at an early age he left home for a life of derring-do. Unlike many writers of adventurous tales, he actually adventured. In eight years at sea as a young man, he traveled around the world three times. Travel remained a favorite pastime during his brief life.

Hodgson specialized in eerie tales of the supernatural, some of which are definitely in the horror genre but partake as well of science fictional elements. He didn't like to be limited by genre expectations. His sole other venture into crime fiction also overlaps with the supernatural—*Carnacki the Ghost Finder.* But Hodgson's reputation rests primarily on two books: his long, faux-archaic novel *The Night Land* and a shorter novel, *The House on the Borderland,* about which horror master H. P. Lovecraft muttered the backhanded compliment that "but for a few touches of commonplace sentimentality," it would be a classic "of the first water." Despite Lovecraft's reservations, this novel has long been acclaimed a classic of literate horror writing.

The Gault stories appear as entries in the ship captain's diary—a damning document for which he presumably has an ingenious hiding place. Naturally he never quite tells all until the final scene. Even in his diary, Gault is judicious about what he reveals and when he reveals it. In some of the stories, he indulges in allegedly humorous asides on the perfidy of women; he can't outwit a villainess without generalizing and moralizing. Most of the stories end with Gault explaining his own cleverness. But the gimmicks are genuinely clever and the tone lively. Gault possesses the artistic thief's primary trait: a gleeful disregard for law and an ungentlemanly pride in his own cleverness.

"The Diamond Spy" first appeared at a tragic time, in the August 1914 issue of *The London Magazine*. Hodgson reprinted it three years later in his collection *Captain Gault: Being the Exceedingly Private Log of a Sea-Captain*. In April of the next year he was killed by a German artillery shell at Ypres.

THE DIAMOND SPY

S.S. Montrose,
June 18.

I am having enough bother with one or two of the passengers this trip, to make me wish I was running a cargo boat again.

When I went up on the upper bridge this morning, Mr. Wilmet, my First Officer, had allowed one of the passengers, a Mr. Brown, to come up on to the bridge and loose off some prize pigeons. Not only that; but the Third Officer was taking the time for him, by one of the chronometers.

I'm afraid what I said looked a bit as if I had lost my temper.

"Mr. Wilmet," I said, "will you explain to Mr. Brown that this bridge is quite off his beat; and I should like him to remove himself, and ask him please to remember the fact for future reference. If Mr. Brown wants to indulge his taste in a pigeon flying, I've no objections to offer at all; but he'll kindly keep off my bridge!"

I certainly made no effort to spare Mr. Brown; and this is not the first time I have had to pull him up; for he took several of his pigeons down into the dining-saloon yesterday, and was showing them off to a lot of his friends—actually letting them fly all about the place; and you know what dirty brutes the birds are! I gave him a smart word or two before all the saloon-full; and I fancy they agreed with me. The man's mad on his pigeon-flying.

Then there's a bore of a travelling Colonel, who's always trying to invade my bridge, to smoke and yarn with me. I've had to tell him plainly to keep off the bridge, same as Mr. Brown, only, perhaps, not quite in the same manner. And there are two ladies, an old and a young one, who are always on the bridge steps, as you might say. I took the opportunity to talk to the oldest about my eighth boy, to-day. I thought it might cool her off; but it didn't; she's started talking to me now about the dear children; and as I'm not even married, I've lied myself nearly stupid, confound her! And the old lady has let the young one know, *of course!* And the young one has left me now entirely to the old one's mercies! Goodness me!

But the passenger who really bothers me, is a Mr. Aglae, a sallow, fat, darkish man, short, and most infernally inquisitive. He seems always to be hanging about; and I've more than a notion he's cultivating a confidential friendship with my servant-lad.

Of course, I've guessed all along he's a Diamond Spy; and I don't doubt but there's need for the breed in these boats; for there's a pile to be made in running stones and pearls through the Customs.

I nearly broke loose on him to-day and told him, slam out, I knew he was a spy, and that he had better keep his nose out of my cabin and my affairs; and pay a bit more attention to people who had the necessary thousands to deal successfully in his line of goods.

The man was actually peeking into my cabin, when I came up behind him; but he was plausible enough. He said he had knocked, and thought I said, "Come in." He had come to ask me to take care of a very valuable diamond, which he brought out of his vest pocket, in a wash-leather bag. He told me he had begun to feel it might be safer if properly locked up. Of course, I explained that his diamond would be taken care of in the usual way; and when he asked my opinion of it, I became astonishingly affable; for it was plainly his desire to get me to talk on the subject.

"A magnificent stone!" I said. "Why, I should think it must be worth thousands. It must be twenty or thirty carats."

I knew perfectly well that the thing was merely a well cut piece of glass; for I tried it slyly on the tester I carry on the inner edge of my ring; and as for the size, I was purposely "out"; for I knew that if it had been a diamond, it would have been well over sixty carats.

The little fat spy frowned slightly and I wondered whether I'd shown him that he was getting up the wrong tree; and then, in a moment, I saw by the look in his eyes that he suspected me as much as ever; and was putting me down as being simply *ostentatiously* ignorant of diamonds. After he had gone, I thought him over for a bit, and I got wishing I could give the little toad a lesson.

June 19.

I got a splendid idea during the night. We should dock this evening, and I've just time to work it. The diamond-running talk came up at dinner last night, as is but natural in these boats; and different passengers told some good yarns, some of them old and some new, and a lot of them very clever dodges that have been worked on the Customs.

One man at my table told an I.D.B. yarn of how a duck had been induced to gobble up diamonds by bedding them in pellets of bread, and in this way the diamonds had been cunningly hidden, at a very critical moment for the well-being of their "illicit" owner.

This gave me an idea; for that diamond spy has got on to my nerves a bit, and if I don't do something to make him look and feel a fool, I shall just get rude; and rudeness to passengers is not a thing that commends itself to owners.

I have a coop of S. African black ring-neck hens, down on the well-deck, which I am taking across to my brother, who makes a hobby of hen-keeping and has bred some wonderful strains.

I sent my servant for a plateful of new crumb-bread, and then I fished out from the bottom of my sea-chest, a box of what we used to call among the islands "native blazers"—that is, cut-glass imitation diamonds, which certainly cleaned up to a very pretty glitter. I'd had the things with me for years, some left-overs, from a sporting trip I made once that way.

I sat down at my table, and made bread pellets; and then I began to bed each of the "stones" into a pellet. As I did so, I became aware that some one was peeping in the window that looks into the saloon. I glanced into the mirror, across on the opposite bulkshead of my cabin, and saw for an instant the face of my servant.

This is what I had expected.

"So ho! my lad!" I said to myself. "I guess this is the last trip you'll take with me; for, though I'll see you aren't dangerous now, you may be some other time."

When I had done coating my "diamonds" with bread, I went forrard to my hen-coop, and began to feed the pellets to the birds. As I turned away from giving the last of the big bread pills, I literally bumped into Mr. Aglae, who had just come round the end of the coop. Obviously, he had received word from my servant, and had been watching me feed diamonds to my hens, so as to hide my illegal jewelry, while the search officers were aboard!

It was rather funny to see the way in which the diamond spy put on a vacant expression, and apologized for his clumsiness, blaming the rolling of the vessel. As a matter of fact, he had no business in that part of the ship at all; and I made a courteous reference to this fact; for I wished him to think that I was disturbed and annoyed by his being there at so (apparently) critical a moment for me.

Later on, when I went into the wireless room, I found Mr. Aglae sending a wireless; and I sat down on the lounge to write my own message, while Melson (the Operator) was sending.

Instead, however, of writing out my own message, I jotted down the dot and dash iddle-de-umpty of the iggle-de-piggle that the Operator was sending; for it was a private code message, and ran: 17 a y b o z w r e y a a j g o o a v o o 1 o w t p q 2 2 3 2 1 m v n 6 7 a m n t 8 t s .17. aglae. g.v.n.

I smiled; for it was the latest official cypher, and I had the "key" in my pocket-book. It is desirable to have what is popularly called "a friend in high quarters." Only my friend is not very high, at least, not highly paid; though his secretarial position gives him access in a certain government office to papers that help him considerably to make both ends meet.

After Mr. Aglae had departed, I took out my "key," and translated the message, while Melson was sending mine. Translated, it was this: "Hens fed on hundreds of diamonds concealed in bread pellets. Better come out in the pilot tug. Shall mark coop. I must not appear in the case at all. Most important capture of years. 17. Aglae. g. v. n."

This was sent to a private address, merely as a blind; for Mr. Aglae would be of little further use as a diamond spy if he began sending cypher messages to the Head Office! The 17, just before his name, I knew must be his official number; and I was interested, and perhaps a little impressed; for I have heard of the unknown "Number 17" before. He had effected some wonderful captures among the diamond smugglers. I wondered what he might look like, minus what I began now to suspect was both false stomachic appendage, and dyed hair, plus his little, vaguely foreign mannerisms, to suit.

The letters "g.v.n.," which followed the signature, were the inner "keys" to the message; for the cypher is really clever, in that a long message can be sent with a limited number of symbols, by a triplicate reading, according to the use of the various combinations—the working of which the main "key" explains, and which are indicated by the combination letters, which are always written, in this cypher, after the signature.

As I went out of the wireless room, I had a second splendid idea. I got some bread-crumbs as an excuse, and had another walk down to the well-deck to look at my coop of prize chickens, and I came slam on Number 17 (as I now called him to myself) just strolling off.

Now, I had made it plain to him that he had no business down there, and I called to him, to ask him what he was doing again in that part of the ship, after what I had told him in the morning.

I must say that Number 17 has got quite a remarkably sound "nerve" on him.

"I'm sorry, Captain," he said; "but I'd lost my cigarette holder. I knew I'd had it in my fingers when I tumbled against you this morning, and I thought I might have dropped it then."

He held it out to me, between his finger and thumb.

"I found it lying on the deck here," he explained. "A mercy it was not trodden on. I'm thankful much; for I prize it."

"That's all right, Mr. Aglae," I said, and hid the smile his tricky little foreign flavour of speech rose in me. As a matter of fact, if what I've heard is correct, the man is Scotch, bred and born and reared. It shows what even a Scotchman can come down to!

After he had gone, with one of his dinky little bows, I overhauled the hen-coop; but in a casual sort of way, so that no one, looking on, could suspect I was doing more than making one of my usual bi-daily visits to my chuck-chucks, and feeding them with bread-crumbs.

If I had not read the cypher message, I should certainly not have discovered the marks that Mr. Aglae had made on the coop; they were merely three small dots, in a triangle, like this . ˙ ., with a tiny 17 in the centre. The thing had just been jotted down on one of the legs of the coops with a piece of sharp-pointed chalk, and it could have been covered with a ha'penny.

I grinned to myself and went to the carpenter's shop for a piece of chalk. I made Chips sharpen it to a fine point with a chisel; then I put it in my pocket and continued my afternoon stroll round the decks.

I wanted first to place Mr. Aglae; for it would spoil part of the amusingness of my plot, if he were on the spy, and saw what I was going to do. I found him, away aft in the upper-deck smoke-room, reading *Le Petit Journal,* and looking most subtly foreign and most convincingly innocent.

"You little devil!" I thought; and went right away to the well-deck. Here, in an unobtrusive way, I copied Mr. Aglae's private signature, faithfully, on to the hen-coop above the one in which I was carrying my brother's black ring-necks. The coop was occupied for the voyage by the bulk of Mr. Brown's confounded pigeons, which, I had insisted, must not be brought again into the saloon.

After I had re-duplicated the mark, I lifted out four of my ring-necks from the bottom coop, and put them into the top one, among Mr. Brown's pigeons. My argument was that, when the searchers boarded us with the pilot, they would find both these coops marked, and both with hens in them, and would act accordingly. They would have to open the upper coop to remove the four hens, and there would be a general exodus of Mr. Brown's pigeons, which would re-double the confusion and general glad devilment of my little plot.

Mr. Brown would be enormously angry and enormously vociferous. I could picture him thundering: "I never heard of such

a thing! Confound you, Sir! I shall write to *The Times* about
this."

And then, it seemed to me, Number 17 would have to come
and make some kind of semi-public explanation, of what he
could never properly explain; and ever after, his value as a diamond spy would be decreased something like twenty-five per
cent.; for quite a lot of people aboard (maybe some of them in
the Diamond-Running business) would be able to get a good
square look at the famous Number 17, and for all time afterwards, in whatever way he might try to veil his charming personality, he would run chances of being recognised at some
awkward and premature moment; at least, from his point of
view!

But, of course, at first, Mr. Aglae (Number 17) would be
only partly involved in my cheerful little net of difficulties. He
would know, all the time, that these curious complications were
only trifling; for had he not made the greatest capture of years.
Let Mr. Brown be apologized to; even compensated, if such
compensation were legally his right. The great thing would be
to reduce the black ring-necks to poultry, as speedily as possible, and then to pick his Triumph from their gizzards!

I wriggled quietly with pleasure, as I saw it all. And then, the
Official Appraiser's brief explanation to the Chief; and the salty
flavour of the Chief's explanation to Number 17, that there
was no law against a sea Captain feeding his pet hens with bits
of glass, cut or otherwise, for the improvement, or otherwise,
of their digestions.

Then there would be the replacing of my five dozen ring-
necks, or their equivalent in good honest dollars, treasury dollars, I presume. I calculated rapidly that even as the prestige of
Number 17 must come down, so the price of my hens should as
infallibly go up.

I snicked the lesser door of the upper coop shut, and watched
my four hens and Mr. Brown's pigeons. The hens clucked, and
walked odd paces in the dignified and uncertain fashion affected
by all hens of a laying age. The pigeons fluttered a bit, and then
resumed their wonted cooing; and after that, all was comfortable in that ark; for the hens discovered pigeon-food to be very

good hen-food also, and set to work earnestly to fill the unfill-able.

The searchers came aboard with the Pilot, and after the usual preliminaries, my presence was requested at the opening of the hen-coop. I noticed that Mr. Aglae was still in the upper smoke-room, as I passed, and there he appeared intent to stay. I admired his judgment.

The officials gathered on the well-deck, and the Chief ex-plained that they had received certain information which they were acting upon; and asked me formally whether I had any di-amonds to declare.

"I'm sorry to say that I've left my diamond investments at home this trip, Mister," I said. "I've nothing I'm setting out to declare, except you've been put on to some mare's nest!"

"We happen to think otherwise, Cap'n," he said. "I've given you your chance, and you've chucked it. Now you've got to take what's coming to you!"

He turned to one of his men.

"Open the lower coop, Ellis," he told him. "Rake out those chickens. Hand 'em over to the poulterer."

As each chicken was taken out, it was handed to the poulterer, and the man killed it then and there. My little plan was making things unfortunate, of course, for my brother's ring-necks; but, after all, they were fulfilling their name, and I felt that, eventu-ally, I should have nothing personally to grumble about.

But, in spite of this pleasant inward feeling, I protested for-mally and vigorously against the whole business, and pointed out that someone would have to pay, and keep on paying for an "outrage" (as I called it) of this kind.

The Chief merely shrugged his shoulders, and told the men to rake out the four hens from the upper coop. The man reached in his hand through the trap; but, of course, the hens side-stepped him in a dignified fashion. Then the man grew a little wrathy, and whipped down the whole front of the coop, and plunged in, head and shoulders, to get them.

Instantly, what I had planned, happened. There was a multi-tudinous, harsh, dry whisper of a hundred pairs of wings; and then, hey! the air was white with pigeons. The man backed out of the coop, with a couple of my ring-neck hens in each hairy fist; and met the blast of his superior's wrath—

"You clumsy goat!" snarled the Chief—"What——" And then the second thing that I had foreseen, occurred.

"Confound you, Sir!" yelled Mr. Brown, dashing in among us, breathless. "Confound you! Confound you! You've loosed all my pigeons! What the blazes does this mean! What the blazes. . . ."

"You may well ask, Sir, what it means," I answered. "I think these officials have gone mad!"

But Mr. Brown was already, to all appearances, quite oblivious of anyone or anything, except his beloved pigeons.

He had lugged out a big gold watch and a notebook and was making frantic efforts to achieve a lightning-like series of time-notes, staring up with a crick in his neck, trying crazily to identify the directions taken by various of his more particular birds.

He had, of course, to give it up almost at once; for already the bulk of the birds had made their preliminary circles, and were now shooting away for the coast, at various angles.

Then Mr. Brown proved himself more of a man than I had hitherto supposed possible in one who flew pigeons. He attained a height of denunciatory eloquence, which not only brought most of the first-class passengers to the spot; but caused a number, even of the married women, to withdraw hastily.

The Chief made several attempts to pacify him; but it was useless, and he made dumb-show then to the poulterer to set about opening up my brother's five dozen ring-necks, which that man did with admirable skill, until the well-deck looked like a slaughter house. And still Mr. Brown continued to express himself.

At last, the Chief sent a messenger, and (evidently much against his will) Mr. Aglae had to come and explain.

Mr. Brown ceased to denunciate for a moment, while Mr. Aglae explained, and the passengers crowded nearer, until the Chief asked me to tell them to retire. But I shrugged my shoulders. It fell in well with my plans for the spy's flattening, to have as many witnesses as possible.

"I never marked your coop, Sir," said Number 17, warmly. "It was the Captain's coop of hens that I marked. . . ."

"Rubbish!" interpolated the Chief; "here's your mark on both coops!"

It struck me, in that moment, that possibly the Chief would not be sorry to weaken Number 17's position; for that man may have been climbing the promotion-ladder a little too rapidly for the Chief's peace of mind; though I knew the Chief would not dare say much, in case the capture proved as important as Number 17 had described.

I never saw a man look so bewildered as the spy, when he saw that both coops were marked. Then he turned and looked straight at me; but I gave him a good healthy back-stare.

"So," I said aloud, for every one to hear, "you're a beastly spy? I don't wonder I've felt crawly every time you've passed near me this trip!"

The little man glared at me, and I thought he was going to lose control, and come for me; but at that moment, Mr. Brown, having rested, began again.

During the fluent period that followed, the poulterer worked stolidly and quickly and I saw that he was resurrecting quite a number of my cut-glass ornaments.

They had brought out the official appraiser with them; so important had they considered the case, from Number 17's message; and that man, breaking himself from the charmed circle of Mr. Brown's listeners, walked over to the poulterer, and began to examine the "diamonds."

I watched him quietly, and saw him test the first one, carefully; then frown, and pick up another. At the end of five minutes, both he and the poulterer finished their work almost simultaneously; and I saw the appraiser throw down the last of the "diamonds" contemptuously on to the hatch.

"Mr. Franks!" he called out aloud, to the Chief, "I have to report that there is not a single diamond in the crops of these— er—poultry. There are a large number of pieces of cut-glass, such as can be bought for ten cents a dozen; but no diamonds. I imagine our Mr. Aglae has made a thumper for once."

I grinned, as I realized that Number 17 was not loved, even

by the appraiser. But I laughed outright, when I looked from the Chief's face to Number 17's, and then back again.

Mr. Brown had halted spasmodically, in his fiftieth explanation of the remarkable and unprintable letter that he meant to write to *The Times,* on the subject of his outrage. And now he commenced again, but, by mutual consent, everyone moved away sufficiently far to hear themselves speak; and there and then, the Chief said quite some of the things he was thinking and feeling about Number 17's "capture."

Number 17 said not a word. He looked stunned. Abruptly, a light came into his eyes, and he threw up his hand, to silence the Chief.

"Good Lord, Sir!" he said, in a high, cracking voice of complete comprehension. "The pigeons! The pigeons! We've been done brown. The hens were a blind worked off on me, to keep me from smelling the pigeon pie. Carrier pigeons, Sir! *What* a fool I've been!"

I explained that he had no right to make such a libellous and unfounded statement, and Mr. Brown's proposed letter to *The Times* grew in length and vehemence. Eventually, Mr. Aglae had to apologise as publicly as he had slandered both Mr. Brown and me. But that did not prevent us from presenting our bills for compensation for damage done. And what is more, both of us got paid our own figure; for neither the Treasury, nor its officers, were eager for the further publicity which would have inevitably accompanied the fighting of our "bills of costs" at a court trial.

It was, maybe, a week later, that Mr. Brown and I had dinner together at a certain very famous restaurant.

"Pigeons——" said Mr. Brown, meditatively—"I like 'em best with a neat little packet of diamonds fixed under their feathers."

"Same here!" I said, smiling reminiscently.

I filled my glass.

"Pigeons!" I said.

"Pigeons!" said Mr. Brown, raising his glass.

And we drank.

SINCLAIR LEWIS

Sinclair Lewis was the first American to win the Nobel Prize in Literature, with a citation praising "his vigorous and graphic art of description and his ability to create, with wit and humour, new types of characters." Lewis is not thought of as a crime writer, but he was no stranger to con men. Glad-handing puffery is the hallmark of many of his best known characters, including the businessman who lent his name to *Babbitt* in 1922, two years after Lewis's breakthrough novel, *Main Street.* Evangelist Elmer Gantry was first and last a con artist. Only a few characters here and there, such as the idealistic young research physician Martin Arrowsmith, have much nobility about them.

During the 1920s Lewis cheerfully joined his friend H. L. Mencken in lampooning the ignorance and credulity that marked the heyday of spiritualists, evangelist Aimee Semple McPherson, and the Scopes trial. His books often lack subtlety and depth, but they aimed much-needed spotlights at dark corners of the American psyche—and did so with the kind of naïve glee typical of gaslight crime writers. *Babbitt,* for example, portrays the law-abiding, business-minded boosters on whom J. Rufus Wallingford preys so successfully.

Lewis's early tales include many duplicitous and opportunistic characters who were not officially criminals. In "The Willow Walk," he edges toward Dostoyevsky's turf, the crisis of conscience. In the best caper-movie mode—and for years Hollywood maintained an option on the story—his protagonist encounters troubles he did not foresee when he was planning his crime. The story first appeared in the August 10, 1918, issue of the *Saturday*

Evening Post and was soon anthologized in *Best Short Stories of 1918*. In 1935 a *Time* reviewer dismissed most of the tales in Lewis's *Selected Short Stories* as "long-winded and mechanical," except for "his brilliant 'The Willow Walk,' a first-rate story in any company."

THE WILLOW WALK

From the drawer of his table-desk Jasper Holt took a pane of window glass. He laid a sheet of paper on the glass and wrote, "Now is the time for all good men to come to the aid of the party." He studied his round business-college script, and rewrote the sentence in a small finicky hand, that of a studious old man. Ten times he copied the words in that false pinched writing. He tore up the paper, burned the fragments in his large ashtray and washed the delicate ashes down his stationary washbowl. He replaced the pane of glass in the drawer, tapping it with satisfaction. A glass underlay does not retain an impression.

Jasper Holt was as nearly respectable as his room, which, with its frilled chairs and pansy-painted pincushion, was the best in the aristocratic boardinghouse of Mrs. Lyons. He was a wiry, slightly bald, black-haired man of thirty-eight, wearing an easy gray flannel suit and a white carnation. His hands were peculiarly compact and nimble. He gave the appearance of being a youngish lawyer or bond salesman. Actually he was Senior Paying Teller in the Lumber National Bank in the city of Vernon.

He looked at a thin expensive gold watch. It was six-thirty, on Wednesday—toward dusk of a tranquil spring day. He picked up his hooked walking stick and his gray silk gloves and trudged downstairs. He met his landlady in the lower hall and inclined his head. She effusively commented on the weather.

"I shall not be here for dinner," he said amiably.

"Very well, Mr. Holt. My, but aren't you always going out with your swell friends though! I read in the 'Herald' that you were going to be star in another of those society plays at the

Community Theater. I guess you'd be an actor if you wasn't a
banker, Mr. Holt."

"No, I'm afraid I haven't much temperament." His voice
was cordial, but his smile was a mere mechanical sidewise twist
of the lip muscles. "You're the one that's got the stage presence.
Bet you'd be a regular Ethel Barrymore if you didn't have to
look out for us."

"My, but you're such a flatterer!"

He bowed his way out and walked sedately down the street
to a public garage. Nodding to the night attendant, but saying
nothing, he started his roadster and drove out of the garage,
away from the center of Vernon, toward the suburb of Rosebank. He did not go directly to Rosebank. He went seven blocks
out of his way, and halted on Fandall Avenue—one of those
petty main thoroughfares which, with their motion-picture
palaces, their groceries, laundries, undertakers' establishments
and lunchrooms, serve as local centers for districts of mean residences. He got out of the car and pretended to look at the
tires, kicking them to see how much air they had. While he did
so he covertly looked up and down the street. He saw no one
whom he knew. He went into the Parthenon Confectionery
Store.

The Parthenon Store makes a specialty of those ingenious
candy boxes that resemble bound books. The back of the box
is of imitation leather, with a stamping simulating the title of a
novel. The edges are apparently the edges of a number of pages
of paper. But these pages are hollowed out, and the inside is to
be filled with candy.

Jasper gazed at the collection of book boxes and chose the
two whose titles had the nearest approach to dignity—*Sweets
to the Sweet* and *The Ladies' Delight*. He asked the Greek clerk
to fill these with the less expensive grade of mixed chocolates,
and to wrap them.

From the candy shop he went to a drugstore that carried an
assortment of reprinted novels, and from these picked out two
of the same sentimental type as the titles on the booklike boxes.
These also he had wrapped. He strolled out of the drugstore,
slipped into a lunchroom, got a lettuce sandwich, doughnuts

and a cup of coffee at the greasy marble counter, took them to a chair with a tablet arm in the dim rear of the lunchroom and hastily devoured them. As he came out and returned to his car he again glanced along the street.

He fancied that he knew a man who was approaching. He could not be sure. From the breast up the man seemed familiar, as did the customers of the bank whom he viewed through the wicket of the teller's window. When he saw them in the street he could never be sure about them. It seemed extraordinary to find that these persons, who to him were nothing but faces with attached arms that held out checks and received money, could walk about, had legs and a gait and a manner of their own.

He walked to the curb and stared up at the cornice of one of the stores, puckering his lips, giving an impersonation of a man inspecting a building. With the corner of an eye he followed the approaching man. The man ducked his head as he neared, and greeted him, "Hello, Brother Teller." Jasper seemed startled; gave the "Oh! Oh, how are you!" of sudden recognition and mumbled, "Looking after a little bank property."

"Always on the job, eh?"

The man passed on.

Jasper got into his car and drove back to the street that would take him out to the suburb of Rosebank. As he left Fandall Avenue he peered at his watch. It was five minutes of seven.

At a quarter past seven he passed through the main street of Rosebank, and turned into a lane that was but little changed since the time when it had been a country road. A few jerry-built villas of freckled paint did shoulder upon it, but for the most part it ran through swamps spotted with willow groves, the spongy ground covered with scatterings of dry leaves and bark. Opening on this lane was a dim-rutted grassy private road, which disappeared into one of the willow groves.

Jasper sharply swung his car between the crumbly gateposts and along the bumpy private road. He made an abrupt turn, came into sight of an unpainted shed and shot the car into it without cutting down his speed, so that he almost hit the back of the shed with his front fenders. He shut off the engine, climbed out quickly and ran back toward the gate. From the shield of a bank of alder bushes he peered out. Two chattering women were going down the public road. They stared in through the gate and half halted.

"That's where that hermit lives," said one of them.

"Oh, you mean the one that's writing a religious book, and never comes out till evening? Some kind of a preacher?"

"Yes, that's the one. John Holt, I think his name is. I guess he's kind of crazy. He lives in the old Beaudette house. But you can't see it from here—it's clear through the block, on the next street."

"I heard he was crazy. But I just saw an automobile go in here."

"Oh, that's his cousin or brother or something—lives in the city. They say he's rich, and such a nice fellow."

The two women ambled on, their chatter blurring with distance. Standing behind the alders Jasper rubbed the palm of one hand with the fingers of the other. The palm was dry with nervousness. But he grinned.

He returned to the shed and entered a brick-paved walk almost a block long, walled and sheltered by overhanging willows. Once it had been a pleasant path; carved wooden benches were placed along it, and it widened to a court with a rock garden, a fountain and a stone bench. The rock garden had degenerated into a riot of creepers sprawling over the sharp stones; the paint had peeled from the fountain, leaving its iron cupids and naiads eaten with rust. The bricks of the walk were smeared with lichens and moss and were untidy with windrows of dry leaves and cakes of earth. Many of the bricks were broken; the walk was hilly in its unevenness. From willows and bricks and scuffled earth rose a damp chill.

But Jasper did not seem to note the dampness. He hastened along the walk to the house—a structure of heavy stone which, for this newish Midwestern land, was very ancient. It had been built by a French fur trader in 1839. The Chippewas had scalped a man in its very dooryard. The heavy back door was guarded by an unexpectedly expensive modern lock. Jasper opened it with a flat key and closed it behind him. It locked on a spring. He was in a crude kitchen, the shades of which were drawn. He passed through the kitchen and dining room into the living room. Dodging chairs and tables in the darkness as though he was used to them he went to each of the three windows of the living room and made sure that all the shades were down before he lighted the student's lamp on the gate-legged table. As the glow crept over the drab walls Jasper bobbed his head with satisfaction. Nothing had been touched since his last visit.

The room was musty with the smell of old green rep upholstery and leather books. It had not been dusted for months. Dust sheeted the stiff red velvet chairs, the uncomfortable settee, the chill white marble fireplace, the immense glass-fronted bookcase that filled one side of the room.

The atmosphere was unnatural to this capable businessman, this Jasper Holt. But Jasper did not seem oppressed. He briskly removed the wrappers from the genuine books and from the candy-box imitations of books. One of the two wrappers he laid on the table and smoothed out. Upon this he poured the candy from the two boxes. The other wrapper and the strings he stuffed into the fireplace and immediately burned. Crossing to the bookcase he unlocked one section and placed both the real books and the imitation books on the bottom shelf. There was a row of rather cheap-looking novels on this shelf, and of these at least six were actually such candy boxes as he had purchased that evening.

Only one shelf of the bookcase was given over to anything so frivolous as novels. The others were filled with black-covered, speckle-leaved, dismal books of history, theology, biography—the shabby-genteel sort of books you find on the fifteen-cent shelf at a secondhand bookshop. Over these Jasper pored for a moment as though he was memorizing their titles.

He took down *The Life of the Rev. Jeremiah Bodfish* and read aloud:

In those intimate discourses with his family that followed evening prayers I once heard Brother Bodfish observe that Philo Judaeus—

whose scholarly career always calls to my mind the adumbra-
tions of Melanchthon upon the essence of rationalism—was a
mere sophist—

Jasper slammed the book shut, remarking contentedly,
"That'll do. Philo Judaeus—good name to spring."

He relocked the bookcase and went upstairs. In a small bedroom at the right of the upper hall an electric light was burning. Presumably the house had been deserted till Jasper's
entrance, but a prowler in the yard might have judged from this
ever-burning light that someone was in residence. The bedroom was Spartan—an iron bed, one straight chair, a wash-
stand, a heavy oak bureau. Jasper scrambled to unlock the
lowest drawer of the bureau, yank it open, take out a wrinkled
shiny suit of black, a pair of black shoes, a small black bow tie,
a Gladstone collar, a white shirt with starched bosom, a speckly
brown felt hat and a wig—an expensive and excellent wig with
artfully unkempt hair of a faded brown.

He stripped off his attractive flannel suit, wing collar, blue
tie, custom-made silk shirt and cordovan shoes, and speedily
put on the wig and those gloomy garments. As he donned them
the corners of his mouth began to droop. Leaving the light on
and his own clothes flung on the bed he descended the stairs.
He was obviously not the same man who had ascended them.
As to features he was like Jasper, but by nature he was evidently
less healthy, less practical, less agreeable, and decidedly more
aware of the sorrow and long thoughts of the dreamer. Indeed
it must be understood that now he was not Jasper Holt, but
Jasper's twin brother, John Holt, hermit and religious fanatic.

John Holt, twin brother of Jasper Holt, the bank teller, rubbed
his eyes as though he had for hours been absorbed in study,
and crawled through the living room, through the tiny hall,
to the front door. He opened it, picked up a couple of circu-
lars that the postman had dropped through the letter slot in
the door, went out and locked the door behind him. He was
facing a narrow front yard, neater than the willow walk at the

back, on a suburban street more populous than the straggly back lane.

A street arc illuminated the yard and showed that a card was tacked on the door. John touched the card, snapped it with the nail of his little finger, to make certain that it was securely tacked. In that light he could not read it but he knew that it was inscribed in a small finicky hand: *Agents kindly do not disturb, bell will not be answered, occupant of house engaged in literary work.*

John stood on the doorstep till he made out his neighbor on the right—a large stolid commuter, who was walking before his house smoking an after-dinner cigar. John poked to the fence and sniffed at a spray of lilac blossoms till the neighbor called over, "Nice evening."

"Yes, it seems to be very pleasant."

John's voice was like Jasper's; but it was more guttural, and his speech had less assurance.

"How's the book going?"

"It is—it is very—very difficult. So hard to comprehend all the inner meanings of the prophecies. Well, I must be hastening to Soul Hope Hall. I trust we shall see you there some Wednesday or Sunday evening. I bid you good night, sir."

John wavered down the street to a drugstore. He purchased a bottle of ink. In a grocery that kept open evenings he got two pounds of corn meal, two pounds of flour, a pound of bacon, a half pound of butter, six eggs and a can of condensed milk.

"Shall we deliver them?" asked the clerk.

John looked at him sharply. He realized that this was a new man, who did not know his customs. He said rebukingly: "No, I always carry my parcels. I am writing a book. I am never to be disturbed."

He paid for the provisions out of a postal money order for thirty-five dollars, and received the change. The cashier of the store was accustomed to cashing these money orders, which were always sent to John from South Vernon, by one R. J. Smith. John took the bundle of food and walked out of the store.

"That fellow's kind of a nut, isn't he?" asked the new clerk.

The cashier explained: "Yep. Doesn't even take fresh milk—uses condensed for everything! What do you think of that! And they say he burns up all his garbage—never has anything in the ash can except ashes. If you knock at his door he never answers it, fellow told me. All the time writing this book of his. Religious crank, I guess. Has a little income though—guess his folks were pretty well fixed. Comes out once in a while in the evening and pokes round town. We used to laugh about him, but we've kind of got used to him. Been here about half a year, I guess it is."

John was serenely passing down the main street of Rosebank. At the dingier end of it he turned in at a hallway marked by a lighted sign announcing in crude housepainter's letters: SOUL HOPE FRATERNITY HALL. EXPERIENCE MEETING. ALL WELCOME.

It was eight o'clock. The members of the Soul Hope cult had gathered in their hall above a bakery. Theirs was a tiny, tight-minded sect. They asserted that they alone obeyed the scriptural tenets; that they alone were certain to be saved; that all other denominations were damned by unapostolic luxury; that it was wicked to have organs or ministers or any meeting places save plain halls. The members themselves conducted the meetings, one after another rising to give an interpretation of the scriptures or to rejoice in gathering with the faithful, while the others commented "Hallelujah!" and "Amen, brother, amen!" They were a plainly dressed, not overfed, rather elderly and rather happy congregation. The most honored of them all was John Holt.

John had come to Rosebank only six months before. He had bought the Beaudette house, with the library of the recent occupant, a retired clergyman, and had paid for them in new one-hundred-dollar bills. Already he had gained great credit in the Soul Hope cult. It appeared that he spent almost all his time at home, praying, reading and writing a book. The Soul Hope Fraternity were excited about the book. They had begged him to read it to them. So far he had read only a few pages, consisting mostly of quotations from ancient treatises on the prophecies. Nearly every Sunday and Wednesday evening he appeared at the meeting and in a halting but scholarly way lectured on the world and the flesh.

Tonight he spoke polysyllabically of the fact that one Philo Judaeus had been a mere sophist. The cult were none too clear as to what either a Philo Judaeus or a sophist might be, but with heads all nodding in a row, they murmured: "You're right, brother! Hallelujah!"

John glided into a sad earnest discourse on his worldly brother Jasper, and informed them of his struggles with Jasper's itch for money. By his request the fraternity prayed for Jasper.

The meeting was over at nine. John shook hands all round with the elders of the congregation, sighing: "Fine meeting tonight, wasn't it? Such a free outpouring of the Spirit!" He welcomed a new member, a servant girl just come from Seattle. Carrying his groceries and the bottle of ink he poked down the stairs from the hall at seven minutes after nine.

At sixteen minutes after nine John was stripping off his brown wig and the funereal clothes in his bedroom. At twenty-eight after John Holt had again become Jasper Holt, the capable teller of the Lumber National Bank.

Jasper Holt left the light burning in his brother's bedroom. He rushed downstairs, tried the fastening of the front door, bolted it, made sure that all the windows were fastened, picked up the bundle of groceries and the pile of candies that he had removed from the booklike candy boxes, blew out the light in the living room and ran down the willow walk to his car. He threw the groceries and candy into it, backed the car out as though he were accustomed to backing in this bough-scattered yard, and drove off along the lonely road at the rear.

When he was passing a swamp he reached down, picked up the bundle of candies, and steering with one hand removed the wrapping paper with the other hand and hurled out the candies. They showered among the weeds beside the road. The paper which had contained the candies, and upon which was printed the name of the Parthenon Confectionery Store, Jasper tucked into his pocket. He took the groceries item by item from the labeled bag containing them, thrust that bag also into his pocket, and laid the groceries on the seat beside him.

On the way from Rosebank to the center of the city of Vernon he again turned off the main avenue, and halted at a goat-infested shack occupied by a crippled Norwegian. He sounded the horn. The Norwegian's grandson ran out.

"Here's a little more grub for you," bawled Jasper.

"God bless you, sir. I don't know what we'd do if it wasn't for you!" cried the old Norwegian from the door.

But Jasper did not wait for gratitude. He merely shouted: "Bring you some more in couple of days," as he started away.

At a quarter past ten he drove up to the hall that housed the latest interest of Vernon society—the Community Theater. The Boulevard Set, the "best people in town," belonged to the Community Theater Association, and the leader of it was the daughter of the general manager of the railroad. As a well-bred bachelor Jasper Holt was welcome among them, despite the fact that no one knew much about him except that he was a good bank teller and had been born in England. But as an actor he was not merely welcome: he was the best amateur actor in Vernon. His placid face could narrow with tragic emotion or puff out with comedy; his placid manner concealed a dynamo of emotion. Unlike most amateur actors he did not try to act— he became the thing itself. He forgot Jasper Holt, and turned into a vagrant or a judge, a Bernard Shaw thought, a Lord Dunsany symbol, a Susan Glaspell radical, a Clyde Fitch man-about-town.

The other one-act plays of the next program of the Community Theater had already been rehearsed. The cast of the play in which Jasper was to star were all waiting for him. So were the worried ladies responsible for the staging. They wanted his advice about the blue curtain for the stage window, about the baby-spot that was out of order, about the higher interpretation of the role of the page in the piece—a role consisting of only two lines, but to be played by one of the most popular girls in the younger set. After the discussions, and a most violent quarrel between two members of the play-reading committee, the rehearsal was called. Jasper Holt still wore his flannel suit and a wilting carnation; but he was not Jasper; he was the

Duc de San Saba, a cynical, gracious, gorgeous old man, easy of gesture, tranquil of voice, shudderingly evil of desire.

"If I could get a few more actors like you!" cried the professional coach.

The rehearsal was over at half-past eleven. Jasper drove his car to the public garage in which he kept it, and walked home. There, he tore up and burned the wrapping paper bearing the name of the Parthenon Confectionery Store and the labeled bag which had contained the groceries.

The Community Theater plays were given on the following Wednesday. Jasper Holt was highly applauded, and at the party at the Lakeside Country Club, after the play, he danced with the prettiest girls in town. He hadn't much to say to them, but he danced fervently, and about him was a halo of artistic success.

That night his brother John did not appear at the meeting of the Soul Hope Fraternity out in Rosebank.

On Monday, five days later, while he was in conference with the President and the Cashier of the Lumber National Bank, Jasper complained of a headache. The next day he telephoned to the President that he would not come down to work—he would stay home and rest his eyes, sleep and get rid of the persistent headache. That was unfortunate, for that very day his twin brother John made one of his infrequent trips into Vernon and called at the bank.

The President had seen John only once before, and by a coincidence it had happened that on this occasion also Jasper had been absent—had been out of town. The President invited John into his private office.

"Your brother is at home; poor fellow has a bad headache. Hope he gets over it. We think a great deal of him here. You ought to be proud of him. Will you have a smoke?"

As he spoke the President looked John over. Once or twice when Jasper and the President had been out at lunch Jasper had spoken of the remarkable resemblance between himself and his twin brother. But the President told himself that he didn't really see much resemblance. The features of the two were alike, but

John's expression of chronic spiritual indigestion, his unfriendly manner, and his hair—unkempt and lifeless brown, where Jasper's was sleekly black above a shiny bald spot—made the President dislike John as much as he liked Jasper.

And now John was replying: "No, I do not smoke. I can't understand how a man can soil this temple with drugs. I suppose I ought to be glad to hear you praise poor Jasper, but I am more concerned with his lack of respect for the things of the spirit. He sometimes comes to see me, at Rosebank, and I argue with him, but somehow I can't make him see his errors. And his flippant ways—!"

"We don't think he's flippant. We think he's a pretty steady worker."

"But his play-acting! And reading love stories! Well, I try to keep in mind the injunction 'Judge not, that ye be not judged.' But I am pained to find my own brother giving up immortal promises for mortal amusements. Well, I'll go and call on him. I trust that some day we shall see you at Soul Hope Hall, in Rosebank. Good day, sir."

Turning back to his work the President grumbled: "I'm going to tell Jasper that the best compliment I can hand him is that he is not like his brother."

And on the following day, another Wednesday, when Jasper reappeared at the bank, the President did make this jesting comparison; and Jasper sighed: "Oh, John is really a good fellow, but he's always gone in for metaphysics and Oriental mysticism and Lord knows what all, till he's kind of lost in the fog. But he's a lot better than I am. When I murder my landlady—or say, when I rob the bank, chief—you go get John; and I bet you the best lunch in town that he'll do his best to bring me to justice. That's how blame square he is!"

"Square, yes—corners just sticking out! Well, when you do rob us, Jasper, I'll look up John. But do try to keep from robbing us as long as you can. I'd hate to have to associate with a religious detective in a boiled shirt!"

Both men laughed, and Jasper went back to his cage. His head continued to hurt, he admitted. The President advised him to lay off for a week. He didn't want to, he said. With the new munition industries due to the war in Europe, there was much increase in factory pay rolls, and Jasper took charge of them.

"Better take a week off than get ill," argued the President late that afternoon.

Jasper did let himself be persuaded to go away for at least a week end. He would run up north, to Wakamin Lake, the coming Friday, he said; he would get some black-bass fishing, and be back on Monday or Tuesday. Before he went he would make up the pay rolls for the Saturday payments and turn them over to the other teller. The President thanked him for his faithfulness, and as was his not infrequent custom invited Jasper to his house for the evening of the next day—Thursday.

That Wednesday evening Jasper's brother John appeared at the Soul Hope meeting in Rosebank. When he had gone home and had magically turned back into Jasper this Jasper did not return the wig and garments of John to the bureau but packed them into a suitcase, took the suitcase to his room in Vernon and locked it in his wardrobe.

Jasper was amiable at dinner at the President's house on Thursday, but he was rather silent, and as his head still throbbed he left the house early—at nine-thirty. Sedately, carrying his gray silk gloves in one hand and pompously swinging his stick with the other, he walked from the President's house on the fashionable boulevard back to the center of Vernon. He entered the public garage in which his car was stored.

He commented to the night attendant: "Head aches. Guess I'll take the bus out and get some fresh air."

He drove away at not more than fifteen miles an hour. He headed south. When he had reached the outskirts of the city he speeded up to a consistent twenty-five miles an hour. He settled down in his seat with the unmoving steadiness of the long-distance driver: his body quiet except for the tiny subtle movements of his foot on the accelerator, of his hands on the steering wheel—his right hand across the wheel, holding it at the top, his left elbow resting easily on the cushioned edge of his seat and his left hand merely touching the wheel.

He drove in that southern direction for fifteen miles—almost to the town of Wanagoochie. Then by a rather poor side road he turned sharply to the north and west, and making a huge circle about the city drove toward the town of St. Clair. The suburb of Rosebank, in which his brother John lived, is also north of Vernon. These directions were of some importance to him: Wanagoochie eighteen miles south of the mother city of Vernon; Rosebank, on the other hand, north, eight miles north, of Vernon; and St. Clair twenty miles north—about as far north of Vernon as Wanagoochie is south.

On his way to St. Clair, at a point that was only two miles from Rosebank, Jasper ran the car off the main road into a grove of oaks and maples and stopped it on a long-unused woodland road. He stiffly got out and walked through the woods up a rise of ground to a cliff overlooking a swampy lake. The gravelly farther bank of the cliff rose perpendicularly from the edge of the water. In that wan light distilled by stars and the earth he made out the reedy expanse of the lake. It was so muddy, so tangled with sedge grass that it was never used for swimming; and as its only inhabitants were slimy bullheads few people ever tried to fish there. Jasper stood reflective. He was remembering the story of the farmer's team which had run away, dashed over this cliff and sunk out of sight in the mud bottom of the lake.

Swishing his stick he outlined an imaginary road from the top of the cliff back to the sheltered place where his car was standing. Once he hacked away with a large pocketknife a mass of knotted hazel bushes which blocked that projected road. When he had traced the road to his car he smiled. He walked to the edge of the woods and looked up and down the main highway. A car was approaching. He waited till it had passed, ran back to his own car, backed it out on the highway, and went on his northward course toward St. Clair, driving about thirty miles an hour.

On the edge of St. Clair he halted, took out his kit of tools, unscrewed a spark plug, and sharply tapping the plug on the engine block, deliberately cracked the porcelain jacket. He screwed the plug in again and started the car. It bucked and spit, missing on one cylinder, with the short-circuited plug.

"I guess there must be something wrong with the ignition," he said cheerfully.

He managed to run the car into a garage in St. Clair. There was no one in the garage save an old Negro, the night washer, who was busy over a limousine, with sponge and hose.

"Got a night repair man here?" asked Jasper.

"No, sir; guess you'll have to leave it till morning."

"Hang it! Something gone wrong with the carburetor or the ignition. Well, I'll have to leave it, then. Tell him—Say, will you be here in the morning when the repair man comes on?"

"Yes, sir."

"Well, tell him I must have the car by tomorrow noon. No, say by tomorrow at nine. Now don't forget. This will help your memory."

He gave a quarter to the Negro, who grinned and shouted: "Yes, sir; that'll help my memory a lot!" As he tied a storage tag on the car the Negro inquired: "Name?"

"Uh—my name? Oh, Hanson. Remember now, ready about nine tomorrow."

Jasper walked to the railroad station. It was ten minutes of one. Jasper did not ask the night operator about the next train into Vernon. Apparently he knew that there was a train stopping here at St. Clair at one-thirty-seven. He did not sit in the waiting room but in the darkness outside on a truck behind the baggage room. When the train came in he slipped into the last seat of the last car, and with his soft hat over his eyes either slept or appeared to sleep. When he reached Vernon he went off the direct route from the station to his boardinghouse, and came to the garage in which he regularly kept his car. He stepped inside. The night attendant was drowsing in a large wooden chair tilted back against the wall in the narrow runway which formed the entrance to the garage.

Jasper jovially shouted to the attendant: "Certainly ran into some hard luck. Ignition went wrong—I guess it was the ignition. Had to leave the car down at Wanagoochie."

"Yuh, hard luck, all right," assented the attendant.

"Yump. So I left it at Wanagoochie," Jasper emphasized as he passed on.

He had been inexact in this statement. It was not at Wanagoochie, which is south, but at St. Clair, which is north, that he had left the car.

He returned to his boardinghouse, slept beautifully, hummed in his morning shower bath. Yet at breakfast he complained to his landlady of his continuous headache, and announced that he was going to run up north, to Wakamin, to get some bass fishing and rest his eyes. She urged him to go.

"Anything I can do to help you get away?" she queried.

"No, thanks. I'm just taking a couple of suitcases, with some old clothes and some fishing tackle. Fact, I have 'em all packed already. I'll probably take the noon train north if I can get away from the bank. Pretty busy now, with these pay rolls for the factories that have war contracts for the Allies. What's it say in the paper this morning?"

Jasper arrived at the bank, carrying the two suitcases and a neat, polite, rolled silk umbrella, the silver top of which was engraved with his name. The doorman, who was also the bank guard, helped him to carry the suitcases inside.

"Careful of that bag. Got my fishing tackle in it," said Jasper to the doorman, apropos of one of the suitcases, which was heavy but apparently not packed full. "Well, I think I'll run up to Wakamin today and catch a few bass."

"Wish I could go along, sir. How is the head this morning? Does it still ache?" asked the doorman.

"Rather better, but my eyes still feel pretty rocky. Guess I been using 'em too much. Say, Connors, I'll try to catch the train north at eleven-seven. Better have a taxicab here for me at eleven. Or no; I'll let you know a little before eleven. Try to catch the eleven-seven north, for Wakamin."

"Very well, sir."

The President, the Assistant Cashier, the Chief Clerk—all asked Jasper how he felt; and to all of them he repeated the statement that he had been using his eyes too much, and that he would catch a few bass at Wakamin.

The other paying teller from his cage next to that of Jasper called heartily through the steel netting: "Pretty soft for some people! You wait! I'm going to have the hay fever this summer, and I'll go fishing for a month!"

Jasper placed the two suitcases and the umbrella in his cage, and leaving the other teller to pay out current money he himself made up the pay rolls for the next day—Saturday. He casually went into the vault—a narrow, unimpressive, unaired cell, with a hard linoleum floor, one unshaded electric bulb, and a back wall composed entirely of steel doors of safes, all painted a sickly blue, very unimpressive, but guarding several millions of dollars in cash and securities. The upper doors, hung on large steel arms and each provided with two dials, could be opened only by two officers of the bank, each knowing one of the two combinations. Below these were smaller doors, one of which Jasper could open, as teller. It was the door of an insignificant steel box, which contained one hundred and seventeen thousand dollars in bills and four thousand dollars in gold and silver.

Jasper passed back and forth, carrying bundles of currency. In his cage he was working less than three feet from the other teller, who was divided from him only by the bands of the steel netting.

While he worked he exchanged a few words with this other teller.

Once as he counted out nineteen thousand dollars he commented: "Big pay roll for the Henschel Wagon Works this week. They're making gun carriages and truck bodies for the Allies, I understand."

"Uh-huh!" said the other teller, not much interested.

Mechanically, unobtrusively going about his ordinary routine of business, Jasper counted out bills to amounts agreeing with the items on a typed schedule of the pay rolls. Apparently his eyes never lifted from his counting and from this typed schedule which lay before him. The bundles of bills he made into packages, fastening each with a paper band. Each bundle he seemed to drop into a small black leather bag which he held beside him. But he did not actually drop the money into these pay-roll bags.

Both the suitcases at his feet were closed, and presumably

fastened; but one was not fastened. And though it was heavy it contained nothing but a lump of pig iron. From time to time Jasper's hand, holding a bundle of bills, dropped to his side. With a slight movement of his foot he opened that suitcase, and the bills slipped from his hand down into it.

The bottom part of his cage was a solid sheet of stamped steel, and from the front of the bank no one could see this suspicious gesture. The other teller could have seen it, but Jasper dropped the bills only when the other teller was busy talking to a customer or when his back was turned. In order to delay for such a favorable moment Jasper frequently counted packages of bills twice, rubbing his eyes as though they hurt him.

After each of these secret disposals of packages of bills Jasper made much of dropping into the pay-roll bags the rolls of coin for which the schedule called. It was while he was tossing these blue-wrapped cylinders of coin into the bags that he would chat with the other teller. Then he would lock up the bags and gravely place them at one side.

Jasper was so slow in making up the pay rolls that it was five minutes of eleven before he finished. He called the doorman to the cage and suggested: "Better call my taxi now."

He still had one bag to fill. He could plainly be seen dropping packages of money into it, while he instructed the assistant teller: "I'll stick all the bags in my safe, and you can transfer them to yours. Be sure to lock my safe. Lord, I better hurry or I'll miss my train! Be back Tuesday morning, at latest. So long; take care yourself."

He hastened to pile the pay-roll bags into his safe in the vault. The safe was almost filled with them. And except for the last one not one of the bags contained anything except a few rolls of coin. Though he had told the other teller to lock his safe he himself twirled the combination—which was thoughtless of him, as the Assistant Teller would now have to wait and get the President to unlock it.

He picked up his umbrella and the two suitcases—bending over one of the cases for not more than ten seconds. Waving good-by to the Cashier at his desk down front and hurrying so fast that the doorman did not have a chance to help him carry the suitcases he rushed through the bank, through the door, into the waiting taxicab, and loudly enough for the doorman to hear he cried to the driver, "M. & D. Station."

At the M. & D. R.R. Station, refusing offers of redcaps to carry his bags, he bought a ticket for Wakamin, which is a lake-resort town one hundred and forty miles northwest of Vernon, hence one hundred and twenty beyond St. Clair. He had just time to get aboard the eleven-seven train. He did not take a chair car, but sat in a day coach near the rear door. He unscrewed the silver top of his umbrella, on which was engraved his name, and dropped it into his pocket.

When the train reached St. Clair, Jasper strolled out to the vestibule, carrying the suitcases but leaving the topless umbrella behind. His face was blank, uninterested. As the train started he dropped down on the station platform and gravely walked away. For a second the light of adventure crossed his face, and vanished.

At the garage at which he had left his car on the evening before he asked the foreman: "Did you get my car fixed—Mercury roadster, ignition on the bum?"

"Nope! Couple of jobs ahead of it. Haven't had time to touch it yet. Ought to get at it early this afternoon."

Jasper curled his tongue round his lips in startled vexation. He dropped his suitcases on the floor of the garage and stood thinking, his bent forefinger against his lower lip.

Then: "Well, I guess I can get her to go—sorry—can't wait—got to make the next town," he grumbled.

"Lot of you travelling salesmen making your territory by motor now, Mr. Hanson," said the foreman civilly, glancing at the storage check on Jasper's car.

"Yep. I can make a good many more than I could by train."

He paid for overnight storage without complaining, though since his car had not been repaired this charge was unjust. In fact he was altogether prosaic and inconspicuous. He thrust the suitcases into the car and drove out, the motor spitting. At another garage he bought a new spark plug and screwed it in. When he went on, the motor had ceased spitting.

He drove out of St. Clair, back in the direction of Vernon—

and of Rosebank, where his brother lived. He ran the car into that thick grove of oaks and maples only two miles from Rosebank where he had paced off an imaginery road to the cliff overhanging the reedy lake. He parked the car in a grassy space beside the abandoned woodland road. He laid a light robe over the suitcases. From beneath the seat he took a can of deviled chicken, a box of biscuits, a canister of tea, a folding cooking kit and a spirit lamp. These he spread on the grass—a picnic lunch.

He sat beside that lunch from seven minutes past one in the afternoon till dark. Once in a while he made a pretense of eating. He fetched water from a brook, made tea, opened the box of biscuits and the can of chicken. But mostly he sat still and smoked cigarette after cigarette.

Once a Swede, taking this road as a short cut to his truck farm, passed by and mumbled "Picnic, eh?"

"Yuh, takin' a day off," said Jasper dully.

The man went on without looking back.

At dusk Jasper finished a cigarette down to the tip, crushed out the light and made the cryptic remark: "That's probably Jasper Holt's last smoke. I don't suppose you can smoke, John—damn you!"

He hid the two suitcases in the bushes, piled the remains of the lunch into the car, took down the top of the car and crept down to the main road. No one was in sight. He returned. He snatched a hammer and a chisel from his tool kit, and with a few savage cracks he so defaced the number of the car stamped on the engine block that it could not be made out. He removed the license numbers from fore and aft, and placed them beside the suitcases. Then, when there was just enough light to see the bushes as cloudy masses, he started the car, drove through the woods and up the incline to the top of the cliff, and halted, leaving the engine running.

Between the car and the edge of the cliff which overhung the lake there was a space of about a hundred and thirty feet, fairly level and covered with straggly red clover. Jasper paced off this distance, returned to the car, took his seat in a nervous, tentative way, and put her into gear, starting on second speed and

slamming her into third. The car bolted toward the edge of the
cliff. He instantly swung out on the running board. Standing
there, headed directly toward the sharp drop over the cliff,
steering with his left hand on the wheel, he shoved the hand
throttle up—up—up with his right. He safely leaped down
from the running board.

Of itself the car rushed forward, roaring. It shot over the
edge of the cliff. It soared twenty feet out into the air as though
it were a thick-bodied airplane. It turned over and over, with a
sickening drop toward the lake. The water splashed up in a
tremendous noisy circle. Then silence. In the twilight the surface of the lake shone like milk. There was no sign of the car on
the surface. The concentric rings died away. The lake was secret and sinister and still. "Lord!" ejaculated Jasper, standing
on the cliff; then: "Well, they won't find that for a couple of
years anyway."

He returned to the suitcases. Squatting beside them he took
from one the wig and black garments of John Holt. He
stripped, put on the clothes of John, and packed those of Jasper
in the bag. With the cases and the motor-license plates he
walked toward Rosebank, keeping in various groves of maples
and willows till he was within half a mile of the town. He
reached the stone house at the end of the willow walk, and
sneaked in the back way. He burned Jasper Holt's clothes in the
grate, melted down the license plates in the stove, and between
two rocks he smashed Jasper's expensive watch and fountain
pen into an unpleasant mass of junk, which he dropped into
the cistern for rain water. The silver head of the umbrella he
scratched with a chisel till the engraved name was indistin-
guishable.

He unlocked a section of the bookcase and taking a number
of packages of bills in denominations of one, five, ten and
twenty dollars from one of the suitcases he packed them into
those empty candy boxes which, on the shelves, looked so
much like books. As he stored them he counted the bills. They
came to ninety-seven thousand five hundred and thirty-five
dollars.

The two suitcases were new. There were no distinguishing

marks on them. But taking them out to the kitchen he kicked them, rubbed them with lumps of blacking, raveled their edges and cut their sides, till they gave the appearance of having been long and badly used in traveling. He took them upstairs and tossed them up into the low attic.

In his bedroom he undressed calmly. Once he laughed: "I despise those pretentious fools—bank officers and cops. I'm beyond their fool law. No one can catch me—it would take me myself to do that!"

He got into bed. With a vexed "Hang it!" he mused: "I suppose John would pray, no matter how chilly the floor was."

He got out of bed and from the inscrutable Lord of the Universe he sought forgiveness—not for Jasper Holt, but for the denominations who lacked the true faith of Soul Hope Fraternity.

He returned to bed and slept till the middle of the morning, lying with his arms behind his head, a smile on his face.

Thus did Jasper Holt, without the mysterious pangs of death, yet cease to exist, and thus did John Holt come into being not merely as an apparition glimpsed on Sunday and Wednesday evenings, but as a being living twenty-four hours a day, seven days a week.

The inhabitants of Rosebank were familiar with the occasional appearances of John Holt, the eccentric recluse, and they merely snickered about him when on the Saturday evening following the Friday that has been chronicled he was seen to come out of his gate and trudge down to a news and stationery shop on Main Street.

He purchased an evening paper and said to the clerk: "You can have the 'Morning Herald' delivered at my house every morning—27 Humbert Avenue."

"Yuh, I know where it is. Thought you had kind of a grouch on newspapers and all those lowbrow things," said the clerk pertly.

"Ah, did you indeed? The 'Herald,' every morning, please. I will pay a month in advance," was all John Holt said, but he looked directly at the clerk, and the man cringed.

John attended the meeting of the Soul Hope Fraternity the next evening—Sunday—but he was not seen on the streets again for two and a half days.

There was no news of the disappearance of Jasper Holt till the following Wednesday, when the whole thing came out in a violent, small-city, front-page story, headed:

PAYING TELLER,
SOCIAL FAVORITE, MAKES GETAWAY

The paper stated that Jasper Holt had been missing for four days, and that the officers of the bank, after first denying that there was anything wrong with his accounts, had admitted that he was short one hundred thousand dollars—two hundred thousand, said one report. He had purchased a ticket for Wakamin, this state, on Friday, and a trainman, a customer of the bank, had noticed him on the train, but he had apparently never arrived at Wakamin.

A woman asserted that on Friday afternoon she had seen Holt driving an automobile between Vernon and St. Clair. This appearance near St. Clair was supposed to be merely a blind, however. In fact our able Chief of Police had proof that Holt was not headed north, in the direction of St. Clair, but south, beyond Wanagoochie—probably for Des Moines or St. Louis. It was definitely known that on the previous day Holt had left his car at Wanagoochie, and with their customary thoroughness and promptness the police were making search at Wanagoochie. The Chief had already communicated with the police in cities to the south, and the capture of the man could confidently be expected at any moment. As long as the Chief appointed by our popular Mayor was in power it went ill with those who gave even the appearance of wrongdoing.

When asked his opinion of the theory that the alleged fugitive had gone north the Chief declared that of course Holt had started in that direction, with the vain hope of throwing pursuers off the scent, but that he had immediately turned south and picked up his car. Though he would not say so definitely the Chief let it be known that he was ready to put his hands on the fellow who had hidden Holt's car at Wanagoochie.

When asked if he thought Holt was crazy the Chief laughed and said: "Yes, he's crazy two hundred thousand dollars' worth. I'm not making any slams, but there's a lot of fellows among our gentlemanly political opponents who would go a whole lot crazier for a whole lot less!"

The President of the bank, however, was greatly distressed, and strongly declared his belief that Holt, who was a favorite in the most sumptuous residences on the Boulevard, besides being well known in local dramatic circles, and who bore the best of reputations in the bank, was temporarily out of his mind, as he had been distressed by pains in the head for some time past. Meantime the bonding company, which had fully covered the employees of the bank by a joint bond of two hundred thousand dollars, had its detectives working with the police on the case.

As soon as he had read the paper John took a trolley into Vernon and called on the President of the bank. John's face drooped with the sorrow of the disgrace. The President received him. John staggered into the room, groaning: "I have just learned in the newspaper of the terrible news about my brother. I have come—"

"We hope it's just a case of aphasia. We're sure he'll turn up all right," insisted the President.

"I wish I could believe it. But as I have told you, Jasper is not a good man. He drinks and smokes and play-acts and makes a god of stylish clothes—"

"Good Lord, that's no reason for jumping to the conclusion that he's an embezzler!"

"I pray you may be right. But meanwhile I wish to give you any assistance I can. I shall make it my sole duty to see that my brother is brought to justice if it proves that he is guilty."

"Good o' you," mumbled the President. Despite this example of John's rigid honor he could not get himself to like the man. John was standing beside him, thrusting his stupid face into his.

The President pushed his chair a foot farther away and said disagreeably: "As a matter of fact we were thinking of searching your house. If I remember, you live in Rosebank?"

"Yes. And of course I shall be glad to have you search every inch of it. Or anything else I can do. I feel that I share fully with my twin brother in this unspeakable sin. I'll turn over the key of my house to you at once. There is also a shed at the back, where Jasper used to keep his automobile when he came to see me." He produced a large, rusty, old-fashioned door key and held it out, adding: "The address is 27 Humbert Avenue, Rosebank."

"Oh, it won't be necessary, I guess," said the President, somewhat shamed, irritably waving off the key.

"But I just want to help somehow! What can I do? Who is—in the language of the newspapers—who is the detective on the case? I'll give him any help—"

"Tell you what you do: Go see Mr. Scandling, of the Mercantile Trust and Bonding Company, and tell him all you know."

"I shall. I take my brother's crime on my shoulders—otherwise I'd be committing the sin of Cain. You are giving me a chance to try to expiate our joint sin, and, as Brother Jeremiah Bodfish was wont to say, it is a blessing to have an opportunity to expiate a sin, no matter how painful the punishment may seem to be to the mere physical being. As I may have told you I am an accepted member of the Soul Hope Fraternity, and though we are free from cant and dogma it is our firm belief . . ."

Then for ten dreary minutes John Holt sermonized; quoted forgotten books and quaint, ungenerous elders; twisted bitter pride and clumsy mysticism into a fanatical spider web. The President was a churchgoer, an ardent supporter of missionary funds, for forty years a pewholder at St. Simeon's Church, but he was alternately bored to a chill shiver and roused to wrath against this self-righteous zealot.

When he had rather rudely got rid of John Holt he complained to himself: "Curse it, I oughtn't to, but I must say I prefer Jasper the sinner to John the saint. Uff! What a smell of damp cellars the fellow has! He must spend all his time picking potatoes. Say! By thunder, I remember that Jasper had the infernal nerve to tell me once that if he ever robbed the bank I was to call John in. I know why, now! John is the kind of egotistical fool that would muddle up any kind of systematic search. Well, Jasper, sorry, but I'm not going to have anything more to do with John than I can help!"

John had gone to the Mercantile Trust and Bonding Company, had called on Mr. Scandling, and was now wearying him by a detailed and useless account of Jasper's early years and recent vices. He was turned over to the detective employed by the bonding company to find Jasper. The detective was a hard, noisy man, who found John even more tedious. John insisted on his coming out to examine the house in Rosebank, and the detective did so—but sketchily, trying to escape. John spent at least five minutes in showing him the shed where Jasper had sometimes kept his car.

He also attempted to interest the detective in his precious but spotty books. He unlocked one section of the case, dragged down a four-volume set of sermons and started to read them aloud.

The detective interrupted: "Yuh, that's great stuff, but I guess we aren't going to find your brother hiding behind those books!"

The detective got away as soon as possible, after instantly explaining to John that if they could use his assistance they would let him know.

"If I can only expiate—"

"Yuh, sure, that's all right!" wailed the detective, fairly running toward the gate.

John made one more visit to Vernon that day. He called on the Chief of City Police. He informed the Chief that he had taken the bonding company's detective through his house; but wouldn't the police consent to search it also? He wanted to expiate—The chief patted John on the back, advised him not to feel responsible for his brother's guilt and begged: "Skip along now—very busy."

As John walked to the Soul Hope meeting that evening dozens of people murmured that it was his brother who had robbed the Lumber National Bank. His head was bowed with the shame. At the meeting he took Jasper's sin upon himself, and prayed that Jasper would be caught and receive the blessed healing of punishment. The others begged John not to feel that he was guilty—was he not one of the Soul Hope brethren who alone in this wicked and perverse generation were assured of salvation?

On Thursday, on Saturday morning, on Tuesday and on Friday John went into the city to call on the President of the bank and the detective. Twice the President saw him, and was infinitely bored by his sermons. The third time he sent word that he was out. The fourth time he saw John, but curtly explained that if John wanted to help them the best thing he could do was to stay away.

The detective was "out" all four times.

John smiled meekly and ceased to try to help them. Dust began to gather on certain candy boxes on the lower shelf of his bookcase, save for one of them, which he took out now and then. Always after he had taken it out a man with faded brown hair and a wrinkled black suit, signing himself R. J. Smith, would send a fair-sized money order from the post office at South Vernon to John Holt, at Rosebank—as he had been doing for more than six months. These money orders could not have amounted to more than twenty-five dollars a week, but that was even more than an ascetic like John Holt needed. By day John sometimes cashed these at the Rosebank post office, but usually, as had been his custom, he cashed them at his favorite grocery when he went out in the evening.

In conversation with the commuter neighbor who every evening walked about and smoked an after-dinner cigar in the yard at the right John was frank about the whole lamentable business of his brother's defalcation. He wondered, he said, if he had not shut himself up with his studies too much, and neglected his brother. The neighbor ponderously advised John to get out more. John let himself be persuaded, at least to the extent of taking a short walk every afternoon and of letting his literary solitude be disturbed by the delivery of milk, meat and groceries. He also went to the public library, and in the reference room glanced at books on Central and South America—as though he were planning to go south, someday.

But he continued his religious studies. It may be doubted if previous to the embezzlement John had worked very consistently on his book about Revelation. All that the world had ever seen of it was a jumble of quotations from theological authorities. Presumably the crime of his brother shocked him into more concentrated study, more patient writing. For during the year after his brother's disappearance—a year in which the bonding company gradually gave up the search and came to believe that Jasper was dead—John became fanatically absorbed in somewhat nebulous work. The days and nights drifted together in meditation in which he lost sight of realities, and seemed through the clouds of the flesh to see flashes from the towered cities of the spirit.

It has been asserted that when Jasper Holt acted a role he veritably lived it. No one can ever determine how great an actor was lost in the smug bank teller. To him were imperial triumphs denied, yet was he not without material reward. For playing his most subtle part he received ninety-seven thousand dollars. It may be that he earned it. Certainly for the risk entailed it was but a fair payment. Jasper had meddled with the mystery of personality, and was in peril of losing all consistent purpose, of becoming a Wandering Jew of the spirit, a strangled body walking.

The sharp-pointed willow leaves had twisted and fallen, after the dreary rains of October. Bark had peeled from the willow trunks, leaving gashes of bare wood that was a wet and sickly yellow. Through the denuded trees bulked the solid stone back of John Holt's house. The patches of earth were greasy between the tawny knots of grass stems. The bricks of the walk were always damp now. The world was hunched up in this pervading chill.

As melancholy as the sick earth seemed the man who in a slaty twilight paced the willow walk. His step was slack, his lips moved with the intensity of his meditation. Over his wrinkled black suit and bleak shirt bosom was a worn overcoat, the velvet collar turned green. He was considering.

"There's something to all this. I begin to see—I don't know

what it is I do see! But there's lights—supernatural world that makes food and bed seem ridiculous. I am—I really am beyond the law! I made my own law! Why shouldn't I go beyond the law of vision and see the secrets of life? But I sinned, and I must repent—someday. I need not return the money. I see now that it was given me so that I could lead this life of contemplation. But the ingratitude to the President, to the people who trusted me! Am I but the most miserable of sinners, and as the blind? Voices—I hear conflicting voices—some praising me for my courage, some rebuking . . ."

He knelt on the slimy black surface of a wooden bench beneath the willows, and as dusk clothed him round about he prayed. It seemed to him that he prayed not in words but in vast confusing dreams—the words of a language larger than human tongues. When he had exhausted himself he slowly entered the house. He locked the door. There was nothing definite of which he was afraid, but he was never comfortable with the door unlocked.

By candle light he prepared his austere supper—dry toast, an egg, cheap green tea with thin milk. As always—as it had happened after every meal, now, for eighteen months—he wanted a cigarette when he had eaten, but did not take one. He paced into the living room and through the long still hours of the evening he read an ancient book, all footnotes and cross references, about *The Numerology of the Prophetic Books, and the Number of the Beast.* He tried to make notes for his own book on Revelation—that scant pile of sheets covered with writing in a small finicky hand. Thousands of other sheets he had covered; through whole nights he had written; but always he seemed with tardy pen to be racing after thoughts that he could never quite catch, and most of what he had written he had savagely burned.

But someday he would make a masterpiece! He was feeling toward the greatest discovery that mortal men had encountered. Everything, he had determined, was a symbol—not just this holy sign and that, but all physical manifestations. With frightened exultation he tried his new power of divination. The hanging lamp swung tinily. He ventured: "If the arc of that moving radiance touches the edge of the bookcase, then it will be a sign that I am to go to South America, under an entirely new disguise, and spend my money."

He shuddered. He watched the lamp's unbearably slow swing. The moving light almost touched the bookcase. He gasped. Then it receded.

It was a warning; he quaked. Would he never leave this place of brooding and of fear—which he had thought so clever a refuge? He suddenly saw it all.

"I ran away and hid in a prison! Man isn't caught by justice— he catches himself!"

Again he tried. He speculated as to whether the number of pencils on the table was greater or less than five. If greater, then he had sinned; if less, then he was veritably beyond the law. He began to lift books and papers, looking for pencils. He was coldly sweating with the suspense of the test.

Suddenly he cried: "Am I going crazy?"

He fled to his prosaic bedroom. He could not sleep. His brain was smoldering with confused inklings of mystic numbers and hidden warnings.

He woke from a half sleep more vision haunted than any waking thought, and cried: "I must go back and confess! But I can't! I can't, when I was too clever for them! I can't go back and let them win. I won't let those fools just sit tight and still catch me!"

It was a year and a half since Jasper had disappeared. Sometimes it seemed a month and a half; sometimes gray centuries. John's will power had been shrouded with curious puttering studies; long heavy-breathing sittings with the ouija board on his lap, midnight hours when he had fancied that tables had tapped and crackling coals had spoken. Now that the second autumn of his seclusion was creeping into winter he was conscious that he had not enough initiative to carry out his plans for going to South America. The summer before he had boasted to himself that he would come out of hiding and go south, leaving such a twisty trail as only he could make. But—oh, it was too much trouble. He hadn't the joy in play-acting which had carried his brother Jasper through his preparations for flight.

He had killed Jasper Holt, and for a miserable little pile of paper money he had become a moldy recluse!

He hated his loneliness, but still more did he hate his only companions, the members of the Soul Hope Fraternity—that pious shrill seamstress, that surly carpenter, that tight-lipped housekeeper, that old shouting man with the unseemly frieze of whiskers. They were so unimaginative. Their meetings were all the same; the same persons rose in the same order and made the same intimate announcements to the Deity that they alone were his elect.

At first it had been an amusing triumph to be accepted as the most eloquent among them, but that had become commonplace, and he resented their daring to be familiar with him, who was, he felt, the only man of all men living who beyond the illusions of the world saw the strange beatitude of higher souls.

It was at the end of November, during a Wednesday meeting at which a red-faced man had for a half hour maintained that he couldn't possibly sin, that the cumulative ennui burst in John Holt's brain. He sprang up.

He snarled: "You make me sick, all of you! You think you're so certain of sanctification that you can't do wrong. So did I, once! Now I know that we are all miserable sinners—really are! You all say you are, but you don't believe it. I tell you that you there, that have just been yammering, and you, Brother Judkins, with the long twitching nose, and I—I—I, most unhappiest of men, we must repent, confess, expiate our sins! And I will confess right now. I st-stole . . ."

Terrified he darted out of the hall, and hatless, coatless, tumbled through the main street of Rosebank, nor ceased till he had locked himself in his house. He was frightened because he had almost betrayed his secret, yet agonized because he had not gone on, really confessed, and gained the only peace he could ever know now—the peace of punishment.

He never returned to Soul Hope Hall. Indeed for a week he did not leave his house, save for midnight prowling in the willow walk. Quite suddenly he became desperate with the silence. He flung out of the house, not stopping to lock or even close the front door. He raced uptown, no topcoat over his rotting garments, only an old gardener's cap on his thick brown hair. People stared at him. He bore it with a resigned fury.

He entered a lunchroom, hoping to sit inconspicuous and hear men talking normally about him. The attendant at the counter gaped. John heard a mutter from the cashier's desk: "There's that crazy hermit!"

All of the half-dozen young men loafing in the place were looking at him. He was so uncomfortable that he could not eat even the milk and sandwich he had ordered. He pushed them away and fled, a failure in the first attempt to dine out that he had made in eighteen months; a lamentable failure to revive that Jasper Holt whom he had coldly killed.

He entered a cigar store and bought a box of cigarettes. He took joy out of throwing away his asceticism. But when, on the street, he lighted a cigarette it made him so dizzy that he was afraid he was going to fall. He had to sit down on the curb. People gathered. He staggered to his feet and up an alley.

For hours he walked, making and discarding the most contradictory plans—to go to the bank and confess; to spend the money riotously and never confess.

It was midnight when he returned to his house.

Before it he gasped. The front door was open. He chuckled with relief as he remembered that he had not closed it. He sauntered in. He was passing the door of the living room, going directly up to his bedroom, when his foot struck an object the size of a book, but hollow-sounding. He picked it up. It was one of the booklike candy boxes. And it was quite empty. Frightened he listened. There was no sound. He crept into the living room and lighted the lamp.

The doors of the bookcase had been wrenched open. Every book had been pulled out on the floor. All of the candy boxes, which that evening had contained almost ninety-six thousand dollars, were in a pile; and all of them were empty. He searched for ten minutes, but the only money he found was one five-dollar bill, which had fluttered under the table. In his pocket he had one dollar and sixteen cents. John Holt had six dollars and sixteen cents, no job, no friends—and no identity.

When the President of the Lumber National Bank was informed that John Holt was waiting to see him he scowled.

"Lord, I'd forgotten that minor plague! Must be a year since he's been here. Oh, let him—No, hanged if I will. Tell him I'm too busy to see him. That is, unless he's got some news about Jasper. Pump him, and find out."

The President's secretary sweetly confided to John:

"I'm so sorry, but the President is in conference just now. What was it you wanted to see him about? Is there any news about—uh—about your brother?"

"There is not, miss. I am here to see the President on the business of the Lord."

"Oh! if that's all I'm afraid I can't disturb him."

"I will wait."

Wait he did, through all the morning, through the lunch hour—when the President hastened out past him—then into the afternoon, till the President was unable to work with the thought of that scarecrow out there, and sent for him.

"Well, well! What is it this time, John? I'm pretty busy. No news about Jasper, eh?"

"No news, sir, but—Jasper himself! I am Jasper Holt! His sin is my sin."

"Yes, yes, I know all that stuff—twin brothers, twin souls, share responsibility—"

"You don't understand. There isn't any twin brother. There isn't any John Holt. I am Jasper. I invented an imaginary brother, and disguised myself—Why, don't you recognize my voice?"

While John leaned over the desk, his two hands upon it, and smiled wistfully, the President shook his head and soothed: "No, I'm afraid I don't. Sounds like good old religious John to me! Jasper was a cheerful, efficient sort of crook. Why, his laugh—"

"But I can laugh!" The dreadful croak which John uttered was the cry of an evil bird of the swamps. The President shuddered. Under the edge of the desk his fingers crept toward the buzzer by which he summoned his secretary.

They stopped as John urged: "Look—this wig—it's a wig. See, I am Jasper!"

He had snatched off the brown thatch. He stood expectant, a little afraid.

The President was startled, but he shook his head and sighed.

"You poor devil! Wig, all right. But I wouldn't say that hair was much like Jasper's!"

He motioned toward the mirror in the corner of the room.

John wavered to it. And indeed he saw that day by slow day his hair had turned from Jasper's thin sleek blackness to a straggle of damp gray locks writhing over a yellow skull.

He begged pitifully: "Oh, can't you see I am Jasper? I stole ninety-seven thousand dollars from the bank. I want to be punished! I want to do anything to prove—Why, I've been at your house. Your wife's name is Evelyn. My salary here was—"

"My dear boy, don't you suppose that Jasper might have told you all these interesting facts? I'm afraid the worry of this has—pardon me if I'm frank, but I'm afraid it's turned your head a little, John."

"There isn't any John! There isn't! There isn't!"

"I'd believe that a little more easily if I hadn't met you before Jasper disappeared."

"Give me a piece of paper. You know my writing . . ."

With clutching claws John seized a sheet of bank stationery and tried to write in the round script of Jasper. During the past year and a half he had filled thousands of pages with the small finicky hand of John. Now, though he tried to prevent it, after he had traced two or three words in large but shaky letters the writing became smaller, more pinched, less legible.

Even while John wrote the President looked at the sheet and said easily: "Afraid it's no use. That isn't Jasper's fist. See here, I want you to get away from Rosebank—go to some farm—work outdoors—cut out this fuming and fussing—get some fresh air in your lungs." The President rose and purred: "Now, I'm afraid I have some work to do."

He paused, waiting for John to go.

John fiercely crumpled the sheet and hurled it away. Tears were in his weary eyes.

He wailed: "Is there nothing I can do to prove I am Jasper?"

"Why, certainly! You can produce what's left of the ninety-seven thousand!"

John took from his ragged waistcoat pocket a five-dollar bill and some change. "Here's all there is. Ninety-six thousand of it was stolen from my house last night."

Sorry though he was for the madman the President could not help laughing. Then he tried to look sympathetic, and he comforted: "Well, that's hard luck, old man. Uh, let's see. You might produce some parents or relatives or somebody to prove that Jasper never did have a twin brother."

"My parents are dead, and I've lost track of their kin—I was born in England—Father came over when I was six. There might be some cousins or some old neighbors, but I don't know. Probably impossible to find out, in these wartimes, without going over there."

"Well, I guess we'll have to let it go, old man." The President was pressing the buzzer for his secretary and gently bidding her: "Show Mr. Holt out, please."

From the door John desperately tried to add: "You will find my car sunk—"

The door had closed behind him. The President had not listened.

The President gave orders that never, for any reason, was John Holt to be admitted to his office again. He telephoned to the bonding company that John Holt had now gone crazy; that they would save trouble by refusing to admit him.

John did not try to see them. He went to the county jail. He entered the keeper's office and said quietly: "I have stolen a lot of money, but I can't prove it. Will you put me in jail?"

The keeper shouted: "Get out of here! You hoboes always spring that when you want a good warm lodging for the winter! Why the devil don't you go to work with a shovel in the sand pits? They're paying two–seventy-five a day."

"Yes, sir," said John timorously. "Where are they?"

EDGAR WALLACE

No author in this book was more successful during his lifetime than Edgar Wallace. He wrote at least 175 novels of, not surprisingly, wildly varying quality. He has the distinction of having had more films made from his books than any other author in history: more than 160, according to one source. Wallace also wrote a couple of dozen plays, as well as uncountable numbers of short stories, newspaper articles, and essays. Somehow he found time to gamble disastrously, to run for political office and fail, and to marry twice. One other item always jumps off his résumé and into any article about Wallace: when he died, he was in Hollywood working on the script for *King Kong*.

Wallace was not above recycling plots from one form to another. Although his characters are entertaining and seldom generic, especially his detective J. G. Reeder and his thief Four Square Jane, his tales are definitely plot-driven. His short stories often follow a favorite series character, but most of his novels are one-time outings. A couple of exceptions include 1905's *The Four Just Men*, about world-class vigilantes who kill people who are otherwise beyond the hand of justice, and a series of African adventures launched in 1918 with *Sanders of the River*.

Wallace's first story about the woman whom news media have nicknamed "Four Square Jane" appeared in the December 13, 1919, issue of *The Weekly News* in London. It was entitled simply "Four Square Jane," and ten years later the entire series appeared in book form under the same title. The narrative progresses from story to story, so for the book publication Wallace replaced story titles with chapter numbers. The following adventure comprises chapter 3. Lord Claythorpe finds himself repeatedly victimized as the book goes on, while Peter Dawes pursues Jane from caper to caper, usually remaining just a step behind.

In this story, a commissioner at Scotland Yard asks about Jane the kind of question that has been asked about every rogue in this book: Did anyone actually *see* the thief? And in reply he gets the same sort of answer that every other investigator gets when these smooth professionals come in and do their work and leave: Well, yes and no.

FOUR SQUARE JANE

Chief Superintendent Dawes, of Scotland Yard, was a comparatively young man, considering the important position he held. It was the boast of his department—Peter himself did very little talking about his achievements—that never once, after he had picked up a trail, was Peter ever baffled.

A clean-shaven, youngish looking man, with grey hair at his temples, Peter took a philosophical view of crime and criminals, holding neither horror towards the former, nor malice towards the latter.

If he had a passion at all it was for the crime which contained within itself a problem. Anything out of the ordinary, or anything bizarre fascinated him, and it was one of the main regrets of his life that it had never once fallen to his lot to conduct an investigation into the many Four Square mysteries which came to the Metropolitan police.

It was after the affair at Lord Claythorpe's that Peter Dawes was turned loose to discover and apprehend this girl criminal, and he welcomed the opportunity to take charge of a case which had always interested him. To the almost hysterical telephone message Scotland Yard had received from Lord Claythorpe Peter did not pay too much attention. He realized that it was of the greatest importance that he should keep his mind unhampered and unprejudiced by the many and often contradictory "clues" which everyone who had been affected by Four Square Jane's robberies insisted on discussing with him.

He interviewed an agitated man at four o'clock in the morning, and Lord Claythorpe was frantic.

"It's terrible, terrible," he wailed, "what are you people at

Scotland Yard doing that you allow these villainies to continue? It is monstrous!"

Peter Dawes, who was not unused to outbursts on the part of the victimized, listened to the squeal with equanimity.

"As I understand it, this woman came here with two men who pretended to have her in custody?"

"Two detectives!" moaned his lordship.

"If they called themselves detectives, then you were deceived," said Peter with a smile. "They persuaded you to allow the prisoner and one of her captors to spend ten minutes in the library where your jewels are kept. Now tell me, when the crime occurred had your guests left?"

Lord Claythorpe nodded wearily.

"They had all gone," he said, "except my friend Lewinstein."

Peter made an examination of the room, and a gleam of interest came into his eyes when he saw the curious labels. He examined the door and the window-bars, and made as careful a search of the floor as possible.

"I can't do much at this hour," he said. "At daylight I will come back and have a good look through this room. Don't allow anybody in to dust or to sweep it."

He returned at nine o'clock, and to his surprise, Lord Claythorpe, whom he had expected would be in bed and asleep, was waiting for him in the library, and wearing a dressing-gown over his pyjamas.

"Look at this," exclaimed the old man, and waved a letter wildly.

Dawes took the document and read:

You are very mean, old man! When you lost your Venetian armlet you offered a reward of ten thousand pounds. I sent that armlet to a hospital greatly in need of funds, and the doctor who presented my gift to the hospital was entitled to the full reward. I have taken your pearls because you swindled the hospital out of six thousand pounds. This time you will not get your property back.

There was no signature, but the familiar mark, roughly drawn, the four squares and the centred "J."

"This was written on a Yost," said Peter Dawes, looking at the document critically. "The paper is the common stuff you buy in penny packages—so is the envelope. How did it come?"

"It came by district messenger," said Lord Claythorpe. "Now what do you think, officer? Is there any chance of my getting those pearls back?"

"There is a chance, but it is a pretty faint one," said Peter.

He went back to Scotland Yard, and reported to his chief.

"So far as I can understand, the operations of this woman began about twelve months ago. She has been constantly robbing, not the ordinary people who are subjected to this kind of victimization but people with bloated bank balances, and so far as my investigations go, bank balances accumulated as a direct consequence of shady exploitation companies."

"What does she do with the money?" asked the Commissioner curiously.

"That's the weird thing about it," replied Dawes. "I'm fairly certain that she donates very large sums to all kinds of charities. For example, after the Lewinstein burglary a big crèche in the East End of London received from an anonymous donor the sum of four thousand pounds. Simultaneously, another sum of four thousand was given to one of the West End hospitals. After the Talbot burglary three thousand pounds, which represented nearly the whole of the amount stolen, was left by some unknown person to the West End Maternity Hospital. I have an idea that we shall discover she is somebody who is in close touch with hospital work, and that behind these crimes there is some quixotic notion of helping the poor at the expense of the grossly rich."

"Very beautiful," said the Chief dryly, "but unfortunately her admirable intentions do not interest us. In our eyes she is a common thief."

"She is something more than that," said Peter quietly; "she is the cleverest criminal that has come my way since I have been associated with Scotland Yard. This is the one thing one has dreaded, and yet one has hoped to meet—a criminal with a brain."

"Has anybody seen this woman?" said the Commissioner, interested.

"They have, and they haven't," replied Peter Dawes. "That sounds cryptic, but it only means that she has been seen by people who could not recognize her again. Lewinstein saw her, Claythorpe saw her, but she was veiled and unrecognizable. My difficulty, of course, is to discover where she is going to strike next. Even if she is only hitting at the grossly rich she has forty thousand people to strike at. Obviously, it is impossible to protect them all. But somehow——" he hesitated.

"Yes?" said the Chief.

"Well, a careful study of her methods helps me a little," replied Dawes. "I have been looking round to discover who the next victim will be. He must be somebody very wealthy, and somebody who makes a parade of big wealth, and I have fined down the issue to about four men. Gregory Smith, Carl Sweiss, Mr. Thomas Scott, and John Tresser. I am inclined to believe it is Tresser she is after. You see, Tresser has made a great fortune, not by the straightest means in the world, and he hasn't forgotten to advertise his riches. He is the fellow who bought the Duke of Haslemere's house, and his collection of pictures—you will remember the stuff that has been written about."

The Chief nodded.

"There is a wonderful Romney, isn't there?"

"That's the picture," replied Dawes. "Tresser, of course, doesn't know a picture from a gas-stove. He knows that the Romney is wonderful, but only because he has been told so. Moreover, he is the fellow who has been giving the newspapers his views on charity—told them that he never spent a penny on public institutions, and never gave away a cent that he didn't get a cent's worth of value for. A thing like that would excite Jane's mind; and then, in addition, the actual artistic and monetary value of the Romney is largely advertised—why, I should imagine that the attraction is almost irresistible!"

Mr. Tresser was a difficult man to meet. His multitudinous interests in the City of London kept him busy from breakfast time until late at night. When at last Peter ran him down in a private dining-room at the Ritz-Carlton, he found the multi-millionaire a stout, red-haired man with a long clean-shaven upper lip, and a cold blue eye.

The magic of Peter Dawes' card secured him an interview.

"Sit down—sit down," said Mr. Tresser hurriedly, "what's the trouble, hey?"

Peter explained his errand, and the other listened with interest, as to a business proposition.

"I've heard all about that Jane," said Mr. Tresser cheerfully, "but she's not going to get anything from me—you can take my word! As to the Rumney—is that how you pronounce it?— well, as to that picture, don't worry!"

"But I understand you are giving permission to the public to inspect your collection."

"That's right," said Mr. Tresser, "but everybody who sees them must sign a visitor's book, and the pictures are guarded."

"Where do you keep the Romney at night—still hanging?" asked Peter, and Mr. Tresser laughed.

"Do you think I'm a fool," he said, "no, it goes into my strong room. The Duke had a wonderful strong room which will take a bit of opening."

Peter Dawes did not share the other's confidence in the efficacy of bolts and bars. He knew that Four Square Jane was both an artist and a strategist. Of course, she might not be bothered with pictures, and, anyway, a painting would be a difficult thing to get away unless it was stolen by night, which would be hardly likely.

He went to Haslemere House, which was off Berkeley Square, a great rambling building, with a long, modern picture-gallery, and having secured admission, signed his name and showed his card to an obvious detective, he was admitted to the long gallery. There was the Romney—a beautiful example of the master's art.

Peter was the only sightseer, but it was not alone to the picture that he gave his attention. He made a brief survey of the room in case of accidents. It was long and narrow. There was only one door—that through which he had come—and the windows at both ends were not only barred, but a close wire-netting covered the bars, and made entrance and egress impossible by that way. The windows were likewise long and narrow, in keeping with the shape of the room, and there were no curtains behind which an intruder might hide. Simple spring roller blinds were employed to exclude the sunlight by day.

Peter went out, passed the men, who scrutinized him closely, and was satisfied that if Four Square Jane made a raid on Mr. Tresser's pictures, she would have all her work cut out to get away with it. He went back to Scotland Yard, busied himself in his office, and afterwards went out for lunch. He came back to his office at three o'clock, and had dismissed the matter of Four Square Jane from his mind, when an urgent call came through. It was a message from the Assistant Chief Commissioner.

"Will you come down to my office at once, Dawes?" said the voice, and Peter sprinted down the long corridor to the bureau of the Chief Commissioner.

"Well, Dawes, you haven't had to wait long," he was greeted.

"What do you mean?" said Peter.

"I mean the precious Romney is stolen," said the Chief, and Peter could only stare at him.

"When did this happen?"

"Half an hour ago—you'd better get down to Berkeley Square, and make inquiries on the spot."

Two minutes later, Peter's little two-seater was nosing its way through the traffic, and within ten minutes he was in the hall of the big house interrogating the agitated attendants. The facts, as he discovered them, were simple.

At a quarter-past two, an old man wearing a heavy overcoat, and muffled up to the chin, came to the house, and asked permission to see the portrait gallery. He gave his name as "Thomas Smith."

He was an authority on Romney, and was inclined to be garrulous. He talked to all the attendants, and seemed prepared to give a long-winded account of his experience, his artistic training, and the excellence of his quality as an art critic—which meant that he was the type of bore that most attendants have to deal with, and they very gladly cut short his monotonous conversation, and showed him the way to the picture gallery.

"Was he alone in the room?" asked Peter.

"Yes, sir."

"And nobody went in with him?"

"No, sir."

Peter nodded.

"Of course, the garrulity may have been intentional, and it may have been designed to scare away attendants, but go on."

"The man went into the room, and was seen standing before the Romney in rapt contemplation. The attendants who saw him swore that at that time the Romney was in its frame. It hung on the level with the eyes; that is to say the top of the frame was about seven feet from the floor.

"Almost immediately after the attendants had looked in the old man came out talking to himself about the beauty of the execution. As he left the room, and came into the outer lobby, a little girl entered and also asked permission to go into the gallery. She signed her name 'Ellen Cole' in the visitor's book."

"What was she like?" said Peter.

"Oh, just a child," said the attendant vaguely, "a little girl."

Apparently the little girl walked into the saloon as the old man came out—he turned and looked at her, and then went on through the lobby, and out through the door. But before he got to the door, he pulled a handkerchief out of his pocket, and with it came about half a dozen silver coins, which were scattered on the marble floor of the vestibule. The attendants helped him to collect the money—he thanked them, his mind still with the picture apparently, for he was talking to himself all the time, and finally disappeared.

He had hardly left the house when the little girl came out and asked: "Which is the Romney picture?"

"In the centre of the room," they told her, "immediately facing the door."

"But there's not a picture there," she said, "there's only an empty frame, and a funny kind of little black label with four squares."

The attendants dashed into the room, and sure enough the picture had disappeared!

In the space where it had been, or rather on the wall behind the place, was the sign of Four Square Jane.

The attendants apparently did not lose their heads. One

went straight to the telephone, and called up the nearest police station—the second went on in search of the old man. But all attempts to discover him proved futile. The constable on point duty at the corner of Berkeley Square had seen him get into a taxi-cab and drive away, but had not troubled to notice the number of the taxi-cab.

"And what happened to the little girl?" asked Peter.

"Oh, she just went away," said the attendant; "she was here for some time, and then she went off. Her address was in the visitor's book. There was no chance of her carrying the picture away—none whatever," said the attendant emphatically. "She was wearing a short little skirt, and light summery things, and it was impossible to have concealed a big canvas like that."

Peter went in to inspect the frame. The picture had been cut flush with the borders. He looked around, making a careful examination of the apartment, but discovered nothing, except, immediately in front of the picture, a long, white pin. It was the sort of pin that bankers use to fasten notes together. And there was no other clue.

Mr. Tresser took his loss very calmly until the newspapers came out with details of the theft. It was only then that he seemed impressed by its value, and offered a reward for its recovery.

The stolen Romney became the principal topic of conversation in clubs and in society circles. It filled columns of the newspapers, and exercised the imagination of some of the brightest young men in the amateur criminal investigation business. All the crime experts were gathered together at the scene of the happening and their theories, elaborate and ingenious, provided interesting subject matter for the speculative reader.

Peter Dawes, armed with the two addresses he had taken from the visitor's book, the address of the old man and of the girl, went round that afternoon to make a personal investigation, only to discover that neither the learned Mr. Smith nor the innocent child were known at the addresses they had given.

Peter reported to headquarters with a very definite view as to how the crime was committed.

"The old man was a blind," he said, "he was sent in to create suspicion and keep the eyes of the attendants upon himself. He purposely bored everybody with his long-winded discourse on art in order to be left alone. He went into the saloon knowing that his bulky appearance would induce the attendants to keep their eyes on him. Then he came out—the thing was timed beautifully—just as the child came in. That was the lovely plan.

"The money was dropped to direct all attention on the old man, and at that moment, probably, the picture was cut from its frame, and it was hidden. Where it was hidden, or how the girl got it out is a mystery. The attendants are most certain that she could not have had it concealed about her, and I have made experiments with a thick canvas cut to the size of the picture, and it certainly does seem that the picture would have so bulged that they could not have failed to have noticed it."

"But who was the girl?"

"Four Square Jane!" said Peter promptly.

"Impossible!"

Peter smiled.

"It is the easiest thing in the world for a young girl to make herself look younger. Short frocks, and hair in plaits—and there you are! Four Square Jane is something more than clever."

"One moment," said the Chief, "could she have handed it through the window to somebody else?"

Peter shook his head.

"I have thought of that," he said, "but the windows were closed and there was a wire netting which made that method of disposal impossible. No, by some means or other she got the picture out under the noses of the attendants. Then she came out and announced innocently that she could not find the Romney picture—naturally there was a wild rush to the saloon. For three minutes no notice was being taken of the 'child.'"

"Do you think one of the attendants was in collusion?"

"That is also possible," said Peter, "but every man has a record of good, steady service. They're all married men and none of them has the slightest thing against him."

"And what will she do with the picture? She can't dispose of it," protested the Chief.

"She's after the reward," said Peter with a smile. "I tell you,

Chief, this thing has put me on my mettle. Somehow, I don't think I've got my hand on Jane yet, but I'm living on hopes."

"After the reward," repeated the Chief; "that's pretty substantial. But surely you are going to fix her when she hands the picture over?"

"Not on your life," replied Peter, and took out of his pocket a telegram and laid it on the table before the other. It read:

> The Romney will be returned on condition that Mr. Tresser undertakes to pay the sum of five thousand pounds to the Great Panton Street Hospital for Children. On his signing an agreement to pay this sum, the picture will be restored.
>
> JANE

"What did Tresser say about that?"

"Tresser agrees," answered Peter, "and has sent a note to the secretary of the Great Panton Street Hospital to that effect. We are advertising the fact of his agreement very widely in the newspapers."

At three o'clock that afternoon came another telegram, addressed this time to Peter Dawes—it annoyed him to know that the girl was so well informed that she was aware of the fact that he was in charge of the case.

> I will restore the picture at eight o'clock tonight. Be in the picture gallery, and please take all precautions. Don't let me escape this time—THE FOUR SQUARE JANE.

The telegram was handed in at the General Post Office.

Peter Dawes neglected no precaution. He had really not the faintest hope that he would make the capture, but it would not be his fault if Four Square Jane were not put under lock and key.

A small party assembled in the gloomy hall of Mr. Tresser's own house.

Dawes and two detective officers, Mr. Tresser himself—he sucked at a big cigar and seemed the least concerned of those present—the three attendants, and a representative of the Great Panton Street Hospital were there.

"Do you think she'll come in person?" asked Tresser. "I would rather like to see that Jane. She certainly put one over on me, but I bear her no ill-will."

"I have a special force of police within call," said Peter, "and the roads are watched by detectives, but I'm afraid I can't promise you anything exciting. She's too slippery for us."

"Anyway, the messenger—" began Tresser.

Peter shook his head.

"The messenger may be a district messenger, though here again I have taken precautions—all the district messenger offices have been warned to notify Scotland Yard in the event of somebody coming with a parcel addressed here."

Eight o'clock boomed out from the neighbouring church, but Four Square Jane had not put in an appearance. Five minutes later there came a ring at the bell, and Peter Dawes opened the door.

It was a telegraph boy.

Peter took the buff envelope and tore it open, read the message through carefully, and laughed—a hopeless, admiring laugh.

"She's done it," he said.

"What do you mean?" asked Tresser.

"Come in here," said Peter.

He led the way into the picture gallery. There was the empty frame on the wall, and behind it the half-obliterated label which Four Square Jane had stuck.

He walked straight to the end of the room to one of the windows.

"The picture is here," he said, "it has never left the room."

He lifted his hand, and pulled at the blind cord, and the blind slowly revolved.

There was a gasp of astonishment from the gathering. For, pinned to the blind, and rolled up with it, was the missing Romney.

"I ought to have guessed when I saw the pin," said Peter to his chief. "It was quick work, but it was possible to do it.

"She cut out the picture, brought it to the end of the room, and pulled down the blind; pinned the top corners of the picture to the blind, and let it roll up again. Nobody thought of pulling that infernal thing down!"

"The question that worries me," said the Chief, "is this—Who is Four Square Jane?"

"That," replied Peter, "is just what I am going to discover."

THE STORY OF PENGUIN CLASSICS

Before 1946 . . . "Classics" are mainly the domain of academics and students; readable editions for everyone else are almost unheard of. This all changes when a little-known classicist, E. V. Rieu, presents Penguin founder Allen Lane with the translation of Homer's *Odyssey* that he has been working on in his spare time.

1946 Penguin Classics debuts with *The Odyssey*, which promptly sells three million copies. Suddenly, classics are no longer for the privileged few.

1950s Rieu, now series editor, turns to professional writers for the best modern, readable translations, including Dorothy L. Sayers's *Inferno* and Robert Graves's unexpurgated *Twelve Caesars*.

1960s The Classics are given the distinctive black covers that have remained a constant throughout the life of the series. Rieu retires in 1964, hailing the Penguin Classics list as "the greatest educative force of the twentieth century."

1970s A new generation of translators swells the Penguin Classics ranks, introducing readers of English to classics of world literature from more than twenty languages. The list grows to encompass more history, philosophy, science, religion, and politics.

1980s The Penguin American Library launches with titles such as *Uncle Tom's Cabin* and joins forces with Penguin Classics to provide the most comprehensive library of world literature available from any paperback publisher.

1990s The launch of Penguin Audiobooks brings the classics to a listening audience for the first time, and in 1999 the worldwide launch of the Penguin Classics Web site extends their reach to the global online community.

The 21st Century Penguin Classics are completely redesigned for the first time in nearly twenty years. This world-famous series now consists of more than 1,300 titles, making the widest range of the best books ever written available to millions—and constantly redefining what makes a "classic."

The Odyssey continues . . .

The best books ever written

PENGUIN CLASSICS

SINCE 1946

Find out more at www.penguinclassics.com

Visit www.vpbookclub.com

CLICK ON A CLASSIC
www.penguinclassics.com

The world's greatest literature at your fingertips

Constantly updated information on more than a thousand titles,
from Icelandic sagas to ancient Indian epics, Russian drama to
Italian romance, American greats to African masterpieces

•

The latest news on recent additions to the list, updated
editions, and specially commissioned translations

•

Original essays by leading writers

•

A wealth of background material, including biographies
of every classic author from Aristotle to Zamyatin, plot
synopses, readers' and teachers' guides, useful Web links

•

Online desk and examination copy assistance for academics

•

Trivia quizzes, competitions, giveaways, news on
forthcoming screen adaptations